The Assassins' Ball

For Mom
—PT

To my good friends,
Tom and Kathie Ruth
—JF

I

"ANOTHER TRIUMPH FOR Gardner Investigations," I announced as I walked into my office, slightly breathless. Behind the reception desk sat a redheaded, green-eyed vision of loveliness that could make a man forget all his troubles. This man, at least.

"You seem out of breath, Jack," she said. "Rough morning?"

"It was fine, for a Thursday," I said between gasps for air. "Just out taking photographs and videos. It wasn't the job that wore me out; it was getting back to the office. Walking up twelve flights takes a little time at my age," I planted my butt on the edge of her desk.

Annie smiled. "All part of my devious scheme to keep you in shape."

"Honey, you disconnected the elevators just for me. How sweet," I said, as I stood and made a mock attempt to get by the desk into my office. Annie rose and blocked my path.

"You're in my way," I said, a smile on my face.

"And what are you going to do about it," she asked, rubbing her front up close against mine. Her movement reminded me of a cat, except I was the one doing the purring. Annie licked her lips, slow and sensual, then capped off her seduction by wrapping her long, well-toned arms around my neck. "Resistance is futile."

"Then I guess my only hope is surrender." Our playfulness ended in a passionate kiss. It was amazing. Every time I kiss her, she makes the rest of the world disappear. The kiss would not have ended but for the "harrumph" that Bill Maple made to try to get our attention. It worked on the fourth try.

"Excuse me, but this *is* a place of business," he said sarcastically, half leaning against a bookcase in his imitation designer suit.

"What's your point," I asked, then added while refusing to let go of Annie, "I mean, business." She hugged me tighter.

"Annie, I'd be more than willing to represent you in a sexual harassment suit against this lout."

"No thanks, Bill," Annie said, "I started it. If anyone should be pressing charges, it should be my husband here." To prove her point, she lifted her right leg off the floor and wrapped it around my back.

Did I mention she's incredibly agile? I bent down, kissed her on the lips, then whispered in her ear. "That pretty much adds up to a confession. I could take you for everything you own."

"Or you could just take me," Annie whispered back.

"Well, in that case, Jack, would you be interested in my representation," Bill asked.

"No, thanks. Don't think it would be a good precedent to set, suing my wife," I answered.

"Your loss," Bill said with a shrug of his shoulders. "You could buy yourself a shiny new hand."

Bill was referring to the fact that the only left hands I have are made of steel, fiberglass, and rubber, and can be taken off at night. I lost the real one a while back, and have to make do with prosthetics.

"Not interested, unless it has a blood supply and nerve endings," I said, leaning over to kiss Annie again.

"Just don't act that way in front of my clients. You might actually give them the idea that marriages can work. If that happened, I'd be out of business."

"We can't make you any promises," I said, as Annie pulled my face to hers for a quick smooch. "You must be pretty desperate to drum up some business if you're hitting up your office mates."

"It's been a pretty slow morning. I guess clients just don't want to walk up stairs. Probably why Sarah called in sick. She's smarter than the rest of us," Bill said, referring to our absent receptionist. He was insinuating she could have come in today. Truth is, she probably could have, but it would have taken her a while. Sarah has spina bifida and is wheelchair-bound, but her determination to do everything possible is impressive. She even did indoor rock climbing at a climbnasium. Sarah has hands that could crush full beer cans.

"That reminds me," Annie said, suddenly serious. "Call building management. Tell them that if the elevators are not fixed by tomorrow, we're suing on behalf of Sarah under the Americans with Disabilities Act. Tell them they're on the hook for her wages, as well as the cost of a temp."

Bill nodded. He liked the idea. "Legal fees as well?"

"Whatever you can get."

"In that case, my hourly rate just doubled."

My wife and I share office space with Bill. It was convenient, as our professions were non-competitive, and we were occasionally able to throw each other some business. What I had actually been working on that day was a case for Bill and one of his clients.

"How did it go," he asked, pouring himself a cup of coffee in a chipped mug he refused to get rid of.

"Amazingly well. Your client was right. His wife was indeed cheating on him as soon as he left for work in the morning. Guy sat in his car until the husband went around the corner, then walked right up to the front door like he owned the place. The wife let him in, but it turns out, it wasn't just with that one guy. About ten minutes later, his two brothers showed up, with, surprisingly, a goat," I answered.

"Really?" Bill said, strangely excited by the prospect to the point of almost spilling his coffee.

"No, not really. I got him going in, a little stuff in the living room, but they moved on to the bedroom which had the curtains drawn. On the way out she hugged and kissed him good-bye half naked. I think it should be enough for your client to make his case." I handed him the SD card onto which I'd copied the pictures and video.

"Thanks. The check is in the mail," Bill said.

"You've tried that one before," Annie said, "The next thing you'll be telling us is we'll do lunch."

"Not today. I have to be in court in thirty minutes, and I still have to climb down the mountain. See you guys later," Bill said as he left.

"All alone at last," Annie said, resuming her position with her hands wrapped around my neck. "Whatever shall we do," she asked in a voice husky enough to pull a sled.

"You, my dear, are insatiable," I said.

"Like you're complaining," she said with a grin. "Man at your age should be happy with whatever he can get."

I had twelve years on my wife. "I'm not that old," I said, trying to sound indignant. I just couldn't pull it off with her so close by.

"No, you're not, and with your age and experience, you can teach me oh so much," she said sarcastically.

"Honey, that sounds like a great idea."

Just then, the phone rang.

Annie looked at me with distress written all over her face. She had forgotten to forward the calls to our answering service. Her expression changed to one of apology. "Damn, I have to get that," she said.

I nodded. We had an agreement to always put business first in the office, and us first at home. Sadly, we were at the office.

"It's okay," I said, as we separated from our embrace. "I'll fill out the paperwork on this case. Give me ten minutes and you'll have yourself a date for lunch."

"Lunch isn't for another three hours."

"Then a brunch date."

"Sounds good. Write fast and make it five minutes," she ordered, as she walked back to the desk and picked up the phone. Annie was normally tough as nails, but she could seduce a monk if she wanted to. Luckily for those boys and their vows of celibacy, she doesn't like bald guys in robes. She just wants me. I'm rather happy about that. I don't understand it, but I'm real happy about it.

I walked into my office, grabbed the form on the video case, and filled out the billable hours, what was seen, and a brief summary of the pictures and video. I was almost done when there was a commotion in the outer office.

"Excuse me," I heard Annie say in her school marm voice. Didn't bode well for whoever was outside. "You can't go in there."

A voice heavy with traces of the Baltimore streets responded. "Listen, sister, I can go anywhere I want. It's bad enough I had to walk up here. Why don't you just go powder your nose?"

First off, I couldn't believe anyone was trying to get by Annie. Obviously, he didn't know what was good for him. Second, I couldn't believe anyone actually talked like that anymore. I started to go out to see what was going on, when a familiar face came in through the door. The face was much older than I remembered it, but it brought back enough bad memories to make me reach in my desk for my gun. Unfortunately, the man with the face was not alone. His companion, also with a face, resembled what I imagine a shaved gorilla would look like if it was shoved into a two-piece charcoal gray suit. He had his hand in his pocket already. That meant his gun was closer than mine was.

"I wouldn't do that if I was you," the gorilla said.

"Why not," I asked, then added, "You shouldn't do that," pointing to the hand in his pocket. "You'll go blind. Or your fur will grow back and they'll put you back in the zoo."

The gorilla pulled his gun out and pointed it between my eyes. "What do you have to say now, wise ass?"

"Put it away, or I'll shove it where it won't ever see daylight again," I promised.

The old man chimed in, "Boys, please. All I want is to have a little chat with you, Jack. And I don't think you're in any position to argue with me."

I sat down, smiled, and proceeded to put my feet up on my desk. The pair looked at me as if I was mad. They must not have read my psych profile. Then it was my turn to be amused.

I watched as the old man's and the gorilla's eyes went wide and the blood ran from their faces. An ominous click had filled the air, followed by the not-so-gentle pressure of the muzzles from a pair of Berettas that were now pressed up against the sides of their heads.

"I would say he is in a great position to argue," Annie snarled, "Put the gun down." The gorilla complied. "Put your hands where I can see them, and no sudden moves or you are both dead."

"Hi, honey," I said, blowing Annie a kiss before picking the gorilla's gun off my desk and putting it in my drawer. "Glad you could join the party."

"Jack, do you know these gentlemen?" Annie said with scorn.

"The gorilla, I have no idea. I'm assuming he's just hired muscle. But this gentleman with the cane is Joseph Mozzano. You remember, the mob capo that I helped put away oh so many years ago, back in my younger days." Mozzano was still looking quite stunned by the turn of events.

"That's one hell of a receptionist you have there, Jack," he said, "Whatever you're paying, I'd double it."

"She's just filling in for our receptionist for the day. That's my wife and partner. Annie, Joseph Mozzano. Joseph, Annie. Annie, gorilla. Gorilla, Annie. Joseph, I'm surprised at you. You've been out of jail for a while now. I didn't think you were the revenge type," I said.

"You got me all wrong, Jack. I'm actually here to hire you."

"I don't work for criminals," I said, leaning back in my chair. I picked up a piece of paper and folded it into an airplane.

"I'm not a criminal any more. I went legit after I got out of the pen," he said.

I thought he had about as much a chance of going legit as a salmon had of swimming downstream during spawning season, but I decided to let him finish his little story. I picked up a "private eye" Barbie knock-off that someone had given Annie, and handed it to the gorilla.

"Hold this," I said to the Gorilla. He acted as if I needed a straightjacket, but he was wrong: I had one. I had saved the one they used on me during a forced vacation from the force a few years back.

"It's family business that I want you for," Mozzano explained, as he leaned forward in his chair, resting his hands on his cane.

"I know exactly what business your family is in. I'm the one who took you down, remember? I'm not interested," I said, throwing the airplane at the gorilla. "You should be grateful you aren't on top of the Empire State Building; you could've fallen to your death."

The gorilla threw the doll at me.

"Oh no! Poor Fay Wray!" I said. Annie actually let a smile slip through. "At least you weren't hard up enough to rip off her shirt for a cheap thrill."

"Wait, wait, hear me out, please."

Joseph Mozzano saying please? That got my attention, even if I didn't show it. I nodded for him to go on.

"My grandson was murdered last night," Mozzano said. A tear in his eye managed to do what he himself had been unable to do in prison: it escaped.

"That's a job for the police, not for me," I said, folding another plane to distract me. I hate the sight of old mob bosses crying.

"No, it's not. The police can't do anything about it. Or should I say, they won't."

"What do you mean the police can't and won't do anything about it," asked Annie, who had still not lowered her guns. Annie pressed the gun into the side of Joseph's head to accentuate her question. She took badmouthing about the Baltimore Police Department personally. Can't say that I blame her. Most of her family is on the force or in the State's

Attorney's Office. Except for her older brother. He's an elementary school teacher. He's considered the black sheep of the family. Not that that bothers him. He always claims that since he teaches in a city public school, he has the more dangerous job. No one disagrees with him.

Mozzano's reaction was cool, the same cool that let him rule his share of the Baltimore mobs for almost twenty years. The gorilla, on the other hand, was sweating and more than a little bit embarrassed. He was going to have trouble living with the fact that a woman got the drop on him, but Annie could get the drop on James Bond if she wanted to. This job keeps her on her toes, and keeping up with her keeps me on mine. I took pity on the ape man, and held off launching the next wave of my pulp air force.

"Just what I said, Miss," Mozzano stated. "It happened during a very unique convention at The Hotel Royale. The sponsor of this event is a very powerful man. His reach is longer than mine was back before my enforced leave. It even extends into the offices of the mayor and governor. There will be no thorough investigation; the matter will not even be filed as a crime."

"I find that very hard to believe," she said. Annie's father was the Police Commissioner, and he was a blind spot with her. Don't get me wrong. We've had our differences in the past, but Buzz McHale is a good man. Problem with Annie is she thinks of her Dad as more than a man, and she forgets that red tape can tie the hands of any mere mortal.

"So why come to us," I asked.

"Two reasons. One, I couldn't trust anyone in the family to do this. None of them would be able to keep their cool long enough to accomplish anything: they would start busting heads, which in this case would only get them dead. I need someone I know is honest, tough as nails, and just unbalanced enough to consider taking the job. You're the only person I could think of that fits that bill," Mozzano said.

I smiled amicably, remembering back to when I was a detective who had uncovered enough evidence to put away the top under-boss. It was my last big case before I transferred into the bomb squad.

"When you brought me in, I offered you two hundred thousand dollars in cash to let me go and make the evidence disappear. You didn't take it. I applied pressure to have your superiors threaten your job. You still wouldn't budge."

What Mozzano forgot to mention was that three attempts on my life didn't have much effect either, other than the fact that I slept wearing Kevlar pajamas for six months. I still remember all of that. One of the reasons I later quit the force.

"Listen, Mozzano, I'm not real fond of you." I said, launching my paper airplane at him and hitting him right between the eyes. He ignored it. "I don't see why I should be doing you any favors."

"Well," Mozzano said. "I can give you fifty thousand reasons. I'll pay you fifty thousand dollars as a retainer, and another fifty thousand dollars to the St. Camillus orphanage."

Prison hadn't dulled Mozzano; he was still as sharp as ever. A while back, Annie and I had been involved in a case where some Jamaicans were trying to use the orphanage to smuggle and deal drugs. It took a lot to shove them down and to save the kids. Ever since then, we've acted as guardian angels, taking the kids out, watching over them, giving them unofficial protection.

"I understand there is a child at St. Camillus who needs some unusual medical treatment for which funds have not yet been raised. Fifty thousand would go a long way toward helping him."

Mozzano had definitely done his homework. There was an eight-year-old boy named Connor who had contracted a rare form of bone cancer, which had an equally rare, and expensive, form of treatment. Along with the local volunteer fire department, we had been raising funds for months, but we were still a long way from being able to foot the bill for the treatment.

"Okay, you have my attention." I nodded to Annie. She frisked both of them, removing a gun from each of them, and a knife holstered inside the gorilla's left trouser leg. I motioned for them to sit down, and Annie took up a position behind them in case the ape tried any monkey business. "So, what do you want me to do?"

"Very simple. My grandson was attending a convention at the hotel. It's a very unique gathering, and I believe that the sponsor either had him killed or knows who did."

"So what you're saying is, Shriners killed your grandson?"

"Not exactly. It's a convention for assassins."

"Excuse me," I said, wondering if I had heard right. "Are you telling me that assassins are openly cavorting in the heart of the Baltimore City?"

"Oh yes. It's been going on for years. This is actually the fourteenth annual convention," Mozzano said, twirling his cane in the air.

Annie looked at the cane and took it from him. "Excuse me, madame, but why are you taking an old man's means of support?"

"Don't even try the indignant act," she said, as she twisted and pulled back the top of his cane to reveal a concealed gun hidden inside the handle. She unloaded five cartridges and popped a sixth from the chamber, then tossed it back at Joseph. He nodded, impressed.

"What do they do at these conventions," asked Annie, dropping the rounds into a garbage pail.

"The usual stuff: network, build up business, learn the latest techniques, update equipment. That sort of thing. Which brings me to the second reason that you are the only candidate for the job. With your background in demolition, you could easily pass for a hitman who uses explosives. You would be able to blend in easily."

It was true. Way back when, I was head of the bomb squad for the Baltimore Police Department. It was rarely a fun job, but I was good at it. The best the East Coast had ever seen, I humbly submit. It's not a job that I've ever wanted to go back to. It cost me a hand and a good portion of my sanity, and I hadn't had much to begin with.

I still did some demolition work for local construction companies. I was licensed and bonded—not only as a private investigator, but as a demolitions expert—so I had to keep current. I know how to blow up a bridge and bring down a building. Much as I hated to admit, the concept of attending a convention of killers was almost intriguing enough to take the job. "Sounds interesting, but what if someone else did it? Someone not at this convention?"

"I thought of that, too, but my people can handle that part of it. Probably do it a lot quicker than you," said Mozzano. I couldn't argue with him there. My methods tended not to involve physical violence unless absolutely necessary. "I'm sure it was somebody at the convention. I want you to go in and check it out."

"There is no way I'd go in there alone. I'd need someone to watch my back."

"No problem," said Mozzano. "I'll send Marty here with you."

Marty apparently was the gorilla's name. I would have preferred Kong, but I guess his Momma didn't know how big he was going to turn out.

"Sorry, but I don't know or trust Marty. I was thinking more along the lines of my partner." Mozzano looked toward my wife as she smiled and nodded. She still held the guns so that they were aimed at our visitors.

"Sure, no problem, she can be included in this."

"I don't come cheap," Annie said curtly, not appreciative of being taken lightly.

"I thought you would be included in his fee," said Mozzano. It was an understandable mistake. His organization isn't one that treats women as equals.

"Why, hardly," Annie said. "I'm better than he is. You're lucky if I even let you pay the same rate."

Mozzano was taken aback, and looked at me to help him out. No chance of that. I shrugged my shoulders.

"My wife is an expert marksman. She's been winning national competitions since she was fifteen. She can take the wings off a fly at fifty feet," I said, which actually was no lie. She did it successfully once on a bet. Of course, we were in Florida, in the Everglades swamps, and the fly was huge, but she still did it.

"How much?" he said, getting down to business.

"Same as Jack here. Fifty grand for me and an additional fifty for the orphanage. Plus expenses, of course."

Mozzano cringed. He'd thought he'd flash some cash and get his way. Normally our rates are a fraction of what we were charging him, but tough. I wasn't doing him any favors, at least not at economy rates. Two hundred grand was more than he was looking to pay, but in the end, he agreed. It wasn't like he didn't have the money, and his grandson was family.

"It would be best if you went tonight. The convention has already started, and is actually more than half over," Joseph said. "Do you have false identification?"

"Of course," I answered.

"What names would you like to be registered under?"

"Annie and Jack Frost," I said. These were names for criminal identities that the BPD had invested much time and effort in establishing as legit. We had used them once on the force, when the department needed a married couple for deep undercover. Since they couldn't be used by anyone else, we sort of took them with us when we left the department. We just kind of forgot to mention it to anyone in authority. They've come in handy in our private enterprise before, and it looked like they would again.

"First, we'll need to check the murder scene," I said.

"Unfortunately, that's impossible," Joseph said. "The body was cleaned up and returned to me on the sly, before the police could even get there. There won't be any traces of evidence left there. It was covered up by professionals."

"Criminal professionals," I said to myself, knowing I'd be calling on my own expert to see just how thorough a job was done.

"We'll need to examine the body," Annie said, "as well as any personal effects that were returned to you."

Mozzano nodded in agreement. "I anticipated you would. It's all been arranged. If you would like to come with me now, I have a car waiting outside."

"No, thanks. We prefer to drive," I said. "Where's the body now?"

"Abott's Funeral Home. Do you know where it is?"

I nodded. I knew of it from my days on the force. It was the place the mobs laid out their dead. Ritzier than the places most people have their weddings.

"We'll meet you there in an hour."

"Make it ninety minutes," Annie corrected.

"Very good, thank you," Mozzano said, standing to leave. He walked over to the garbage pail and looked down.

"Leave them," Annie said.

"Those are custom bullets," he said.

"Consider them expenses," she said with a grin. Mozzano nodded, and walked to the door. The gorilla stood in front of my desk, waiting.

"Sorry, rules of the establishment. You pull a gun, you don't get to leave with it," I said.

"It was a gift from my father," Marty said. "It has sentimental value."

"Didn't know Mighty Joe Young was a handgun fan," I quipped. He fumed, but remained silent, letting it soar over his head, which was no small feat. He was not happy as he stomped toward the exit. "You can always scale down the side of the building if you don't want to take the stairs."

Marty turned back, looking as if he wanted to teach me a lesson. Mozzano put a hand on his huge forearm. The ape man left without another word.

Annie made sure the pair of them made it to the staircase, then locked the door.

"You didn't hear him complaining about the climb up here," Annie joked. "Maybe I am on the wrong side of the tracks. Bad guys must have better stamina."

"The gorilla must have carried him up the stairs," I said.

"Then maybe I should check out someone lower on the evolutionary tree."

"You once told me there was no one lower on the evolutionary tree than me," I shot back.

"That's true," she said. "Sorry I missed the cane."

"Don't worry about it. I never would have picked up on it."

"Pretty standard model. He got it out of a catalog."

"Same catalog that sells sword and drinking canes?"

"Yep."

"Always wanted one of those sword canes."

"I'll get you one for Christmas," she said, plopping her pretty posterior on a chair at the front of my desk, and putting her feet up next to mine. She kicked her shoes off and started playing footsie with me. My feet were naked in seconds.

"Why did we just take that case? We certainly don't need the money."

She was right. As far as private eyes go, we're lucky. We did a lot of security work, enough that we had to subcontract quite a bit of it. We were good, and a lot of people figured it was a good idea to throw work toward the Commissioner's daughter. Didn't carry much weight with Buzz McHale, but we never mention that.

We had never struck it rich, but we had made enough that we could pick and choose our cases and go a while without work. Of course, we were lucky enough not to have to.

"One, it will definitely help Connor with his treatments, not to mention put the orphanage on financially stable feet for the first time in its existence. Two, this thing sounds too bizarre not to take a look at."

"Yes," Annie said. "It does sound enticing. Plus, we could get a lot of information for Daddy."

"Can't he gather his own intelligence?"

"Nobody can do it alone," she said, as she squeezed my hand. It was something she made sure she reminded me of when I needed to hear it.

"Well, I suppose you'll probably want to head home. I know you'll have trouble deciding which guns to wear and what ammunition to bring," I quipped.

"Yes, I suppose I will, but not just yet," she said with a smile, as she walked over to the phones and set the call forward function. "I think we have some other business we need to take care of first. If you thought you were breathless before, you ain't seen nothing yet."

II

BACK IN THE '20s, when booze was illegal and gangsters began to organize, Abott's Funeral Home was *the* place to die. Well, not die, because, like today, few criminals get to choose when or where the bullet will find them. But it was the place for a crook with any status at all to be laid out. Back then, Abott's was on Belair Road, down where it ran into Gay Street. Time went on, and while the custom of holding gangland wakes at Abott's didn't change, the neighborhood did. The local youths weren't as respectful of the rich, white men in their fancy cars as they had been. Incidents occurred. Sometimes the police were called, and when that happened, it cost money, favors, and respect to fix. There was talk of taking fallen comrades to another establishment.

When this talk reached the ears of Tiberius Abott, he did exactly what every other successful, white businessman did in the face of changing urban conditions—he moved to the county.

Abott's second location was still on Belair Road, only just outside the city line, where there were still some farms, lots of trees, and plenty of open spaces. But when urban sprawl made its inevitable way into the suburbs, Abott's moved again, and again. These days, Abott's is located just outside the city of Bel Air, about an hour's ride from Baltimore, in a very exclusive part of Harford County, where no one cares what you do, as long as you do it quietly and with good taste.

It was a beautiful day, so Annie and I decided to take our Harleys for a spin. As we headed north up Route 1, we chatted over the headsets and microphones we had built into our helmets. They worked on CB frequencies. When we got to the funeral home, Marty was waiting outside. The guy was standing in front of the door in the standard bodyguard position—stone-faced, legs spread shoulder width apart, with his arms crossed in front of his waist. I wondered if they taught that in a school somewhere.

I could see from the look in his eye that he didn't approve of his boss's choice. I suspected that he had an idea that he could do it better than we could. Worse, he felt it was a sign that Mozzano didn't have as much faith in him as he should. Not necessarily true, but if that's what you believed, truth didn't really make a difference.

We walked up, and Annie gave him her thousand-watt smile. Despite himself, he smiled back.

"Is everything ready for us," Annie asked.

"Yeah," he said. He started out trying to act like a tough guy, but under the gaze of Annie's green eyes, he just couldn't hold out. I had fallen under the power a long time ago and I never have gotten free. "Go inside. He's waiting. Second room on the right."

We entered. The place had the look of all funeral homes, only more expensive. It was incredibly neat, wall to wall carpeting, oak furniture, nondescript pictures on the wall, with a very somber color scheme. Mozzano's grandson was laid out in an elaborate mahogany coffin. The top half was open. I was constantly amazed at how lifelike morticians make the dearly departed seem. Always wondered why they didn't hire themselves out for some of the living. Might be able to do wonders without plastic surgery.

Mozzano was kneeling in front of the coffin, his hands folded and his head bowed in prayer. Annie and I stood in the background, waiting respectfully. After a moment, he noticed we were there. He crossed himself, stood up, and came to us. Mozzano shook our hands as if we were old friends.

"Came to pay our respects," I said. As opposed to making an examination of a corpse.

"I assume there is no medical examiner's report," Annie asked.

"No," said Joseph. "Nor will there be. I had one of my own doctors look him over, and I can get you the results of that, but the cause of death was quite simple. A bullet straight to the heart," said Joseph.

"I'm amazed they were able to get away with this," I said, looking down at the corpse.

"Have you ever heard of Hanson Bach?"

I almost made a crack about him being a dead composer, but out of respect, kept it to myself.

Annie and I both shook our heads.

"I'm not surprised. He likes the shadows. Runs things from the background. Hanson Bach has a placement agency for assassins and hitmen, basically brokers the deals for a cut from both sides. He's sponsoring this gathering of killers. Lets him impress the talent and the buyers. Part of his sales pitch is to guarantee the safety of all participants. My grandson, Joey—yes, he was named after me—threw a monkey wrench into his promises by getting killed. Bach did not want to make a scene at his precious convention, especially if it made him look like his promises weren't worth squat. He wants the entire thing covered up, not only from the police, but from the killers. He managed to have my grandson's cause of death listed as natural causes, despite the gaping gunshot wound."

"And you don't want to change that," I asked.

"No," said Mozzano. "Unfortunately, there are forces that I am too old to control. It would only make trouble for myself and my family, and that we don't need. I know Bach is covering up something, and I want to know what. I want to know who killed my grandson and I want them to pay."

Annie and I looked at each other.

"Let's get something straight," I said. "If we find out who killed your grandson, we are not setting anyone up for a hit."

Mozzano looked up at us, not used to having the terms dictated to him. "What difference does it make to you? You just point him out. I'm not asking you to kill him."

"We don't work that way," Annie said. "And if that's what you are going to do, then the deal is off."

"Well, I can see who wears the pants in this family," Mozzano said, trying to antagonize me. In regards to my wife, it'll never happen.

"Yes, and actually, I find the dress to be comfortable. I look rather good in it, if I do say so myself. I refuse to wax my legs and back, though. Annie likes the natural look. It is oh-so European," I quipped.

"I can't believe you ever got the goods on me," Mozzano moaned, looking down on me. Didn't bother me none. I had finally broken his cool. "You are a buffoon."

"I resent that. I don't have a big red butt. I don't even have hemorrhoids."

"He said buffoon, dear, not baboon," Annie said with a grin.

"Oh, that I can live with. Listen, Mozzano, how I deal with life is my business. You don't like it, step off. As to your comments about Annie's refusal to take part in a hit, I agree with her completely. We're not going to be used to have somebody else killed. If we do this, it's being done by the book. We'll find them, we'll get enough evidence, and we will make sure they are put away. That's our deal: take it or leave it."

Mozzano looked over at his grandson, lying unmoving. I could tell he was weighing his options. He leaned heavily on his cane, slumping his shoulders, his body hunched over. From that angle, the bald spot on his head became much more prominent, and the gray hairs seemed to stick out more. For a moment, he was no longer a mob boss, just a withered, very old man with a great sadness permeating his soul. His eyes barely held back tears. He wanted to make sure that the person who did this to his family paid the ultimate price, but as he said, he was getting old.

"All right. We'll do it your way," he finally said.

"Give me your word on that," I asked.

He said, "What?"

I replied, "Give me your word, your solemn oath."

"You think that will make a difference?"

"I'm not sure, but I've got to have something."

"Okay, fine. I swear that I will not have the scum who killed Joey killed, if you can find enough evidence to get him convicted."

I looked at Annie, she nodded. "Good enough."

"Do you want to be here when we examine your grandson?" Annie said.

"Yes," said Mozzano.

Annie and I put on rubber gloves. She started unbuttoning Danny's shirt and coat while I opened the coffin all the way. Unfortunately, we didn't learn much. The mortician had sewn up the wound, so all we saw were stitch marks on his left chest. We rolled him over. There was no exit wound, so the slug had stayed inside of him, and because of the stitching, there was no way to tell the angle at which the bullet had entered.

"About five to fifteen feet, if it was a handgun. Up to three hundred if it was a rifle," said Annie.

We continued to look. I asked Mozzano, "Did he have any personal effects that were returned with him?"

He nodded and handed me a bag. Inside the bag was a small booklet entitled "KCON at a Glance," a wallet with some credit cards, and about

$1,200 in cash, one gold necklace, a gold watch, and two gold rings: one was a simple gold band with a black onyx stone jutting out slightly; the other had the initial "J" carved onto it. The only other things in the bag were a set of keys with a separate car alarm beeper. From this evidence, Sherlock Holmes would of course be able to put it together. Figure out everything, including the man's date of birth. Well, actually I could do that by looking at the driver's license. It only gave us the basics of what might have happened.

Annie had almost finished her examination when she turned to Mozzano. "Would you please wait outside, Mr. Mozzano?"

"Why?"

She looked at him, then at Joey's body. "You don't want to know."

Mozzano was about to object, but something in Annie's eyes and tone of voice told him that he really didn't want to know. As he turned to leave, she added, "Would you ask Mr. Abbot to step in here, please?"

There was no question as to which Mr. Abbot. This was Joseph Mozzano. He only dealt with the owner.

A few minutes later, Augustus Abbot came in. Like all funeral directors, he was impeccably dressed and carried with him the attitude of helping with your every need while at the same time maintaining an air of slight superiority.

Abbot looked down at Joey's body, frowning at his disarranged clothing. Having made his displeasure known, he deigned to address us. "Mr. Mozzano said that you wanted to speak with me," he said in that quiet whisper they must teach in mortician's school.

Annie didn't waste time. "Where's the bullet," she asked.

"I beg your pardon?"

"Don't beg, it's not seemly when a man's dressed as nice as you."

A look from Annie, and I decided it was time to keep quiet and let her work.

"There's an entry wound but no exit. Either the bullet was removed, or it's still in him. Which is it?"

"I couldn't say. I was not the one who—"

"That is Joseph Mozzano's grandson," Annie interrupted. "You may not have gotten your hands bloody, but there is no way you did not supervise the process. Now, where is the bullet?"

"No bullet was removed from Mr. Mozzano's body," Abbot answered with as much dignity as he could muster.

"We need it."

Disbelief slowly spread across Abbot's face. "Madame, he is ready for viewing. There is no way—"

"Mr. Abbot, you have three choices. One, you or one of your employees will retrieve the bullet. Two, I go out to the lobby and inform Mr. Mozzano that you are refusing to assist in finding his grandson's killer. Three, I get it myself."

From somewhere, Annie produced a knife more than capable of slicing Joey into mobster bits. Where she keeps it I've never figured out. Whenever I ask, she tells me to find it myself. Since searching her is so much fun, and inevitably leads to something else, I've yet to find where she keeps the knife.

There was really only one choice. "It might take some time," Abbot said, surrendering to the inevitable.

"You've got thirty minutes."

And without giving Abbot time to object, Annie made the knife disappear and went out to join Mozzano in the lobby. I followed closely behind, wondering what she did with the knife.

Thirty-one minutes later, Abbot called us back into the viewing room. Joey was dressed again, his shirt buttoned and his tie straight. He handed Annie a small envelope, and bowed himself out.

A quick peek in the envelope, and Annie turned to Mozzano to give her report. "The gun used was probably a nine millimeter of some sort." She didn't explain how she knew. Maybe Mozzano would assume she could tell by the size of the wound that had to be stitched up. Maybe he guessed what was in the envelope. It didn't matter. "If it was done in the hotel room, he probably knew his shooter. Were there any signs of forced entry?"

Mozzano looked at her, impressed. "As it was explained to me, there was no forced entry, but one window was shattered."

"Possibly a sniper. The wound doesn't look right, but maybe it's the way they put it back together. Plus, with a high powered rifle, there should have been an exit wound," said Annie. Mozzano nodded.

"Do you really think you can find out who killed my grandson?"

Annie replied, "I'll be honest with you. The evidence has been moved, the scene has been cleaned, and everyone who may know anything adheres to a code of silence that makes those who adhere to your code look like blabbermouths. All the conventioneers are known to be killers. Each of them is a suspect. It is a detective's nightmare. At best, we're going to be stumbling around in the dark, poking around, making some trouble. We might get lucky, but in all honesty, we probably won't be able to find out who did it. Regardless, we will try. We get paid the same either way. It's up to you if you still want to hire us. We'll understand if you want to back out."

Joseph nodded approvingly. "You're honest. I like that. Look, I'm an old man, and what I'm paying you is only money. I have plenty of that. I can't take it with me. I want to know what happened. You both are trained detectives, so you have a better shot than me or my people of finding anything. At least by doing this, I'll know I tried to do something. You understand?"

"Yes, I do," said Annie. She liked to tilt at windmills. Amazing part was, occasionally the windmills came falling down.

"It's almost two now. You should get to the convention as soon as possible, but you can still register up until nine tonight."

"Okay, we'll pack and head to the hotel," I said to Mozzano.

"I know you prefer to do things on your own, but you're going in there under my name. I'm your sponsor. Why don't you do things in style? The Harleys are a nice touch, but you want to show up with class. I have a limo that I would like you to use. Marty will act as your driver and attaché."

"You mean he is going to be our briefcase?" I joked.

Mozzano didn't even crack a smile. "I'll have him pick you up at your office in two hours. The limo's bulletproof. It might come in handy."

"All right," Annie said with a smile. "Just make sure the bar is filled up."

Joseph smiled back. Her charms worked even on him. Guess you're never too old, and I can look forward to my old age after all.

"I'll make sure it's done," he said. It really didn't make a difference. Neither one of us would drink something out of that limo that we hadn't prepared and brought ourselves.

"I'd like to thank you both again. Regardless of what happens, I've already made the payments to the orphanage."

"Thank you," I said.

"No problem," he said. "It's a good cause, not to mention that it's tax deductible." The nuns were a non-profit organization.

We shook hands and left. We passed Marty on the way out. He was still in the ever-vigilant guard position. I walked up to him and unbuttoned his coat, looking on his inside pocket. "Okay, you're going to be our attaché case, so I guess this is where I put my pens. Do you have a combination lock I should know about?" I said, before closing his coat and stepping back. He looked at me as if I had just escaped, and he was hoping the men with the butterfly nets would show up already.

"Behave," Annie said, playfully slapping me on the shoulder, "We'll see you later," she said to Marty.

"Think we should have asked Mozzano to stock the bar with bananas for him," I asked on the trip back.

"Be serious. We've a lot to do. The first thing being having this bullet compared to the gun that's in your desk."

"Good point. Marty might now be working for someone else and simply have failed to mention it to Mozzano."

"Or Mozzano may have had Marty do it, and is just using us for an elaborate and expensive cover-up."

My wife. I love the way she thinks.

III

THE LIMO ARRIVED early, and the bar was stocked to the gills, just as Joseph had said it would be. No bananas, though. I guess I should have asked. Annie and I sat in the back and laid out our battle plan.

"This is going to be like searching for a needle in a haystack," I said.

"True, but I thought you liked a challenge," said Annie.

We went through a checklist of items we had brought. We had weapons, listening devices, tracking beacons. We were the yuppie version of the private eye. When we had extra money, we spent it on toys for the business. They actually even have spy stores and catalogs that sell this stuff. Of course, the CIA and FBI could always have a garage sale. We would be more than willing to pick up their leftovers, but that's probably not going to happen.

"So what's the game plan," Annie asked.

"The usual," I answered.

"You mean, go in and make pests of ourselves until someone tries to exterminate us?"

"Pretty accurate," I said. "With one exception. If we can, we'll need to bring in someone to look over Joey's room."

"I thought Mozzano said the room had been cleaned?"

"Since when do we trust mob bosses?"

"Good point. Who do we get?"

"I was thinking of Maggie Lopez."

There was a sudden silence, one I had expected. Maggie and Annie had never gotten along. No, it wasn't what you're thinking. Ever since I first laid eyes on Annie, she was the only one for me. It's just that Maggie did not play well with others. She was rude to the point of insulting, did not suffer fools gladly or at all, and was sure that despite what anyone else thought, she was always right. To make matters worse, most of the time she was.

Maggie was one of the best crime scene technicians on the streets of Baltimore. That is, she had been until the year the city decided not only to cancel promised raises, but to cut all civilian salaries by two percent. Maggie considered that a breach of trust, and like a few others, sought greener pastures elsewhere. Unlike those few others, Maggie did not take a job with one of the surrounding jurisdictions. Instead, she went private, offering her services to defense attorneys in the area. She's been a thorn in the side of the BPD ever since. Many a seemingly solid case has fallen apart after Maggie's testimony as to something that should have been done but wasn't, or about something that was done but not properly. To be fair, each mistake she's caught has been corrected, and in the long run made for a more effective and efficient crime lab.

That doesn't stop many people, my wife included, from seeing her as some sort of traitor to the cause.

"She works for the enemy," Annie said in a voice so cold that the temperature in the limo dropped five degrees.

"Think about it, honey. In this case, so do we. And if she's working for us now, she can't work against us in trial."

"Good point. Make the call, but don't be surprised if she's the one Bach hired to clean up after the killer."

Marty dropped us off at the front of the Hotel Royale. Bellhops came out to pick up the luggage. Mozzano had already made the arrangements, so we didn't need to check in. We just told the bellhops the room numbers, and off they went with our luggage. Marty pulled the limo into the hotel's parking garage. Annie and I walked in through the gold-trimmed revolving doors. Annie insisted we wait for gorilla boy to catch back up to us. I used the time to check out the lobby.

It had seen better days. The Hotel Royale had been built sometime in the last century, back when Howard Street was the center of Baltimore's downtown. The Belvedere on Charles Street, the Albion on Cathedral, the Emerson on Calvert, the Rochambeau on Franklin—hotels like these and the Royale were the places to be stay and be seen. The epitome of class and elegance. Now most of the grand old ladies have been torn down or else renovated into something else, with the Belvedere being the latest to go condo. Only the Royale remains, and she wasn't in the best of shape.

Her lobby was still impressive, with carved moldings and marble pillars. At first glance it looked good... no, it looked great. But that second glance told you that things weren't being taken care of as well as they should be, and were falling apart around the edges.

Maybe, I thought, this was the way Bach wanted it. Who pays attention to a once grand lady now past her prime? Who would stay here when there are more modern, more attractive hotels down by the Inner Harbor? Not that many. Which made it the perfect place for shady dealings, illicit affairs, and the occasional gathering of killers.

We strolled around hand in hand. Perhaps it wasn't a stereotypical way for assassins to behave, but we didn't care. Unfortunately, Marty had arrived and was following behind us. I didn't really want him around, but that was the one point Joseph was quite firm on. Although he believed I was a man of honesty and integrity, he knew I would have my own agenda and would not tell him everything. Marty, on the other hand, he felt he could trust to keep him informed.

We walked over to the far side of the marble tiled lobby, where there was a table with someone was handing out name tags. The convention was listed as "Mortuary Assistants." Not actually false advertising, and appropriate enough. There was a woman at the desk with big curly hair and a very loud floral patterned dress. She looked like she could be taking names for a plumbers' convention.

"Hi," she said, smiling wide with all the sincerity of middle class America. "Are you here for the convention?"

"Yes, we are," Annie said.

"Oh, very good," the woman said. "May I have your names?"

"Mr. and Mrs. Frost," I said. "And this is our trained monkey, Marty." The woman looked up and raised an eyebrow. Behind us, I could feel the muscles in Marty's neck tighten, and I could almost hear his teeth grind. "Would you like to give him some peanuts? If you play some music, he'll dance." I turned to Marty, smiled, and gave him a wink. He didn't smile back. If looks could kill, then he would have smiled in rapid fire fashion. He did his best to ignore me, and pointed at the list. "My name is right here." The woman checked off his name and nodded.

"Who is your sponsor," she asked, pulling out another list. I guess checking to make sure we weren't undercover cops or—worse—reporters.

Marty answered her, "Joseph Mozzano."

His name was on the list. "Very good." She gave us very nice name tags. Next to our names on each of them was a tombstone with R.I.P. written on it. At least these folks had a sense of humor.

"Step inside there," the other woman said. "You'll have to go through security, of course. Then they'll give you a program of scheduled events for the remainder of the weekend." We did as she said. We had been forewarned about the security check. I had left my guns in my luggage. Annie was packing a plastic handgun. I wasn't sure exactly where, but she promised to let me try to find it later. Maybe I'd find her knife.

Once we were inside the door, the entire atmosphere changed. Outside, it was made to look as if any Tom, Dick, or Harry was going to this convention. Inside, everything became business and high-tech. The first thing we did was walk through a metal detector. They made me take my hand off and verify I had a stump instead of fingers. Then a guy in a dark suit with dark sunglasses approached me and told me he was going to frisk me.

"Not in front of my wife, please. She's very jealous," I mock whispered. The security man, dressed in a suit and tie, ignored me. He got a bit intimate. I would never even think of having a weapon in some of the places he checked. What if it accidentally went off?

"You should have at least bought me dinner first, big boy. Does this mean we're engaged?" I quipped. He had no reaction. Put a big fuzzy hat on him, and he was ready to stand guard in front of Buckingham Palace.

"Thank you for your time and patience, sir. I hope you enjoy your stay," he said before moving on to search Marty. Considering the people he was frisking, it was probably healthy for him to be very polite. A rather large, matronly woman was frisking Annie.

"Honey," I called. "Who's your girlfriend?"

"I don't know her name, but she must have a warm heart," Annie said.

"Why's that?"

"Because her hands are freezing," she answered.

"I thought he was bad enough," chimed in Marty, as security cleared both of them to enter. Annie had successfully smuggled the gun. "With the two of you acting like comedians, I'll never survive until Monday."

"Marty, you can talk, in full sentences even," I said, feigning amazement.

"I have had enough of your mouth, wiseass, and your damn gorilla jokes."

"You're saying you want me to stop monkeying around," I asked.

Marty brought his fist up, pulled back, and punched. I blocked with my left hand, the artificial one. The prosthetic is made of a good deal of metal.

When Marty's hand collided with it, Marty was left in a great deal of pain. The pain wasn't enough to deter him, but Annie was.

"Stop it," she said in a harsh whisper.

"Thank you, dear," I said.

"I meant both of you," replied Annie. "Jack, you provoked him and you know it. We have a job to do, so I want both of you to play nice, understand?"

Marty nodded. So did I. Turning to Marty, I said, "Marty, Annie is right. I was wrong. I apologize. I don't like your boss, and was allowing my feelings to spill over onto you. I can be childish like that. It's part of my charm."

"That's debatable," said Annie, struggling not to grin.

"We are in enemy territory, and it's a dangerous place. We'll need to depend on each other, and constant gorilla jokes are not going to help that."

"So you'll stop them?"

"I can't promise that. Superman has kryptonite. My one weakness is the total inability to pass up a good straight line. I'll try to cut back. Fair enough?"

"No, but it will have to do," said Marty. We shook hands. Marty cringed when I squeezed. He had punched me with his right fist. "What's your hand made out of anyway," Marty asked, rubbing his knuckles.

"Stainless steel, mostly. You're lucky I didn't wear my hook," I said.

"You really have a hook," Marty asked.

"Yep. A mean left one," I said. "I did warn you about my weakness."

"How'd you lose the hand," asked Marty.

"I was on vacation in Las Vegas, and made the mistake of volunteering for a magic trick. The magician asked me to put my hand in a tiger's mouth. A big noise from a slot machine that had just hit the big jackpot in the casino scared it, and it bit off my hand."

"Really?"

I smiled. "Just glad it wasn't my head. Let's get going."

Inside, I was expecting something amazing, instead, I found a normal hotel hall. There was a man and a woman sitting behind a long wooden folding table, handing out programs from large piles of the same.

"Enjoy the convention," said the woman as she handed me mine.

"Thanks."

The program had a color cover with a picture of the Grim Reaper in a long, black robe. Instead of his traditional scythe, he held a high-powered rifle with a scope. The only words on the cover were "KCON Baltimore 14", apparently short for the fourteenth Killer's Convention held in Baltimore. Inside was a schedule of events.

"We should be in for a fun-filled weekend. Something for everyone to do. Check this one out," said Annie. "'It's only murder if you get caught. We'll teach you how not to.'"

"Here's one. 'The first rule of assassination is getting paid. How to get the best prices,'" I said. "'Know the going rates. Prices vary by method, place, and subject. Learn how to assess the whole equation.'"

"How about 'Murder by hypnosis'?" suggested Marty. "'Learn how to be hundreds of miles away from your hit in just ten easy lessons. Videos available.' What do we do first?"

"Examine the murder scene," said Annie.

"Easy enough. You'll be staying in the same room," Marty said, with a smile the devil would have been proud of, not to mention most dentists.

"What?" I said. "We're staying in the same room that the murder happened in?"

It was Marty's turn now to try to make a monkey out of me. "What? Are you squeamish?"

Maybe I was squeamish, but I sure wasn't going to admit it. "I'm just not thrilled by the prospect. Why can't we stay in another room?"

"Simple: hotel's booked solid. Joseph's grandkid had two rooms: I got one, you got the other."

"Then you take the one with the chalk outline."

"Nope, it was just the luck of the draw. Quit your whining. I don't hear your wife complaining."

"That's 'cause Annie is a lot tougher than I am," I said.

Annie grabbed my arm with her hands. "It's true. I even eat nails for breakfast."

"Well, technically you chew your fingernails in the morning," I said, and got a good-natured elbow jab in my ribs.

"Tattletale. Let's just go check into our room."

"The carpet is probably still soaked in blood."

"C'mon, don't wimp on me," pleaded Annie.

"Fine, but I'm not sleeping on the wet spot."

THE ROOM WAS no different than any other hotel room. A king-sized bed in the center. A desk, dresser, table, and easy chair spaced out along the walls. A door that, if opened, would connect this room with the one next door. The bathroom had a large tub, perfect for two.

"Hon, did you bring the bubble bath," I asked.

"Sure did," Annie said, walking by and pinching my butt.

"Firm enough to bounce a quarter off," I said.

"I don't know about that, old man, but we can try later," purred Annie, pulling a quarter out of her pocket and flipping it at me. I caught it and dropped it on my butt. It hit, then bounced to the floor. "I said later," she said, beginning her inspection.

What the room didn't have was any spots of blood or chalk outlines. It was perfectly clean, practically spotless. The room reeked of fresh paint and new carpeting. Using one of our electronic toys, Annie swept for bugs and other listening devices. She found three, wrapped them in a towel, and put them in a drawer.

I checked out the mirror on the far wall, the one not shared with Marty's room. In the old days, it would have been made of two-way glass, probably with a camera behind it. But that was then. This was a real mirror, with just a tiny flaw in the glass, where the micro-camera was installed, the one we were supposed to find. There was probably another. To be safe, I put another towel over the whole thing.

Nothing else in the room was out of the ordinary.

"Guess they cleaned up," I said, thinking maybe we should save some money by calling Maggie back and telling her not to bother. Then I thought, what the hell, let her come, Mozzano's paying all expenses.

"Mr. Mozzano told you they did," said Marty.

I ignored him as Annie and I continued to review the scene. It was bereft of clues. I opened the window. It overlooked an office building that was about three stories higher than the hotel room. We were on the seventh floor, which made that building ten stories. A dead end alley lay in between. This was the window Mozzano had said had been shattered by the bullet that took out Joey.

"Gunman was probably set up on that roof," I suggested.

Annie walked over to the window. "No. Angle's all wrong for a shot from above. Bullet in Joey came in more or less straight on. More likely from the seventh floor of the building across the street, maybe the eighth. One thing still bothers me. The size and shape of the wound, and the lack of an exit wound, point to the gunman being much closer with something less powerful than a rifle."

"Right outside the window," I asked. Annie nodded. "Window washing rig?"

"Maybe the gunman rappelled down from the roof," Annie said.

"What happened to the ropes," I asked, leaning out the window and looking up toward the roof.

"What happened to the blood and police investigation? If what Mozzano said is accurate, the guy running this could make them disappear very easily," said Annie, still disturbed by the concept, but not naive enough to dismiss it.

Marty laughed a biting laugh. "Hanson Bach could make any of us disappear."

"Then we'll need to talk to him, find out what he knows," I said.

"You're joking, right," asked Marty. His face went pale, and his eyes went wide.

"No. This time I'm serious."

IV

WE WERE MET at the door of Bach's penthouse by a brunette.
"The Frosts to see Mr. Bach," I said.
"Yes, come in. He's expecting you," she said. No surprise there. I had called ahead and set up this little get together.

The brunette had on a slinky black number. It was cut low enough that if she took a deep breath, certain outstanding attributes would probably have popped out. The hemline was high enough to protect her back. There was no way she would be able to bend at the waist, a common way to injure the back, without mooning the world. Judging by the outline of the top of her dress, the poor girl was freezing.

"Honey, is it cold in here? Maybe I should have worn a heavier coat," I said. Annie slapped the front of my shoulder.

"Be good," Annie scolded, as we were led inside. If the brunette heard or cared, she gave no sign.

If our room was the typical hotel room, Bach's suite was the poster room for decadence. In the receiving room, leather easy chairs and a marble coffee table awaited our arrival. The wall had large mirrors trimmed in gold. The carpet was thick enough to hide a nest of squirrels. The wet bar had open bottles of liquor whose names I couldn't pronounce, much less afford. Bach had a second young thing manning the bar, or rather, working the bar. With a small waist, big chest, and long blonde hair down past her shoulder blades, "*man*ning" was the wrong word for this one.

The ladies seemed to be around as combination eye candy and servants. Or maybe bodyguards. One would definitely be distracted by either one, giving them time to strike. Neither lady apparently believed in underwear, a fact that seemed to have entranced Marty. Monkey boy was distracted to the point of letting his guard down. If either lady wanted him dead, it wouldn't have taken much. Hell, it wouldn't have taken much for either of them to get anything they wanted from him. I was immune to their charms, at least mostly. Neither held a candle to Annie, even in her underwear.

"Mr. Bach will be out in a minute," said the brunette. "Please have a seat."

"Thanks," said Annie, as the three of us planted our butts in the easy chairs. Very comfortable. The kind that conforms to your body.

"I want one of these for the house," I said to Annie, as I reclined the chair.

"I'll see if I can get you one," said Hanson Bach, strolling out of the bedroom in a black silk robe, doing his best impression of Hugh Hefner. Behind him in the bedroom was a redhead in a matching pink robe. Bach apparently had himself a matched set of ladies.

Talk about your contrasts. The women were all gorgeous, super model quality. Bach himself looked ordinary. Slim, maybe five nine, with a mildly receding hairline. Out on the street, Bach would not have drawn attention. That is, unless you looked into his eyes. When you stare into most people's eyes, you see some trace of warmth. Bach's eyes were stone cold. I had seen eyes like that once before, back when I was still on the force. They belonged to a teenager who had just killed his girlfriend and her entire family over an argument: her father had changed the channel during his favorite TV show and wouldn't change it back. His eyes had that same look. No pity, no remorse, just a smug satisfaction. This was not a guy to be messed with. Which, of course meant I probably would.

"Great. Have it delivered to my room," I said.

"I'll see what I can do," said Bach, shaking my hand and kissing Annie's. He looked down at my prosthesis. "Mr. Frost, how did you lose the hand? A hit gone bad?"

"Nothing so glamorous. You know how garbage disposals have little signs saying don't put your fingers or hand in? I didn't pay attention to it. Very messy business," I said.

The broker of death wasn't amused. "I assume you have a reason for bothering me," asked Bach, as he lazily dropped into the remaining easy chair. He draped one leg over the side, and it instantly became clear that he didn't believe in underwear either.

"Yep," I said. "We are looking for who killed Joseph Mozzano, the younger. We were hoping you might be able to help us with that."

"I was under the impression you were here for the convention, Mr. Frost," said Bach.

"I am, but Joseph Mozzano the first has asked me to see if I can find out who killed his grandson."

"So, you are a good Samaritan, Mr. Frost," asked Bach. The mister was beginning to bug me, to say nothing of the condescending tone in his voice.

"Hardly, Mr. Bach. Mr. Mozzano has offered my wife and me a great deal of money to get this information. The convention itself is just a bonus."

"Money for services rendered. That I can understand. Donna, get the Frosts and their guest some drinks," Bach said to the blonde.

"None for me," said Annie.

"I'll have what she's having," I said. Donna turned to Marty.

"Screwdriver, please," he said in a voice that was a couple of octaves lower than his normal tones. Trying to show how manly he was, I guess. Donna seemed unmoved by the display as she handed him his cocktail.

"Now, why bother me with your problems," asked Bach.

"Simple. We all know who you are. I doubt anything goes on at KCON that you don't know about or can't find out about. We need to know," I said.

"That's well and good, but what's in it for me," asked Bach.

"Ten percent?" I suggested.

"Of what?"

"Fifty grand," I said.

Bach laughed. "Five thousand? I spend more than that in a day. Not interested, and if I was, what's to stop me from going straight to Mozzano and eliminating the middlemen?"

"Nothing," said Annie. "Except for the fact that, as the sponsor of this little event, you guaranteed the safety of all attendees. It says so in your little brochure. Word about this death has to have leaked out, especially to this group. The cops might be able to be bought off into thinking a gunshot wound is a natural cause, but none of your guests will." I was impressed. Annie's expression remained unchanged as she spoke of bribes, and as his silence confirmed her words. "You gave your word. In this business, if people can't trust your word, you'll loss business."

"What's your point," asked Bach.

"I don't think you know who did this, or you would have made a gift of him or her to Mozzano as a peace offering. But maybe, with our help, we can find out who did this. Mozzano gets his revenge. You enforce your guarantee. We get our money. Everybody wins," said Annie, giving Bach her look and tossing in her smile for free. Even with the hair color squad there, willing to do his bidding, he couldn't take his eyes off Annie. That's my girl. Emphasis on the "my".

Bach nodded. "I'll see what I can do for fifty percent."

"Ten percent," said Annie. "And that's only if you deliver."

"Sixty percent."

"You'd do it for free. We need the money more than you do. Hell, if we find the killer, you should be paying us more than Mozzano. Surely your good name is worth a few hundred grand. We are only offering the ten percent out of respect," said Annie.

"Respect? Or a chance for some high-paying work," asked Bach.

"Maybe a little of both," lied Annie. We'd starve in the street before either of us took the kind of work he brokered. We weren't killers. At least, not for hire.

"Okay. I accept your offer. I'll give you any information I come across," said Bach. "If you are interested in money, I have another offer."

"Which is," I asked.

"Sorry, Mr. Frost, the offer is only for Mrs. Frost," said Bach, spreading his legs even further. "The offer has four zeroes after it. If you are interested, Mrs. Frost, we could discuss it alone over dinner."

I raised my eyebrow, then started to raise my voice and my fist when Annie stood, and gave me a wink. That was our little signal to let the winker handle it.

"Thanks, but you don't have enough money," said Annie, still smiling.

"There are other things I can offer besides money. Ask any of these ladies," said Bach.

Annie walked over to him, picked up the corner of his black robe and tossed it over his exposed crotch.

"Sorry, but compared to my husband, you still don't have enough," said Annie. Now the hair color squad and Marty were staring at me with a new-found respect. Of course, Annie could just be being kind, but I'll never tell. "We'll be in touch."

Annie turned toward the door, and I did the same. Marty hadn't finished his screwdriver, and stood with it in his hands. Unsure of what to do with it, he walked over and handed it back to Donna.

"Thank you," said Marty. This time his voice was higher than usual. I don't think Donna noticed. Marty followed behind us.

Bach bit down his anger and smiled though clenched teeth. "Very good. Enjoy the convention. Be sure to take in the lecture on not offending clients."

I started to open my mouth, but Annie sensed what I was doing and turned. She gave me the double raised eyebrow look. That was our signal for "keep your trap shut." I deferred to her judgment, at least until we got out the door.

"What," I said, annoyed. "I was just going to—"

"Piss him off more than I did. We don't need that," said Annie, pushing the down elevator button. Marty was pacing nervously back and forth, not looking up from the floor.

"You don't even know what I was going to say," I replied.

"Want to bet?" she said, extending her pinky. I extended mine, and we made a pinky bet.

"Sure. Dishes for a month," I said.

"Done," said Annie. "First you were going to say 'Don't bother showing us out. We can find the door.' Then you were going to make a suggestion that he use the money he offered me to go see a surgeon about enlargement surgery."

"Damn. I hate it when you do that. Am I that predictable?" I said.

"Yes, but that's part of why I love you," Annie said, kissing my cheek. One of four elevator doors binged and opened. We stepped inside. It was wall-to-wall mirrors. Marty rested his head against the walls.

"A month of dishes. My poor hands," I said with a smile. "You know how delicate my skin is."

"What are you complaining about? One of your hands is waterproof. But don't worry, I'll pick you up a pair of yellow rubber gloves. I wouldn't want my honey to get dishpan hands," said Annie, picking up my hands and kissing them.

Marty started to speak, mostly to himself. "Shit." He kept repeating it.

"Marty, you have to go to the bathroom," I asked.

"No, you idiot! Do you have any idea of what you just did? You just pissed off Hanson Bach! We are so dead," whined Marty. Monkey boy looked like he was about to cry, he was so frightened.

"Marty, you worry too much. First off, he can't afford to have anyone else at this thing turn up dead. It would really ruin his rep. Second, if we catch whoever did this, he won't care about anything else," said Annie.

"Are you sure," asked Marty.

"Yes," said Annie, putting a comforting hand on his arm. What he couldn't see was that the hand she put behind her back had the fingers crossed.

It was just a little after two. We had plenty of time, so we decided to explore. Our next stop was the dealers' room.

V

ANNIE AND I were like two kids in a candy store. The dealers' room, to put it mildly, was amazing. James Bond could have happily done his shopping here. One guy was selling the latest in night vision goggles and night scopes. Somebody else was selling computer programs that did anything you wanted, including hacker programs to bypass passwords. There were books on how to pick your target, devices to help you pick locks. Heck, for the right price someone would even pick your nose.

There were more guns and firearms in one place than I had ever seen before in my life. Annie was in heaven. She was checking out a high-powered sniper rifle. As she was testing it and lining up the sights, the dealer who was running that table decided to show just how ignorant he was of the fairer sex.

"Careful there, little lady. That's not a toy. I don't want you to hurt yourself," said the guy with a condescending smile. I was surprised that the guy could stay in business with an attitude like that. True, about eighty percent of the convention seemed to be male, but you don't want to alienate a full twenty percent of your possible customers.

This guy had sandbags set up at the end of a homemade rifle range so his customers could try out his wares. Annie had been aiming at a target in the back. She put the gun down and looked the dealer in the eyes.

"I can use this better than you can. And if you keep up with that attitude, you're the one who's going to be hurting," Annie said with a smile and just a little bit of an attitude. That's my sweetie.

"Whoa, take it easy there, miss. I just don't want no accidents. And besides, there is no way that you could be as good as me with a rifle," he said smugly.

"Why is that? Because I'm a woman," asked Annie.

"Well—yes," said the dealer, actually surprised that she didn't know this.

"Okay, then. I propose a little contest. We both shoot one clip at the target. Best shot wins and gives the other one an apology," said Annie.

The man laughed. "Why sure, and if you beat me, I'll throw in the gun for free."

"Deal," said Annie. "You go first."

She handed him the rifle, and he went to the shooting end of his own target range. The guy was using the scope to line up the target. Annie walked over and took the scope off.

"Wait a second. We're going by skill, you don't need a scope for that, do you, you big strapping man?" Annie said sarcastically.

A crowd was gathering by this point, and it was obvious that he couldn't say no, so he just nodded his head and acquiesced. The dealer lined up his shots and fired ten rounds. He did pretty good. On this particular target there were three rings of the bull's-eye. He got one shot in the center ring and eight more in the next two rings. He used little clothesline-type ropes attached to the paper target to pull it back. He took it off and handed it to Annie.

"Beat that lady."

"No problem."

He put a new paper target in and handed the gun to Annie. She took a new clip and reloaded. It was obvious that he had planned for her to be at a loss as to how to put the clip in. Annie lined up and took three shots. All three were in the center bull's-eye. She pulled the clothesline set up for the target and showed it to the dealer. He was not a happy camper. She took a pen out of her pocket and using dots, drew a smiley face on the target, with each drawn dot being about the same size as the pen. Annie then used the clothesline to put the target back and took aim, fired and hit each dot perfectly, making a smiley face with the rest of her ammo. She saw it in a movie once and practiced for two weeks solid until she could do it. She then pulled it back and handed it to the dealer. The assembled crowd applauded.

"Where did you learn to shoot like that," he asked.

"It's my job," she said with a smile she imagined a hitwoman might use. Worked for me.

Annie had been a crack shot ever since she was a kid. At 16, with her father's blessing, she ran off and joined her uncle's carnival as a sharp-shooter. She was proud to say that she had mastered every one of Annie Oakley's trick shots and invented a few of her own. She made enough money to pay for college while working summers with her uncle, and then she got even better when she joined the Baltimore PD Quick Response Team.

Annie handed him back the gun. "I would like that gift wrapped with a few rounds of ammo throw in," she said, giving him a wink and a clicking sound with her tongue.

The dealer wasn't angry, just embarrassed. He put out his hand to shake hers; it was the sportsmanlike thing to do.

"That was some fancy shooting there."

"Thanks," Annie said, returning the handshake.

"Could I by any chance interest you in demonstrating some of my products here? With skills like yours, I might be able to double my sales. I'll give you ten percent commission," the dealer said hopefully.

"Maybe I'll do a couple of demonstrations for you in exchange for some guns. You have some high quality product here, and there are a couple of these that I would love to try out. How does that sound?"

"Sounds good to me. Let me know when is good for you."

"I will. I'll pick up the rifle later."

"You have to. I'm not allowed to give weapons to my customers inside KCON."

I walked over to Annie and gave her a big hug and kiss. "Have I ever told you you're my hero?"

"Not today," she replied.

"Ah, the day is still young, it could happen," I said with a smile.

The vendor offered me his hand to shake. I took it, and could now make out the name on his name tag. It was Jacob Holland.

"So tell me, are you as good a shot as your wife, ah, girlfriend here," he asked.

"She's my wife, and no, I'm not," I said. "I could probably hit the target, but she's the sharpshooter. My expertise lies more in things that go boom."

"Afraid I can't help you there," he said, noticing my prosthesis. "How did you lose the hand?"

"I was visiting a wealthy client, and I was standing over a fish tank. I dropped my favorite pen in and reached in to get it, not realizing it was filled with piranha. It was a messy business," I said.

"So what does it do," he asked.

"Huh? It's a prosthetic hand: it opens, it closes. It's got bioelectric sensors, which movement of my stump activates," I said, confused as to why he would ask.

Jacob had a huge smile. "I'm a custom gunsmith, and among the best, if I do say so myself. I've made everything from cameras to cell phones into guns. I could make you a prosthetic hand that was really a gun. It would probably hold up to four bullets. I could even stick in a spring blade loaded stiletto and have it come out the middle digit."

"Really give somebody the finger that way," I said.

"Exactly. The bullets could come out the index finger. It would be a great secret weapon, and no one would ever know you were armed, no pun intended. Think about it," he said.

I did. It was actually a great idea, and I love toys. "You'd put safeties in so I don't blow my own head off?"

"No problem."

"How much would something like that cost me? Any chance my wife's ten percent commission would cover it?" I said.

"No, but I enjoy a challenge, so I wouldn't charge you more than a twenty-five percent mark-up above cost. I could probably have it done in two days. The whole thing would run you maybe twenty, twenty-five thousand," he said.

The price wasn't unreasonable, and I had the money. I looked at Annie, and she looked back and smiled.

"Go ahead, you haven't bought any toys in a while," she said.

"Okay, you've got a deal," I said.

"Fine. I'll need a thirty percent deposit. Why don't we call it seven thousand dollars."

"I don't carry that much cash around with me," I said.

"No problem. As soon as you get me the money, I'll start work," Jacob said.

"Actually, since you're holding my gun and we have a deal for commissions, that amount is in excess of the deposit you want, so why don't you just hold onto my things until we can get the money, and start work on it now," suggested Annie.

She was turning on the charm, using her feminine style. Jacob was no match for those green eyes.

"Normally I wouldn't, but all right, you've got a deal," Jacob said.

"Thanks," I said.

"Don't mention it," he said.

Marty had moved over to join us, and was checking out a couple of the handguns. I was moving down the table when I noticed something, a small tube as thick as a magic marker and about three inches long. It looked like it could be hammered into a wall like a nail.

"Jacob, what's this thing over here," I asked, holding up the cylinder.

"That's my pride and joy, and one of my biggest sellers. I call it the pocket assassin. It's a remote controlled one shot minisniper shot."

"Say what," I asked.

"You can nail it or suction cup to the wall, you can put it into a floor or ceiling, behind a mirror or lighting fixture, and when a target moves in front of it, you hit a tiny remote control button and it fires. Then it self-destructs and melts into slag. It's a weapon that gets rid of itself. I also sell a video attachment if you want to be further away. The regular remote has a fifty to one hundred foot range, depending on conditions. I can fix it up with a long range radio remote, which allows you to be up to one mile from the murder scene and still safely trigger it. But for that, I definitely recommend the video hook-up."

"It's brilliant," said Annie.

Jacob bowed his head modestly. "You're right. I must have sold fifty of them so far this week. You guys interested?"

"No, something like that would take all the fun out of shooting," Annie said, trying to keep in character. Annie loves to shoot, she's just not crazy about aiming at people. She was torn up inside every time she had to sniper down some perp for QRT. She was able to fool the shrinks into believing it never bothered her, but she never fooled me.

I walked over to the far side of the table. Marty looked up at me.

"Time to move on, mo… Marty." I had almost said "monkey boy," but caught myself in time. Annie came over to us, and the three of us left the dealers' room.

"Looks like everything is pretty slow. Maybe most of the attendees are at panels. According to the program, there's a bunch going on and they all end at four," Annie said, as we got on the elevator. Miracle of miracles, one was waiting, and the door opened as soon as I pushed the button. As we weren't the only passengers, we decided silence would work better than conversation.

We got to the seventh floor and got out, then walked the hallway to our room. Annie took out the key card and put it in the lock. The door swung open and Annie went in. Marty started to follow, but I stopped short in the door way.

"What do we do now," asked Marty.

"You can do whatever you want. Annie and I have some connubial business to attend to," I said. Apparently the big word confused Marty.

"Huh?"

Annie came to the door, snaking her arm around my chest.

"What my husband is trying to say is, we're going to take a break for an afternooner. Just to warn you, we're very enthusiastic and loud. You may want to go out for a late lunch."

Annie pulled off my belt and dragged me inside.

"Marty, if you don't hear from us in an hour, be very, very happy for me," I said, closing the door. Marty was still standing there, his mouth agape—or, dare I say it, an ape.

I'm too much of a gentleman to relate what happened next. Hell, who am I kidding? Let's just say life is good when you can make mad, passionate love to the woman you love in the middle of the day.

VI

FOUR O'CLOCK ARRIVED. Annie and I had finished our, eh, business and Marty had rejoined us. We were just about to leave the room when there was a knock.

"Are you expecting someone," Marty asked, his hand instinctively going for the gun he wasn't allowed to wear at the convention.

"It's her, isn't it," Annie asked coldly (and she had been so warm just an hour ago). At my nod, she turned to Marty. "You may want to wait in the other room. It may be better if she didn't know who we were working for."

"And she is?" Marty clearly wasn't pleased about this sudden change in the agenda.

More knocking on the door.

"About to leave if you don't get in the other room." Then I added, "Please."

That mollified the big ape. He nodded and disappeared. Annie answered the door, and in walked Maggie Lopez.

She hadn't changed much in two years. A woman of average height and weight, above average looks, with hair and eyes as dark as the clothes she habitually wore.

"Hides the fingerprint powder," she once told me, when I asked why she only wore black.

"There are strange things going on in this place," Maggie said by way of greeting.

"You should have been here an hour ago. There were some strange things going on right in this room."

This comment got me a punch on the arm and a nasty look from Annie, who then turned to Maggie and said formally, "Yes, there are some strange things going on, Ms. Lopez. But they're not why you're here. A crime was committed in this room, and we would like your professional opinion as to…"

Annie would have gone on, but Maggie was no longer paying attention. Instead, her eyes scanned the room—the walls, the ceiling, the windows. She turned her head one way and then the other, and then of all things, she sniffed loudly before saying, "New pane of glass, new carpet, smell of paint. Someone get killed, or just very badly hurt?"

I said she was good.

"He's in the care of Mr. Abbot," I explained, giving her all the information she needed.

"That would explain why I didn't read anything in the paper. Now, would you explain why you didn't call me in until after the crime scene was…" she searched for an appropriate word, choked back a few inappropriate ones and settled on "…obliterated?"

"Not our choice, Ms. Lopez," Annie said. "You see it as we found it." She then relayed all that we knew about the shooting, leaving out only the names of the victim and our client.

"And of course there's no video or photos?"

I thought about the cameras, microphones, and other devices we'd found. Maybe Joey hadn't been as thorough as we had. Bach may have held out on us.

"If so, they're not accessible."

Maggie barely nodded at me as her eyes glazed over and she started picturing the room as it might have been just before and after Joey was shot. She wandered the room, staring at the floor, looking out the window, putting herself in the place of first the victim then all possible shooters.

"The carpet I understand," she finally said, "but why repaint the room? Only the one wound, right, and it wouldn't have bled much?"

When we told her that described the victim, she shook her head. "I'd like to help, especially for what I'm charging you. But there's nothing here to work with."

"There is one other thing." Annie reached into her purse, and brought out the envelope with the bullet. "This was removed from the body. Go to our office, talk to Sarah. Ask her for the gun that's in Jack's desk. Compare this bullet to it."

If Maggie was puzzled by our method of weapon storage, she didn't show it. "I can do that. It'll take a day or so."

"Good, leave your report when you return the gun and bullet. Call us only if there's a match. Anything else, Jack?"

I shook my head. "That's it."

And it was. Maggie quoted us a price, and we paid without haggling. Why should we? Mozzano was paying. As she left, Maggie paused by the door just long enough to say, "Tell your friend in the other room he can come out now."

Like I said, she was good.

VII

AFTER MAGGIE LEFT, it was time for Annie, Marty, and me to head downstairs, splitting up to cover more ground and check everything out. First thing tomorrow, we would be going back to school, attending some seminars. For tonight, it was more of a people-watching kind of gig. I went into the main ballroom, where a sizeable crowd had gathered around one of the demonstrators. Curious to see what the commotion was about, I eased my way to the front, only to find a bunch of grown men dressed in black pajamas. A bunch of bozos were playing ninja, and people were taking them seriously. First the intimate weapon search, now this. This place was getting too weird for me.

"Amateurs," spat a thirty-something Oriental man who suddenly appeared to my right. He hadn't been there a moment before. The head ninja gave him a dirty look with his eyes. Normally that would go without saying, but normally a look is done with the whole face. In this case, other than his eyes, the guy's face and head were covered by a black hood.

"Looks like a pajama party to me," I said, getting a few laughs from the crowd, and a glare from the head ninja. The rest stood at military attention, not reacting to anything.

"You have something to say," asked the man, fully expecting to be taken seriously, even though he was dressed like a B-movie reject. His attitude and tone would have started a fight in most barrooms. Lucky for him, they weren't serving drinks, at least in the ballroom.

"I didn't realize we were having a costume party. I feel underdressed. Can I be a pirate," I asked sarcastically.

"These are not costumes. They are uniforms of the ninja. We are the night warriors, the ultimate assassins," said the ninja. I was amazed he could talk like that and not crack a smile.

"You are no more ninjas than I am a dragon," said the Oriental man standing next to me.

"I'll have you know that I studied ten years with ninjutsu grandmaster Dosai," bragged the ninja.

"You should get your money back, because he cheated you."

"Do you feel you know more about ninjas than I do?" dared the ninja.

The man shrugged. "I certainly know that no real ninja would walk around dressed like that. The art of the ninja was to blend in with his surroundings. The only time a ninja would dress like that would be at night, in the past. What if he were spotted? How would he explain his appearance? No, only a fool or an amateur would dress like that. When I called you amateur, I was giving you the benefit of the doubt." This last was said in a tone that was half disgust and half disappointment.

"As I've stated," the ninja explained, "these are uniforms, not necessarily our working clothes."

"Then why are you wearing them?"

I wasn't about to let my new-found companion have all the fun. "Did something happen to your face? Are you hiding terrible scars? Can't bear to see the light of day? Or just embarrassed to wear PJ's in public?" My questions were not making ninja-man happy.

"Why we are here today, is to choose a select few to be taken on as students of ninjutsu," said the ninja with great solemnity.

"What does the honor run," my Oriental friend asked.

"A mere thirty thousand dollars for a three-month course, in which the student will be taught how to move like a shadow, fight like a tiger, and kill as silent as a whisper in the darkness. We were about to perform a demonstration. Perhaps you two naysayers would care to join us," asked the ninja.

"No, thanks," I laughed. As stupid as they may have looked, I had no idea how well or poorly they fought. I was a good scrapper, but I also knew enough to choose my own fights.

The Oriental man next to me simply smiled and stepped out into the circle.

"My pleasure. I would be glad to test your students," he said, bowing his head ever so slightly. From what I knew of the martial arts, the deeper the bow, the greater the sign of respect. If a master and a novice face off, the master bows his head while the novice is expected to bend practically to the floor. Most bows were somewhere in the middle. A bow that small was a huge insult to the ninja.

The ninja was not hiding his anger well.

"I will have my lowest student teach you some manners," said the head ninja, snapping his fingers. The ninja on the end jumped forward.

"Wait," said the Oriental man, walking up to the wall of ninjas. There were twelve of them, plus the leader. "Do all of you agree to this battle of your own free will?"

They remained silent until the leader nodded his head, and then screamed out together, "Yes!"

"Fine. Just checking," said the Oriental man, moving into a match position. "Let's begin."

The leader nodded again, and the ninja attacked without warning. His opponent laughed, sidestepped the attack, and lashed out once with his right hand so fast I didn't even see the punch land. The ninja fell to the floor, unconscious.

I was impressed. I had never seen anyone move that swiftly before. Apparently, neither had the ninja leader, and he could see his school's profits for the quarter plummeting. He had to turn this around quickly.

"Attack him! All of you!" he spat. The ninjas moved without hesitation, and the eleven tried to attack the one man. Problem was, there were too many of them, and they were getting in each other's way. I had learned group attack tactics back in the academy. The optimal number to surround a perp for unarmed takedown is six. It doesn't allow the perp to get away, but the officers aren't tripping over each other. Apparently, they didn't teach this in ninja school.

I was amazed at the man they were attacking. In movies when martial artists square off, it's with a big show of arm and leg moves, lots of feints and dodges. Not so in this fight. The man remained still, until he suddenly uncoiled. The result was a fallen and unconscious ninja. I could barely follow his movements, but I could tell he didn't waste more than one punch or kick per ninja. One was all he needed to knock them out. It was like watching an artist. I made a mental note not to tick this guy off. He'd be able to kill me before I could even think about pulling a gun. Hell, the way he moved, I was wondering if he could dodge bullets, or maybe catch them with his teeth.

It hadn't been half a minute, and more than half the ninjas were down. Of the five left, only one had any brains. He turned and ran. The ninja leader was not happy, and decided to enter the battle himself, but from a distance. He suddenly had a blowgun in his hands, and had it aimed at the man's back. That's when I stepped in and lent a hand, literally. I stepped in front of him and put my left hand in front of the blowgun.

"This isn't very sporting of you," I said.

"Get out of the way," he ordered.

"No," I said.

"It's your funeral," he said and blew. The dart tried to fly out, but impaled itself on my hand instead. The ninja leader stared at my hand, his dart sticking out if it, then at me. "That's impossible! There's curare on that dart. You should be dead."

"I get that a lot," I said. I laughed as I pulled the dart out of my prosthetic hand. I turned the point toward the head ninja. "I believe this is yours."

He stepped backward. I stepped forward, bringing my knee high enough into his crotch to crack the pelvic bone. He collapsed, holding his groin, tears streaming out his eyes. I didn't feel any pity for him. He had just tried to kill me, after all, and who knew what other surprises he had.

The rest of the ninjas lay strewn around the floor. The audience broke into applause. The Oriental man stood smiling, silently acknowledging the applause with a simple nod. Eleven men had been knocked out, and he hadn't even broken a sweat.

He walked over to me and extended his hand. I shook it. Man had a strong grip.

"Thanks for your help, but I could have handled him," he said.

"I don't doubt it, but I figured I'd lend a hand, just in case," I said. "That was impressive."

"Thanks." He laughed. The man had a glow, kind of like a man in love, but I sensed the affection had more to do with the fighting than a woman. I couldn't help but like the guy, but I still had a job to do.

"My name's Rao," he said. He pronounced it "Ray-o".

"I'm Jack. Can I buy you a drink," I asked. Might as well see what he knew.

"Why not?" he said. The crowd was already moving on. As we stepped over the fallen ninja leader, Rao stopped and bent down.

"You are a coward and a fraud. I suggest you take some more lessons before you try to teach others," Rao said, as he pulled the hood off the ninja's head and tossed it on the floor.

KCON had its own makeshift bar in a boardroom off the main ballroom. The sign over the door said "Cantina". Guess the conventioneers didn't want to be mixing with the regular folks. Or Bach didn't want to risk a guest assassin having one too many in the hotel bar and spilling the beans about what was going on.

It was a nice setup. Top shelf open bar. From what I had gathered, convention membership was five thousand apiece for the week (and twenty thousand for a dealer's table), so I guess Bach could spring for the booze. Saved me from having to. I got a beer; Rao went with spring water. I tipped the bartender, a pretty blonde.

"Don't do alcohol," I asked, as we found an empty table in the corner. People were making deals all around us. I tried hard not to think on the nature of those deals.

"Only on rare occasions. It tends to slow me down, dull my reflexes. So tell me, Jack, why are you here? You don't seem the type," said Rao.

"What type is that," I asked.

"Killer."

"What makes you say that?"

"Your eyes. I can read eyes. Yours aren't those of an assassin," said Rao.

"I've killed people." That much, at least, was true.

"But it gave you nothing."

"What do you mean?"

"Assassins all get something from a kill. It can be anything from satisfaction to joy to feeding hatred or for vengeance. Your eyes tell me killing would take something away from you. Your eyes make you stand out," said Rao.

"Maybe I should wear sunglasses," I said jokingly.

"Maybe you should, at least to hide your true purpose. I wouldn't worry much. Most people don't get much from eyes. So why are you really here," asked Rao.

"Well, I do have a side job going." I showed him a picture of Joey Mozzano. "Do you recognize this man?"

Rao took the picture.

"Yes. He was here earlier in the week, but I have not seen him lately. I assumed he left," Rao said.

"You could say that," I muttered.

"Dead," he asked.

"Killed in his room by a sniper," I said.

"Ah," said Rao. "A killer dead among killers. Ironic. You seek his killer."

"Yes," I said.

"Why? What is he to you?"

"A reward," I said.

"Money? Is that all?"

"Curiosity. Justice."

"Curiosity I can understand, but justice? A killer is killed. Sounds like justice to me," Rao said.

"Interesting viewpoint for a hitman," I said.

"I'm not a hitman. I am an assassin."

"What's the difference," I asked.

"A hitman kills for money. An assassin kills for a cause or an ideal."

"What's your cause?"

"Justice."

"A just assassin. Wait a second. Rao," I said, pulling out my pocket program. "I saw your name. Here it is. 'The Honorable Assassin. Guidelines for the ethical killer in an unethical world. Plus tips on finding out who is bad enough to kill and how to get paid for it.' You're giving that course."

"Guilty as charged. You strike me as a man who might benefit from it. You should come."

"Maybe I will. An honorable assassin, huh?"

"Yes."

"Who do you kill? Drug dealers?"

"Sometimes. My prey are those who victimize the helpless innocent. Those beyond the reach of the empty justice of law," Rao said.

"Seems to me that most of your colleagues here could be on your hit list."

"Could be. I'm taking notes."

"So what about me?" I said.

"I haven't decided about you yet. I don't believe you are a gun for hire. Until you explained the murder investigation to me, I had no explanation. Now explain how finding a killer's murderer is justice."

"Strictly speaking, I suppose it isn't. I'm partly doing it for his grandfather."

"A friend of yours?"

"More like an old enemy."

"Curiouser and curiouser. Compassion for an enemy. A rare thing. I may learn to like you, Jack… What's your last name," Rao asked.

"Depends on the day," I said. "Right now, it's Frost. What about you?"

"A surname is given by one's parents. As I had no parents, I kept no surname."

"You were an orphan?"

"No. Just abandoned. My mother feared my father, so, pregnant, she left him. She gave birth to me on a Navajo reservation in Arizona, and left me there."

"Why was she afraid of your father?"

"He was Yakuza."

"Japanese mafia."

"Yes."

"Did he ever find you?"

"Yes."

"What happened?"

"Who are you really?" Rao asked with a smile.

"I told you."

"Of course you did. When you tell me the truth, perhaps I will tell you that story."

"Fair enough," I said.

"Your puzzle intrigues me. Tell me more, and maybe I'll help you find the killer."

What passed for my investigative mind told me that Rao might consider a potential heir of a criminal family a proper target for an "honorable assassin." However, my gut told me Rao wasn't the killer we were looking for. There was something about him that inspired me to trust him. "What the heck."

I gave him the details, then asked, "The times you saw Joey, was he alone? Did he get into any fights or arguments, have any trouble with anyone?"

Rao closed his eyes, thinking. "I saw him twice," he said, opening his eyes to look at me, "No, three times. Once in the dealers' room, and in two of the seminars. He was alone, and kept to himself. But I'll ask around." Rao smiled. "I love a mystery."

"You haven't asked about the reward," I said.

"Don't care about it. Money isn't everything."

"Interesting attitude."

"Worry too much about anything, money included, and you become a slave to it."

"True enough. I appreciate your help."

"Don't appreciate it too much. Wait and see it if does you any good."

VIII

"**S**O YOU WENT and told a total stranger just about everything," Annie asked in near total amazement that night back in our room.

While I understood the need for the question, it was the amazement that puzzled me. Surely we'd been married long enough for her to understand the difference between practicality and my brand of stupidity.

"If he's not the killer, then he may prove to be a valuable resource."

"And if he is?"

"I doubt that he is. Joey was shot to death; Rao wouldn't have needed a gun. But if I'm wrong, I'm counting on you two to stop him before he breaks my neck."

"Hope your wife is a good shot," Marty said from the sofa, where he watching some kind of reality show on the TV. "I might have a banana in my hand and not be able to reach my gun. Oh, yeah, you've got my gun, don't you?"

I was starting to like Marty.

"I think we can trust Rao, at least with this. Anyway, there are some other questions that need to be answered."

"Such as?" Annie cocked her head in a way that made her look very cute and delectable, and made me wish that Marty wasn't in the room. I looked at the TV, and saw that the host was about to throw someone off the show, so I knew there was no way I was going to throw Marty off his sofa island.

"Such as, motive. Why kill Joey? He wasn't currently involved in any serious family business. Was he?" I looked over at Marty, who shook his head no. "As for killing a potential family heir, it's too soon. Plenty of time to train a new one."

"Makes sense," Annie agreed. She glanced at the TV, a commercial was on. "Marty, why do people in your… organization… get killed?"

"Mostly, it's just business. Guy's moving in on you. Either you make him gone or you're gone. Guy's gonna rat you out: you gotta keep him quiet. Someone's switching sides: you can't let that happen, makes you look bad. Like I said, business."

The commercial over, the previews for next week's show came on. Marty took a time out to watch them. Then he continued. "Sometimes extreme discipline's needed, you know, an example for others. You tell someone to do something, he doesn't, that's disrespect. Or the guy can't do his job. Ain't no layoffs in our business."

"What about personal beefs," I asked, amazed at Marty's honesty.

He shook his head. "Guys who can't handle personal problems without blood got no future in our… organization. Hell, they got no future. So if it's personal, it's no 'friend' of mine. Course, given who all's here, Joey might have overheard something he shouldn't have. Or someone thought he did."

"Does that answer your question," Annie asked, joining Marty on the sofa. Another reality show, this one with models and fashion. Something for both of them. Annie liked it for clothes, Marty liked it for when the models didn't wear too many of them.

"Not really, but I do have another one."

I got two stares that said, "Shut up and let us watch the show." Of course I didn't. The show didn't interest me. Not one of the models looked half as good as Annie, and anyway, the one I liked got voted off last week.

"Why did Joey need two rooms? If he had a companion, he'd need only one. So why two? Marty?"

"That one's easy: guy was paranoid. Didn't want anyone sneaking in on him through the adjoining door. Also didn't want anyone to know exactly which bed he was sleeping in," Marty said.

"How well did you know Joey," Annie asked.

"Not real well. He was coming up in the ranks, and figured what he learned here might give him the edge he needed to take over the spot his grandfather used to have," said Marty.

"Who has it now," I asked.

"I ain't that stupid," said Marty. "Besides, I'm out of the loop. I just do bodyguard work for Mr. Mozzano."

"That's it," asked Annie.

"Yeah, mostly. I do the chauffeur bit and run errands."

"Seems like a cushy job," I said.

"It is."

"What's it pay?"

"Fifty a year, plus benefits."

"How'd you get it," I asked.

"Mozzano owes my family. My dad took a bullet for him back in the eighties, so he gave me the job. That's part of the other reason my job's so straight. My mother made Mozzano promise he wouldn't have me do anything illegal. He feels guilty enough about my dad to keep it."

"You like it," asked Annie.

"It's a job. I don't have any training or college. It's more money than I'd make anywhere else."

"Money's not everything," said Annie.

"Easy to say when you don't need any; much harder when you do. Now, if you don't mind, the swimsuit part is coming on."

I had another question, but couldn't think of it right then. What the hell, I thought, and sat down next to Annie to watch the show. After all, they were very nice swimsuits.

IX

"I HAVE TO admit, so far it's been interesting," said Annie, munching on a bread stick. We had spent Friday morning in seminars, and then regrouped for lunch in the hotel's restaurant. The food hadn't arrived yet.

"That's an understatement. Your husband almost got us kicked out," said Marty.

"Of the 'Murder by Hypnosis' lecture," asked Annie.

"No, of the whole convention," complained Marty.

"Honey, what did you do now," asked Annie. We had split up to cover more lectures. Marty and I had gone together to the hypnosis lecture, a decision he appeared to regret.

"It was no big deal," I said.

"No big deal? He volunteers to be hypnotized. The lecturer, who introduces himself as 'Doc', puts Jack under and tells him he's a chicken. Jack runs all over the room, flapping his arms and crowing like a rooster. Doc had to chase him down. Then Doc puts him back in a trance and he wakes up thinking he's a monkey. He runs all over again, climbing over chairs and beating his chest."

"I would have thought you'd have liked that part," I said.

"Wait a second, Jack. You can't be hypnotized," said Annie.

"What do you mean he can't be hypnotized," asked Marty.

"Jack was forced to go to the department shrink several times," said Annie.

"Some people thought I was unstable," I said.

"Gee, I wonder why," said Marty.

"That's what I said."

"Anyway, the shrink thought hypnosis might help, and tried it on Jack, several times. Jack played along at first, pretending to be under and making stuff up," said Annie.

"Hey, those two weeks were the best I ever spent in therapy."

"Eventually, the shrink caught on, and figured out that Jack is one of the small percentage of people who can't be hypnotized," explained Annie.

"You mean you were faking the whole time?" asked Marty.

"I would have told you sooner, but I didn't want to hurt your feelings, or insult your manhood," I said in an effeminate tone.

"What about at the end part?" asked Marty.

"That, too," I said.

"What happened at the end," asked Annie.

"While Doc had Jack under, he gives him a post-hypnotic suggestion. He would wake Jack up and he would be normal, or what passes for normal. Doc would end by saying 'thank you ladies and germs.' Jack would be possessed by an overwhelming desire to attack this other guy on the stage with a baseball bat."

"That doesn't seem all that nice," said Annie.

"The guy was in one of those padded suits they use in self defense classes, so the people get the feel of beating on someone without anyone getting hurt. Plus, it was a plastic bat."

"That doesn't seem quite as bad. I sense that's not quite what happened," said Annie.

"Hardly. Doc wakes Jack up and sends him back into the audience, then says the line. Jack gets up, grabs the plastic bat, and rushes the stage. Instead of going after the guy in the padded suit, Jack rushed Doc. Doc takes off running, with Jack on his heels."

"You think this guy would have put a word in the post-hypnotic suggestion to stop Jack," said Annie.

"I thought you said he couldn't be hypnotized?" said Marty.

"But he was pretending to be, so he would have to pretend the word worked. How'd you get around that one, Jack," asked Annie.

"The word was 'Aloha.' As soon as I heard the first syllable, I would scream at the top of my lungs and start swinging the bat," I said.

"You couldn't actually hear the word, so you couldn't be expected to stop," said Annie.

"You know me so well," I said.

"I know. It scares me sometimes," said Annie.

"Well, he scared Doc. Doc ran with Jack hot on his heels, the whole time trying to scream 'Aloha,' and Jack cutting him off by screaming and swinging. The chase spilled over into the hotel proper, through the lobby and the bar."

"I let him get the word out before we had to leave the hotel," I said.

"Why would you do that in the first place?" asked Marty.

"Sabotage."

"Sabotage?"

"Yep. Remember, when he began, he bragged about reaching triple digits in victims using his methods?" I said.

"Yes."

"If he taught his method to the hundred or so killers at his lecture, and they all reached triple digits, how many dead?" I said.

"At least ten thousand," said Marty, without missing a beat. I was impressed.

"By the time I was done, did anybody in there take him seriously?"

"No."

"Are any of them going to try 'Murder by Hypnosis,' or buy Doc's DVD?"

"I doubt it."

"There's your answer."

Marty took a moment to consider what I said.

"So there was a method to your madness. You weren't just playing a fool."

"Don't get me wrong. I love clowning around, but for something like that, even I would need a good reason. Also, your ten thousand estimate doesn't include the ten thousand additional innocents hypnotized into killing."

"Wait a second. I thought you couldn't hypnotize someone into doing something they wouldn't do if they were in control," said Annie.

"According to this Doc guy, that's not true. It's a lie the mental health professionals tell their patients so they will trust them. Actually, it's not entirely false. He says it would be hard to hypnotize someone into killing a person if they find the act repugnant, but there is a way around it. Hypnotize them to see the situation differently, like a video game, for instance. You can kill in a video game and nobody gets hurt, so if the person thinks they're in a game, there is no moral conflict. It also means that some people who have actually killed may in a way be innocent," I said.

"Scary stuff," said Annie.

"Almost as scary as your husband's chicken act," said Marty. "How was your lecture?"

"You mean 'It's only murder if you get caught. We'll teach you how not to. Get the best alibis money can buy'? Very interesting. They had some intriguing ideas which would definitely make the police's job harder," said Annie.

"Like what?" I said.

"Basics, like how not to leave behind fingerprints or DNA evidence. They even went a step further and suggested bringing fake DNA evidence to plant, like hair and blood. They went over disguise basics. Change your hair color, skin tone, add scars or facial hair," said Annie.

"You'd look adorable in a goatee," I said.

"If I ever go back to the carnival, it isn't going to be as a bearded lady. They also went over ways to add height or weight, use a lisp or limp to confuse witnesses. Escape routes were big, even to go as far as having two or three ready. The lecturer even runs a service where he provides you with witnesses who would swear under oath that you were with them at the time of said crime. You can set it up before the crime or after the fact, for about ten times the price," said Annie.

"How's that work, after the fact," I asked.

"The guy employs these people around the clock at a private club, members and guests only, so the witnesses' whereabouts are easy to verify. They do the menial stuff and get bonuses for the alibi stuff. Claims it's a million dollar business, and he was selling franchises," said Annie.

"Got to love the entrepreneurial spirit. Did you happen to do any work?"

"I asked around, mentioned having set up a meet with Joey, but that he hadn't shown. Like your new friend Rao, a few had seen him earlier. No one mentioned any trouble."

"Anybody who could be our shooter?" I said.

"If there was, they've probably bought an alibi by now. How about at yours," asked Annie.

"I was a bit busy, but nobody stuck out. What do you think, Marty," I asked.

"You want my opinion?" Marty was taken aback.

"Sure. You were there, and might have noticed something I didn't."

Marty chewed on his lip for a minute before answering. "No. Nobody comes to mind. And while you were monkeying around with the doc, I did think to ask a few people about Joey, the ones that I recognized. About how I was told to keep an eye out for him, but couldn't find him. "

I pretended not to notice Marty's "monkeying around" comment. "Any luck?"

"Naw. So, what are we doing next?"

"We should check out the 'It's Only Murder' guys. See where they were after Joey got shot."

Marty and Annie both gave me the "Why?" look, then she caught on. Great wife that she is, she let me explain.

"Bach's got a body to get rid of and a crime scene to clean. Who better than someone who's made a study of it? Be nice to know if any of them were on Joey's floor."

"I got that one," Marty volunteered. "I'll check with the hotel staff. Trust me on this. To most people, the help are invisible, but they usually know more than most people realize. I'll hit the night shift right before bed, and the early shift just after breakfast. Besides, one of them probably had to carry the carpet to the dumpster."

Marty's idea to question the staff was a good one. Made me wish I had thought of it. I decided to swallow the next monkey joke I thought of.

"So now what," I asked.

"Take in some more lectures and hope we trip over some clues," said Annie.

"I think I'll take the explosives seminar," I said, handing the program to Annie.

"Here's one I want to check out. Here's what the program says. 'Learn how to do your taxes from a professional CPA. Are bullets deductible? Which is the better foreign bank: Switzerland or The Caymans and why.' Maybe I can figure out a way to save us some money. Then I'm going to hit the 'Entrepreneurial Killer' seminar at four. Maybe I can get some new marketing ideas. Marty, you are welcome to join me," said Annie.

"For an accounting and marketing lecture? I don't think so," said Marty.

"Then you're with me again," I said.

"Suddenly, accounting doesn't seem so bad," said Marty.

"C'mon, it's on explosives: my specialty. It'll be fine. These are the only two lectures to choose from," I said.

"All right, I guess," said Marty. The waitress finally brought us our meal, when I noticed a familiar face come into the restaurant.

"Annie, that's the guy from the hypnosis lecture. Watch this," I said, standing up and walking over to the hostess podium where he was waiting to be seated.

"Hey, Doc," I said, waving my hand. Before I could say anything else, he shoved the woman behind him out of the way and bolted out of the restaurant, practically tripping over his feet.

"Wonder what's wrong with him," I asked aloud to no one in particular. Returning to the table, I gave Annie our "excuse yourself" signal.

As I sat down, she stood up. "You boys will have to pardon me. I have some calls to make before the next session starts."

When Annie had gone, I leaned in close to Marty. "Now that it's just us guys, I have to ask, what have you heard about Joey's love life? Was he big with the girls, or the guys, for that matter?"

Marty looked horrified. "Nah, he wasn't like that. He liked the dames."

"Anyone steady, or did he spread the wealth?"

Marty gave me a "guy to guy" smile. "He spread it every chance he got. Wasn't no broad gonna nail him down. Sure, he talked about getting married one day, but was waiting for an offer from one of the other families." I must have looked confused, so he explained. "Like in the old days over in Europe. Uniting two families either to make peace or strengthen connections."

I nodded understanding. "So did Joey like his women single or married? Or didn't it matter?"

"If he messed with married women, they were on the outside. Fooling with another wiseguy's wife or girl, that's like wearing red: it just ain't done."

"What's wrong with red?"

"Bad luck, but I see where you're going. Joey laid the wrong broad and somebody figured this as a good place for payback. But the stories I heard about him didn't mention no names that I knew. But there was this one time in Vegas…"

Marty's story would have to stay in Vegas. Lunchtime was over. It was time to get back to work.

X

Explosives—Learn the basics from how to blow up a car to how to destroy a skyscraper. Discover how to make explosions look like an accident. How to make or become a property assassin and supplement your income by getting rid of unwanted real estate for a fee.

"THE BOMBER IS the most misunderstood assassin. Many people consider him a coward because he kills from hiding and from a distance, but nothing could be further from the truth. A good bomber is an artist. Without being there, he must be able to foresee all contingencies," Arthur Glemmer droned on, extolling the virtues of bombers. It was weird, listening to him lecture. This was the type of psycho that I had spent years facing off against, defusing their handiwork before it could blow up. Problem was, I was undercover as his peer, and had to consciously restrain myself from smashing the guy in the face.

Glemmer claimed to be the biggest bomber on the East Coast. I had never heard of him, and what I could see of his bomb designs was fairly generic. Nothing original, nothing you couldn't find on the dark side of the Internet. The room was pretty crowded, maybe because of the horror of what the plane hijackers had done in New York. A lot of people had a morbid curiosity, and this was one way to satisfy it.

"Often, the best way to go about business is to make it look like an accident. Say you get a contract on a bakery that hasn't been paying protection money. The amateur bomber might lob some Molotov cocktails through the windows and let the place burn down. This is not the wisest course. It alerts the local police that it was arson and puts the heat—no pun intended—on your employer or client, which in the end is counterproductive. The professional bomber has more skills than just knowing explosives. He can pick locks and deactivate alarms on a par with the best cat burglar. Otherwise, he could never get in to do his work.

"The best way to have taken out that bakery is to use the boiler as your bomb. With a few minor adjustments, the boiler will blow up better than dynamite. To make sure the place burns, liberally dose it with gasoline," lectured Glemmer. Maybe I couldn't hit him, but I could make his life difficult. I started to laugh. Glemmer was insulted and incensed.

"You find this amusing, Mr.…"

"Frost. And yes, I do," I said.

"You are going to do it again, aren't you?" whispered Marty in my ear. He hadn't gotten over the embarrassment from the bit with Doc.

"Yep," I whispered back.

"After this, you're on your own. I'm not going to any more lectures with you," whispered Marty.

"Suit yourself," I whispered.

"You have something to share with the rest of us?" asked Glemmer, like some pompous high school teacher. I decided to treat him as such.

"Am I going to get detention? Or are you going to make me spit out my gum?" I said. It went over Glemmer's head. "I'm sorry, I just find you amusing."

"You think you could do a better job up here?" he asked.

"Even if I was stone drunk. You're complaining about amateurs, but, from where I sit, you're the amateur. Use a boiler as a bomb? Pour gasoline on the place? The gasoline leaves traces the fire marshals can detect. It is an oil burner? Why not use treated oil? Or find out what kind of oils they use in baking that are flammable and use them. The chemical traces won't arouse any suspicions, but the whole boiler thing will," I said.

"No, it won't. It's perfect," whined Glemmer.

"Perfect? Maybe in a fool's paradise. Boilers and fuel tanks don't just blow up. There are too many safety precautions built in. That'd be a red flag right there," I said.

"Okay, smart guy, how would you do it?" challenged Glemmer.

I thought about it a minute. I didn't want to give a room full of bomber wannabes a brilliant idea that might literally blow up in my face some day.

"Well? Either put up or shut up. We're waiting," mocked Glemmer, feeling confident I wouldn't think of anything.

Then it came to me.

"You're talking about a bakery, right? You want it to look like an accident, so why not a freak accident? The place has got to have fans and flour. Pour out the flour and let the fans put it up into the air. A spark will blow the whole thing up," I said.

"You think flour is flammable, and you're calling me an amateur?" mocked Glemmer cluelessly. I had him.

"You've never heard of dust explosions? Pretty sad," I said.

"Dust explosions?"

"Dust explosions happen when the air is filled with finely powdered particles. It doesn't have to be flour. For the bakery, it could be any sugar or starch, but flour would just be the easiest. Sawdust, soap, charcoal, or coal would work just as well. It often happens in coal mines. A spark or flame ignites the particles which start a blaze that travels through the cloud so fast, it causes a blast at least as destructive as your boiler. The baking oils could still be used to help the flames. It would be so bizarre, investigators would have no choice but to rule it an accident. Of course, this would take real skill," I said, knowing it would take more skill than anybody in the room possessed to do it without blowing themselves up, Glemmer included. "Not like your method. Of course, your method could be learned by watching almost any cop show arson episode. Probably where you learned it. You probably put bombs in cars to blow them up," I said.

"Best way to do it. Hook up the starter wire to the bomb, and once they turn the key, thar she blows," said Glemmer.

"Putting a bomb in is stupid, if you want it to look like an accident. The explosives leave traces. All you need is a full tank of gas. Stick a wire from the ignition in the tank, and instant bomb," I said.

"Many times car bombings aren't meant to look like accidents," said Glemmer.

"I suppose. It's just that so far, I haven't heard any original ideas out of you. I'm feeling kind of ripped off," I said.

Glemmer smiled. "You want to see original? I'll show you original. I am offering for sale the IBS 2000."

"I suppose I'm supposed to exclaim in wonder, 'What's the IBS 2000?'" I said.

"IBS stands for Instant Bombing System. It's ready to use right out of the box," said Glemmer.

"But does it make Julian fries," I asked.

"If you aren't going to be quiet, I'm going to have to ask you to leave," said Glemmer.

"Ask away, but unless you plan to move me yourself with the help of about five friends, I wouldn't get your hopes up," I said.

"Security, remove him," ordered Glemmer. Four guys in suits stepped forward. Each of them was about the size of a linebacker. This wasn't going to be fun.

They grabbed me and yanked me right out of my seat. I didn't resist. No point to it. A fight wasn't going to help anybody. Besides, I was way outnumbered by the steroid boys.

One turned to Marty. "You with him?"

"No," I said, before Marty could say anything. They left him alone, and dragged me back toward the exit. My soles weren't even touching the ground. "Hey, this is great. Saves wear and tear on my shoes. Once around the park, and then home for tea."

Before we made it to the exit, the four steroid boys stopped short.

"Hands off, gentlemen," said a voice. I looked back. It was Rao.

"Step aside, sir," said one of the steroid boys.

"No. Take your hands off Mr. Frost," said Rao.

"If we don't?" said the same steroid boy.

One of his large friends whispered, "That's the guy who took out the ninjas."

The first steroid boy was taken aback. The story had grown in the gossip mill. Last time I heard it told, Rao had taken out twenty ninjas blindfolded.

"He was causing a commotion," said steroid boy, but he let go. I got up on my own feet.

"That's what I do," I said.

"What Mr. Frost also does is explosives. He is an expert. I am here to learn, but Mr. Frost seems to feel Mr. Glemmer is not qualified to teach. I have paid a great deal of money to be here, but if what I am being taught is substandard, I will want a refund."

There was some mumbling of agreement from the crowd.

"I would prefer it if Mr. Frost was here to verify Mr. Glemmer's information. If he knows his craft, he has nothing to fear from Mr. Frost's presence. If not, he saves us from using bad information."

"I have to escort Mr. Frost out," said steroid boy.

"You'll have to go through me. If you want to try, I suggest reinforcements," said Rao.

"That would be unfortunate," said steroid boy.

"Yeah, for you. Rao will rip you to shreds," I said.

Steroid boy looked to be deep in thought. I half expected his lips to move.

"If this information is not up to date or accurate, Hanson Bach has a lot to answer for, doesn't he?" said Rao to the crowd. There were several cries of agreement from the killers in the audience. "Why don't you get him, so we can discuss the problem?"

"Mr. Frost can stay. I don't think we need to bother Mr. Bach with this," said steroid boy, nervously.

"I agree," chimed in Glemmer, just as nervous.

"We don't. Get Bach," said Rao.

"Yeah, get Bach to where you dunces belong," I said. Rao gave me an unflattering look. "Too much?"

"A bit," said Rao. The steroid boys left, presumably to get their boss.

"By the way, thanks," I said.

"My pleasure."

"Sorry, for the interruption. Please, tell us more about your bomb in a box," I said, as I retook my seat. Marty moved in, and Rao sat next to me.

Glemmer decided to make the best of things.

"I designed the IBS 2000 myself. It is a self-contained system that uses your victim's own movement as the trigger for the explosion," said Glemmer.

"So you invented the trip wire," said Rao.

"Hey, I was going to say that," I said.

"Great, Tweedledee and Tweedledumber," complained Marty.

"Trip wire? Hardly. A trip wire requires the victim to physically activate the method of his own destruction. The IBS uses motion detectors—"

"Which send an electric impulse to the bomb. It's been done," I said.

"Not like this. Sure, the IBS can use motion detectors to activate the bomb, but it can do much more than that. It can imprison the victim, so you can question them via remote. You can get fake confessions, suicide notes on video. You can get the victim to take the blame for his own death. Plus, it's plug and play. Comes with three camouflaged explosives. My personal favorite is the framed picture, like this one here," said Glemmer, holding up a large landscape painting.

"You hang it in a hall or an office and it doesn't look out of place. Under the innocent looking artwork is a half inch thick layer of C4 plastic explosives." That was overkill. It could take out a small building, not just a room. "C4 should be the explosive of choice. It can be molded and shaped into anything, plus it's safe. Several other explosives detonate if you just drop them. Not C4. You can drop it, stomp on it, and it won't blow until you run an electrical current through it. I will show you a simple example of what the IBS can do here today. First, I'll need to set up a simple motion detector at the back door. Everyone follow me," said Glemmer, with the painting in hand as he walked to the back of the room, to stand beside the only door. The motion detector was the same type used by most home security systems, white plastic with a tiny red light "eye", except it had a suction cup for easy mounting. Glemmer attached it to the wall and flipped a switch on it. The little red light went on, indicating it was active.

"This little baby is wireless, so there is no need to run a line. If someone opens the door, it can either blow or start a timer. I prefer the timer. Gives them a chance to get in, so the door doesn't shield them from the blast," said Glemmer.

Just then, the door opened, knocking the painting from Glemmer's hands. Bach and the steroid boys walked in. The electric eye flashed.

"Frost—" scolded Bach, but I cut him off cold.

"Glemmer, that painting doesn't really have C4, does it? It just a demo, right," I asked.

"No, it's ready to sell."

"It wasn't actively receiving was it? The motion detector just lit up," I said.

"What do you think, I'm stupid?" said Glemmer. I didn't answer. I heard a beeping from the painting. Glemmer looked down at the back of the painting, and his jaw dropped. "Oh, shit."

"What?" I said, afraid I already knew the answer.

"The timer started," said Glemmer.

"Well, shut it down," Bach ordered.

"What he said," I echoed.

"I can't. It's designed so it can't be turned off," said Glemmer.

"We're gonna die," said Marty.

"Nobody's going to die. I need everyone to remain calm." I started assessing the situation. "I thought you said it wasn't active."

"It wasn't. The fall started the timer, not the motion detector."

"How long do we have?" I asked.

"It's counting down from two minutes."

"Great. What happens if the motion detector goes off now?" I asked.

"Boom."

"Nobody move," I said. Glemmer must have thought I meant everyone but him, because he started to run. I cold cocked him with my left hand. With all the steel in the prosthetic, it must have felt like a crow bar smashed his face. He hit the floor. I held back just enough so he wasn't knocked out. I needed him conscious.

"What kind of timer is it? Any other motion detectors, mercury switches, or such? Radio backup against the wires being cut?" I asked. If it did, I couldn't move it without a risk of setting it off.

"No, none of that. Just a timer," Glemmer said. I was already on my knees, checking things out. The digital clock was counting down. It read 00:43, then 00:42, then 00:41. You get the picture.

I pulled my tools out of my left sleeve. I never leave home without them. It's an idiosyncrasy that has saved my life on more than one occasion. I kept them on my prosthetic wrist in a wrap-around wallet type case. I needed the mini-scissors. There were wires to be cut.

"Can you shut it down?" asked Bach. Sweat was forming on his forehead.

"If I can't, you'll be among the first to know," I said, but I was playing with his head. The timer was down to 00:27.

This job was simple. The timer was pretty standard for bomb making, nothing fancy or complex. This was the type of bomb the bomb squad never saw before the fact, so the timer had nothing to befuddle a specialist of my experience.

There were two wires leading from the timer to the C4 under the painting. There was none of the "cut the red wire, not the blue wire" crap. I snipped then both. No wires, no circuit. No circuit, no spark. No spark, no explosion, but Glimmer didn't know that.

I turned and yelled, "Boom!"

He pissed in his pants.

"Not," I said, holding the timer in my hand as it harmlessly reached 00:00. "This has been a test of the emergency bombing system. If this had been a real explosion, we'd all be dead. I return you now to your lives, already in progress."

"You did it?" said Rao, patting me on the shoulder.

"We're not going to die?" said Marty.

"Yes. No," I said. Marty lifted me up in a bear hug.

"Marty, I didn't know you cared," I said.

Bach was staring at the painting.

"It this thing harmless now?" he asked.

"Not exactly, but it won't be going off accidentally," I said. Bach reached down to pick it up. I beat him to it. "I think I'll hold on to it, if you don't mind."

The look in his eyes told me he did, but he wasn't in a position to argue. The painting held at least five figures worth of C4. From my point of view, I was doing a public service by making sure the painting didn't end up in the wrong hands.

"If it had gone off, how big would the explosion have been?" asked Bach.

"Big enough to wipe out all of the KCON sections of the hotel, probably part of the lobby. Not to mention the ceiling and floor. If we are within thirty feet of a support beam, this part of the hotel would have collapsed in on itself," I said, adding, "And brought in the police, the FBI, and Homeland Security."

Bach turned on Glemmer.

"We need to talk," Bach whispered. Glemmer stood up, wet pants and all. There was still fear in his eyes.

"My work here is done," I said, walking out with the painting. Marty and Rao followed behind me.

"I need a drink," said Marty.

"Me too. C'mon, I'm buying," I said.

XI

"**J**ACK, MAN, YOU were so cool in there," said Marty, as he downed a double shot of whiskey. We had taken up a table in the Cantina.

"Makes Jack Frost an apt name, wouldn't you say?" added Rao slyly. He was still trying to figure me out.

"The Ice Man was taken too many times over," I said.

"So Jack Frost isn't your real name?" asked Rao.

"Is Rao yours?" I countered, knowing that at some point he had to have a last name.

"Point taken," said Rao. He was still drinking bottled water. I was drinking a fuzzy navel, so I got the calming effects of the alcohol and something healthy from the O.J.

It's funny, back when I was on the force, they used to call me Jack Frost because I was cool under pressure. Part of why they set me up under that name. Shrink said I had a subconscious death wish, but I wasn't suicidal, so I put myself in situations that were dangerous. Typical shrink BS, although I will admit I never felt more alive than I did when I was in danger. Danger was more of a drug than a death wish. Sure, it was always in the back of my mind, but I wasn't overly worried about getting hurt, so I would go into situations that other cops would only go into at gunpoint. Falling in love with Annie changed all that.

I still got the same thrill from danger, but fear was now part of the equation. Not fear of being hurt and dying, but fear of not being able to be with Annie. I still was the best on the bomb squad, but I did it more from a sense of duty than for the thrill of solving a puzzle and beating the odds. Today was no different. I got a thrill from defusing Glemmer's IBS, but my big worry was never seeing Annie again. I used to tell her I loved her every time we parted, because I knew there was the chance that would be the last time I saw her. I had gotten out of that habit. That was going to change. When I saw Annie again, I was going to give her a big kiss and tell her I loved her.

"I've never been that scared in my life. Does it always feel that intense?" asked Marty.

"It varies, but yes, pretty much," said Rao.

"Man, Jack, I wouldn't want your job for all the money in the world," said Marty. The booze and the post-traumatic euphoria were loosening up his tongue

"Jack's job?" asked Rao, his interest perked.

Marty looked panicked, realizing he had said more than he should have.

"You know, dealing with bombs all the time. I'd be afraid they'd blow up on me or something," covered Marty.

"That is a worry," I said, holding up the painting. Marty looked very uneasy.

"That thing won't blow up now, will it?" asked Marty.

"Not unless we zap an electric current through it," I said.

"It's just creepy, you holding onto it," said Marty.

"Don't worry, I'll put it up in the room," I said.

"Hey, your room's next to mine. If that thing explodes, won't it get me, too?" asked Marty.

"Only if it explodes, which it won't. Besides, I have an idea of how to use it in a practical joke on Annie," I said.

"Practical joke?" asked Rao.

"I'll rig it up so it looks like it's a bomb again, and pretend to find it in the room," I said.

"That's a sick joke to play on your wife. Why does she put up with you?" asked Marty, not bothering to hide his genuine amazement.

"Because I'm cute. There won't be any risk of it going off. Besides, it will only fool Annie for about two seconds, before she realizes it's a fake. Kinda like taking the point off a dart and then throwing it at somebody. Annie's done worse to me," I said.

"Like what?" asked Marty.

"She shot me," I said.

"I can understand that. She use blanks," asked Marty.

"No, real bullets," I said.

"I heard about your wife's contest with Jacob the gunsmith. She couldn't have missed you, unless she wanted to," said Rao, defending Annie.

"She didn't miss. Got me right in the chest."

"And you're still breathing?" asked Marty.

"I was wearing a bulletproof vest." Plus, she was kind enough to use a .22. A lot less bruising, than way.

"Why?" asked Rao.

"We were in a bad situation." Actually, we were undercover as the Frosts. "We were both surrounded by five people with guns. It was more people than we had a chance of taking out. We needed something to shock and confuse the people who had us in their sights. Annie felt shooting me was it. I fell, then she shot out a fuse box. Everything went dark. The five fired. Annie got four of them, I got the fifth."

"That's not exactly a practical joke. Sounds more like she saved your life," said Rao.

"Yeah, he's right," said Marty.

"Okay. Another time she pretended to accidentally pull the pin on a hand grenade. The grenade was a dud, but I didn't know it," I said. That was back before we were an item. We had kind of a love/hate thing going. She thought she was being cute, but I actually thought it was real.

"What did you do?" asked Marty.

"I grabbed it and dove to the ground, throwing myself between her and the grenade, until I could depress the pin lever with my finger. I had both hands back then. I grabbed the pin from her and put it back in," I said. Annie had done it in the squad room the QRT and bomb squad shared, as members of the city's crisis squad. She had expected me to freak and throw it. What I did shocked the hell out of her. Also made her look bad when she confessed it was a dud, and that she had done it on purpose as a joke. I had been asking her out for what seemed like forever. To make up for it, she finally said yes, so that time I turned her down. She started sending me flowers and asking me out after that. I ended up relenting, and the rest is history.

"Well, I guess it's no worse than that," said Marty.

"Actually, it's much nicer," I said.

"How do you figure?" asked Rao.

"She at least knows there is a chance I could defuse it," I said.

"Any luck finding your killer?" asked Rao.

"He knows?" stammered Marty.

"Sure. Rao even offered to help us out. Unfortunately, no answers yet," I said.

"I have been nosing around, but so far, nothing. I'll keep looking. I have an appointment I have to keep. Are you going to the Assassins' Ball tomorrow night?"

"Wouldn't miss it," I said. The brochure listed the Assassins' Ball as the social highpoint of KCON 14.

"Good. I'll see you there," said Rao, as he got up to leave.

Once he was gone, I turned to Marty. "What do you want to do now," I asked.

"I'm not going to any more seminars with you," said Marty.

"You mean you're not having a good time? I've been told I'm more fun than a barrel of monkeys," I said. Marty gave me a dirty look.

"Sorry. Annie's in her seminars until six, and the other seminars don't interest me."

"What are they?" asked Marty.

"Let's see. At four, opposite the 'Entrepreneurial Killer' seminar is 'The second rule of Assassination is leave no witnesses. What to do when you're a witness.' At seven, the choices are: 'Assassin Law: When a contract is written in blood, you have to read between the lines. How to read the fine print,' and 'Who really killed JFK? Come and meet him.'"

"The JFK thing sounds interesting," said Marty.

"Not for me. With my luck, I'd wind up in the middle of the whole conspiracy thing," I said.

"You're probably right about that. There's a demo in the dealers' room for body armor that just started. That sounds interesting," said Marty, looking at the program.

"Body armor demo?" I said.

"Yeah. They dress some guy up in it and let the audience take pot shots at him," said Marty.

"Sounds like fun. I'll go. Annie's gun demo is at eight. Might as well see what they're like," I said, finishing my fuzzy navel and picking up the painting bomb.

"You're not bringing that thing, are you," asked Marty.

"I told you, it's safe."

"It still makes me nervous," said Marty.

"Okay, I'll run it up to the room, then meet you at the demo," I said.

"Thanks," said Marty.

XII

BACK IN THE room, I called Sarah to make sure that Maggie had picked up Marty's gun. I then gave her some homework, offering her double time for working into the night. With Mozzano covering expenses, I should have made it double time and a half, but I didn't want to spoil her. After that, I rigged the fake timer and hung the painting on the wall. I hid the painting that was already up there behind the dresser, then headed down to the body armor demo. It had already started.

One of the venders had dressed up some poor sap like the Tin Woodsman from *The Wizard of Oz*. He had metal bolted on him like he was some boiler-plated knight, including what looked like a military issue metal helmet with a welder's visor attached to the front. The whole set up reminded me of a couple of nuts who had put on a couple of homemade versions of this armor to rob a bank. The cops arrived before they got away. Problem was the cop's bullets were bouncing off the guys, and they were walking calmly down the street taking pot shots at anything that moved. The cops ended up commandeering every firearm from a nearby sporting goods store to take them down.

Some of the killers were getting their jollies by shooting at the guy, but from a distance and behind sandbags. The area had been cleared because of the risk of ricocheting bullets.

I found Marty watching the whole thing, enthralled.

"So, you want one for Christmas," I asked.

"This is incredible. The guy's bulletproof. Nothing could stop him. Why doesn't the army use these things," asked Marty.

"Limited visual range. The guy can barely turn his head, and the armor weighs so much, he moves at the speed of a hyper turtle. Send a guy into battle like that, the enemy would sneak up behind him and tip him over. Bet you he can't get off his back any better than a turtle can," I said.

"But they couldn't hurt him," said Marty.

"Sure they could, just rip the armor off. Gas is an option, but then they could just put in a gas mask. I got it. If you don't want to waste time, pour napalm over him and cook him like a lobster in his shell. Still, almost nobody outside of the military has napalm, and as long as he has enough bullets and the good sense to keep turning around to check his back, he'd be pretty hard to take down. I sure wouldn't want to be the one to do it," I admitted.

"Me neither," agreed Marty.

The demo was over, and the Tin Woodsman left, presumably to go back to Oz. The dealer began extolling the virtues of more traditional body armor.

"It doesn't offer as complete protection as the metal armor, but it can be worn underneath clothing," said the dealer. True enough. I had a Kevlar vest. It was lighter, sure, but it was at best bullet resistant. A true bulletproof vest is bulky, hot, and weighs a ton. Not exactly the last word in comfort. I figured I might as well check out what he had.

"This seems much thinner than my Kevlar vest," I said.

"That's because it isn't Kevlar, it's Twaron. It's made in Europe, and is thinner and stronger than Kevlar. For that reason it's used a lot for women's vests. Can even mold it for the feminine shape. Could do that with Kevlar, too, but Twaron is more comfortable. The one you're holding is rated II-A, which means it will stop ninety percent of all handgun fire. You can get III, but it's twice as thick and heavy, which defeats the advantage over Kevlar. Of course, a III Kevlar is also twice as thick as a II Kevlar. I can get you rifle vests with titanium, steel, or ceramic plates, which ups the rating to III-A. That'll stop assault rifle and medium battle rifle rounds. You can go up to IV-A, which is the best, but you'll feel like you're lugging around a filing cabinet. The problem with the plates is the ricochet factor is increased. We can wrap Kevlar around it, to help absorb the bullets and the fragments somewhat, but that again adds to the weight," he said, all without taking a breath.

"Wow, everything you wanted to know about body armor, but were afraid to ask," I said.

"Exactly. Now which one can I wrap up for you? Or would you prefer to wear it home?" he asked.

"Neither right now, thanks. Just browsing," I said.

"How about this," he said, holding up a black overcoat.

"A trenchcoat? Why would I want that?" I asked. Trenchcoats are a bit stereotypical for PI's.

"It's made from Twaron, so it's bullet proof, and it even has inside pockets, so you can add on titanium, steel, or ceramic plates. Button it up and it covers you from neck to ankles."

"But is it machine washable?" I asked.

"No, not even dry cleanable. Hand wash only, but the fabric covering the Twaron is waterproof, so you can wipe it clean with a sponge. Here, try it on."

I did, and it fit well enough.

"It's still heavy, and it doesn't move like a normal coat," I said.

"True, but a normal coat won't stop a nine millimeter slug. It moves like stiff leather, which is the look we were going for."

The coat did look like a decent imitation leather.

"It's on special for the show only, thirty-five hundred dollars."

"That vest was only five hundred," I said, pointing to the price tag.

"Lot more material, and a lot more goes into the coat. You gonna take that with you?" he asked, using the hard sell. I never responded well to it.

"A little pricey for me, but I got a friend here who might like it. Maybe he's been by." I described Joey to him. The dealer shook his head.

"But if you bring him by and both buy a coat, I'll give you a good deal."

"Let me think about it," I said, handing him back the coat.

"No problem. Take my card, in case you change your mind. We also do armored cars, yours or ours."

"Already got one on loan, but thanks," I said.

I decided to try to find where Marty went. I thought he might have wandered off, when I saw him being dragged out the back door toward a stairwell by two teenagers in gang colors. It didn't look like he was going willingly. I moved close enough to see that one had what looked like a ceramic knife. Just as deadly as steel, but it didn't set off metal detectors.

I didn't have anything resembling a weapon. I ran to Jacob's table.

"Jacob, you wouldn't happen to have my hand ready yet, would you?"

"Not yet, but it should be done by Sunday morning."

"I need to borrow a gun. Just for a couple of minutes," I said, regretting not following Annie's advice to pick up a plastic one like she had.

Jacob smiled. "What's your pleasure?"

"Nine millimeter," I said. Jacob handed me one of his custom models.

"It's not loaded. Five minutes, and if security catches you with it, you are waiting to use the range, got it?"

"Got it," I said. I moved toward the stairwell as fast as I could without drawing attention.

I opened the door and heard fist hitting gut. As I stepped in, the pounding stopped, and one of the pair moved toward me.

"Move on, this is none of your business. It's Chieftain business," he said, accentuating his point by pointing the knife at me. I hit the blade with my left hand, and heard a satisfying clink. That's the disadvantage to a ceramic knife. It will stab and slice flesh, but hit it with something denser and it shatters like glass. A real hand would have been sliced open by that move. I followed up with a quick left roundhouse to the side of his head. The effect was equivalent to using a blackjack. The guy hit the floor like a sack of potatoes.

"Wrong. That's my friend you're using as a punching bag, so I'm making it my business," I said. Punk number two turned toward me with the intent of doing me bodily harm. The sight of the 9mm taught him the error of his ways.

"Smash the knife," I said. He tried five times before he succeeded.

"Hey, you're the guy who defused the bomb. That was so cool. We got no beef with you," he said. "How'd you get the gun in here?"

"I refused to give it up," I lied. Marty had been propped up against a wall for support, and he used this break to stand up. He was holding his stomach in a painful fashion.

"And they let you keep it?"

"I didn't give them a choice. What's your problem with my friend?" I said.

"He didn't give us our props," he said. I knew what the slang meant, but I couldn't resist the straight line.

"Props? You in a play?"

"Play? No man, props is slang for—"

"I know, proper respect," I said.

"That's right. He dissed us."

"How?"

"He bumped us."

"Did he apologize?"

"Yeah, but he looked at us funny when he did it, so we decided to teach him a lesson."

"Consider school closed," I said.

"No way, man. This isn't done until we say it is," he said, with the bravado of youth.

"Two problems with that. One, I got the gun. Two, I know where you live." Or where the Chieftains did. "Your Lombard Street crib may go boom some night unless this ends here. I ain't no local boy. You'll never find me, but I'll find you. This business is done. You take your buddy out of here and leave. Don't come back."

"But we got the rest of the weekend."

"Don't care. I see you or any Chieftain again, I'll shoot you, then blow up the rest of you. Any questions?"

"No, man. You made yourself crystal." He picked up his buddy, who was groggily coming to, and headed out the door.

"You okay?" I asked.

"Yeah. Thanks," said Marty. "I didn't know what to do."

"It happens, even to me. You're young yet, you'll learn, or you won't get any older."

"Not that I'm complaining or anything, but why'd you help me? Those guys could have hurt you."

"You're here with Annie and me. We take care of our own. You've been straight with helping us, so I wasn't about to let someone else make a monkey out of you. That's my job," I said. Marty let the monkey crack go without comment.

"You stuck your neck out for me. I won't forget it," said Marty, sticking his hand out. I shook it. "How did you get the gun?"

"Borrowed it from Jacob. I better get it back to him before he freaks."

XIII

S O FAR, WE had not learned anything useful in figuring out who had killed Joey. When I hit a brick wall, I usually sit and review the facts thus far. It didn't take long. I still had more questions than answers. I figured one place was as good to sit as another while I thought about all I didn't know, so I was back to hanging out in the Cantina.

For free booze, the beer was good. The peanuts were just okay. Annie was at her lecture. Marty was doing his best to be anywhere I wasn't. So far, he was doing a very good job, and had gone up to his room to calm down after the incident with the Chieftains.

Putting aside the big question of who killed Joey, there was the slightly smaller one of who knew he was dead. Annie, me, Marty, Rao, and, of course, Bach. Maybe whoever he got to clean up the crime scene. Find him or them and they might tell us something we needed to know.

And the clean-up—big job for a little scene. Judging from what I saw of Joey's body, there should not have been that much blood. Maybe whoever Bach got to do it was trying to impress the boss.

Then I had to wonder about the gangbangers. Punks whose idea of a hit was to drive by their victim spraying bullets. Or approach the mark and cap him up close and personal. Nothing fancier than that was needed on the street.

So why were they there? If word of the convention had trickled down to them, then one of the many CI's the drug unit used would have dropped the dime, and QRT would have closed the show the first day. Plus, they weren't what Bach would consider ideal guests. That stunt they pulled in the stairwell could have been messy and noisy and attracted way too much attention.

Adding it all up, it was exactly that—a stunt. One designed to look like a gang killing. By now, half the convention knew that we—or someone—were looking for Joey Mozzano, including the killer. Marty had been asking questions below stairs. Step one was complete. We had attracted someone's attention, made someone nervous. Now all we had to do was stay alive until we figured out who.

With that thought, I made a mental note to pick up a few things in the dealers' room that might help us survive the weekend. Maybe a Twaron gown that Annie could wear to the Assassins' Ball.

I was still dumbfounded by the enormity of it all. Every cop gets involved in murder investigations. Despite what people might think, a lot of them never get solved. With those that do, usually the suspects can be narrowed to a handful of people. Of all the conventioneers, the only ones I could confidently eliminate as suspects were Annie and me. I didn't think Rao had done it, but he was still under consideration. Marty wasn't high on the long list, but he was still on it. So was Mozzano. And the doorman, not to mention the maids. Hell, maybe the assassin misread the room number and shot the wrong guy.

"Is this seat taken?" said a voice. I looked up, and was surprised to be staring into the face of Hanson Bach. It took me a minute to answer, after I realized I was in no immediate danger.

"You're buying the drinks," I said, waving him to the chair. Bach snapped his fingers twice, and with his fingers indicated to the bartender to bring something to the table. The bartender jumped and brought a bottle of brandy and two glasses.

"We got off on the wrong foot. You saved my life, and saved me much aggravation by cleaning up Glemmer's mistake." He was slick, never mentioned the bomb. "I wanted to try to make amends. Will you drink with me?" Bach asked.

"Actually—" I started, but Bach cut me off.

"I insist on it. You will drink with me."

I crossed my arms over my chest and leaned back. "Really?"

"I could make you," Bach threatened.

"Or you could just say 'please'," I suggested. That caught him up short. It was not a thing he would normally do, but I guess he figured he owed me.

"Would you *please* have a drink with me?" The "please" came almost as easily as pulling teeth.

"Sure," I said. "You sure have an interesting way of making amends."

"I'm not used to people… disagreeing with me. Most find it unhealthy."

"I imagine they would. If you had only let me finish, you would have heard me say that actually I was partial to good brandy."

Bach laughed. "This is the very best." He poured us each a small glass. Handing me mine, Bach raised his.

"To your health," he toasted.

"I'll drink to that," I said. I let him swallow first. Bach was right about one thing. "This is good brandy."

"Thank you," said Bach. We sat in silence, sipping the brandy. "There is something about you that gets under my skin. Very few men have ever stood up to me, and almost no women. You and your wife are unique in that. You must be very good."

"We are the best at what we do," I said.

"I'm inclined to believe you. I've heard about Mrs. Frost's contest with the gunsmith in the dealers' room, and I saw your little episode at the explosives workshop. You know your stuff."

"Thank you," I said.

"It is I who should be thanking you. Had you not, shall we say, defused the situation, it would have made my life much more difficult." Explosions have that effect. "Despite our earlier problems, I find myself in an unusual position. In your debt."

I nodded sagely, trying to figure out where this was going.

"By way of saying thank you, I have a job offer."

"Is this anything like the job offer you had for my wife?" I said, harshly and foolishly.

"I was out of line. Of course, usually it doesn't matter what I do. It's good to be king," said Bach. "Anyway, I have been approached by a client who is offering one hundred million for an explosives job. It's the chance of a lifetime. Terms are ten percent now, the balance held in escrow until completion. The hundred million is after my twenty percent commission."

"That's a lot of money. Who do I have to kill?" I said. I had used the line before as a joke. There was nothing funny about it this time.

"A representative of some Mideast interests, whom confidentiality prevents me from mentioning by name, is offering the fee in exchange for a single American target."

"After 9/11? Why would you even consider such a thing? You're an American," I said.

"My first loyalty is to myself. After that, my loyalty can be rented," said Bach.

"What do they want blown up? The White House?"

Bach laughed at me. "Dear God, no. I'd never broker that deal," Bach said.

"Glad to hear it," I said.

"Not at that price. That would be a ten figure deal, minimum. No, the target they have picked out is the Statue of Liberty. They want it reduced to smoking rubble. I have a man I would normally offer this to first, but I hate being indebted to anyone, so the job is yours. You interested?"

"No."

"No?! Did you hear the money involved?"

"Yes," I said.

"Why on Earth wouldn't you do it?"

Damn good question. What self-respecting hitman would turn down a hundred million bucks? "I don't hit American targets. At least, not civilian ones."

"A patriot? How droll."

"That's part of it. The other is that whoever does the job will be subject to the second largest manhunt in American history. In my opinion, getting caught is almost assured, unless he wants to live out his life in a cave in Afghanistan. Once caught, there would be no plea bargain, unless you consider life without parole a bargain. I'll blow up cars and the people in them. I'll take down a building for a cut of the insurance. I may even do some pro bono work on a pedophile or two. But I'll leave the political stuff to the fools and fanatics."

Bach shrugged. "Whatever. I made the offer, so we're even. I still get my commission, whoever does it."

"If you really want to do me a favor, help me find Joey Mozzano's killer."

Bach finished his brandy and poured himself a second.

"I have made certain inquiries, but thus far, I have not learned anything worthwhile. The rumors have spread. I want the killer caught and eliminated, so the confirmed 'rumor' of his death will counteract the other rumors. I will share any information I learn with you. Furthermore, if you learn the killer's identity, I will triple what Mozzano is paying you if you bring me the information first. I will even give my word that the old man will be brought in on the kill."

"I'll keep that in mind," I said. Bach stood, taking the bottle of brandy with him.

As he left, I noticed that all eyes in the barroom were covertly trained on me, like they were trying to figure out who I was. Drinks with Bach was apparently very impressive. I was more worried about stopping whoever Bach was going to pass that job along to.

A lone man at an adjacent table did more than stare. He came over.

"May I join you?"

"Sure," I said. "Why not?"

XIV

T HE GUY TALKED too much, like a little kid who had no friends. The conversation was fascinating and frightening, like watching a train wreck. You know what's happening is terrible, but you still can't turn away.

"I love this profession. I mean, I get to do what I really love, and get paid for it. Don't you love it," he asked me. Guy had introduced himself as Charlie. He was in his mid-twenties, but already going bald. Someone might accuse him of murder, but no one would ever accuse him of being in shape. Charlie had enough of a belly to play Santa at Christmas without any padding. If a movie killer looked like this guy, it would have to be a comedy, but there was nothing funny about this guy. I looked at his eyes. Those orbs weren't the same as the killers' eyes I had seen before. The stone cold killers I had seen were real ice men, with eyes that were dark and somehow dead, like nothing mattered, even if they killed you. Charlie's eyes were different. He had trouble keeping eye contact, but his eyes were bright, almost happy. Charlie enjoyed killing, and those eyes scared me more than any ice man.

"It's a living," I replied, trying to impress myself with how long I could keep eye contact.

"It's more than that. It's an avocation. Heck," he said. Interesting. He could kill, but wouldn't swear. He also didn't drink, apparently. He was sipping a cola. I still had my brandy and a half-finished beer. He gave off the impression that being in a bar was something "naughty". I'm sure my former shrink would have had fun with this one. "If I didn't get paid for it, I'd do it for free. Heck, sometimes I do it for free. What about you?"

"For free?" I said, unsure exactly how to reply. "I don't do much for free."

"I hear you, but I don't mean a job. I meant a random victim, just for kicks. You ever do that," he asked, excited.

"No," I said. I could not keep looking at this guy. If I did, I'd either get sick or hit him. Neither would be a good idea at the moment, so I stared into my brandy.

"Oh, man, you should try it. Nothing like it in the world. Hits are usually so cold and impersonal. When you do it on your own, you can take the time to get to know your victim. Give them personal service, you know what I mean?"

Unsure of what to say, but getting a cold, sick feeling in the pit of my stomach, I grunted. Charlie took it for whatever answer he wanted to hear.

"You do any freebies lately," I asked.

"Naw. Last time was about eight days ago. I finished my last job day before that, so it was a good week. Getting itchy, though. Trying to pick up some work. You know anyone who's looking?"

"Lots of people looking, but lots of competition, too," I said.

"I hear you. You must be big time to be meeting with Bach," said Charlie. I shrugged my shoulders, playing it cool. "You do a lot of work for him?"

"You might say we're in the negotiation stage," I said.

"I'd love to get in with Bach. Think you can arrange a meeting," asked Charlie.

"Honestly, I don't know. I barely know him, and don't want to screw up what I got going with him. Negotiations are tricky, especially with a guy like Bach. You know what I'm talking about," I said. I wasn't sure I knew what I was talking about, but Charlie nodded like he was in the know.

"Been there. Didn't mean to impose," he said.

"No problem," I said.

"You think maybe later…?" Charlie said, letting the question hang in the air. The answer came to me in a flash.

"Why not? It may be a few weeks before I can set up a meeting…"

"Sure, sure," Charlie said, pulling out a pen and writing on the back of a cocktail napkin. "When the time's right, drop me an e-mail," he said, handing me the napkin. I now had a way of finding this serial killer. Let me just state that Charlie wasn't the first killer here I wanted to see behind bars, and sadly, he probably wouldn't be the last. Problem was, I wasn't a cop anymore and, even if I was, there was nothing even resembling proof of a crime. Bar room bragging tends not to hold up in a court of law. When KCON was over, and I had passed along Bach's plans for Lady Liberty to the Feds, it would be time for a little sting operation with some friends in the BPD.

"By the way, what's your specialty," Charlie asked.

"Things that make you go boom," I said, pocketing the napkin.

"Explosives man? That's cool. That how you lost the hand?"

"Naw. That was a freak accident with a bottle of tequila and a snow blower," I said.

"You got drunk and your hand got too close, huh?"

"No. I was trying to catch the worm and didn't pull back in time," I said. Charlie couldn't tell if I was serious or not.

"That sucks. Not a bomb man myself. You don't get to see your work up close and personal. Ever kill face to face?"

"When I've had to," I said, truthfully.

"You ever do it with a partner?" Charlie asked.

"By *it*, you don't mean sex, I take it?" I said.

"Heck, no." He giggled, he actually giggled. "I mean the big *it*. The hunt and the kill," said Charlie, his eyes aglow.

It was time to drop into character. "I work with the missus sometimes, but we usually have separate targets."

"You're married? And she's one of us?" said Charlie, impressed. I wasn't exactly sure of everything being one of us entailed, but I knew it wasn't good. "That's amazing, man. You found a real lady killer. You are so lucky. I've never met a woman who understood me, not for long, anyway." Charlie gave me a wink, implying he killed his ex-lovers.

"Remind me never to fix you up with my sister," I said, using the joke to cover my nervousness. Charlie convulsed with fits of laughter. I was glad he hadn't been drinking, or the cola would have come out his nose.

"Your sister! You're hilarious," Charlie said, slapping my back. Great, I finally find someone who likes my jokes, and he's a serial killer. The universe seems to get a little more twisted every day. "What's the little woman do?"

"Guns," I said. "What's your specialty?"

"I make people disappear without a trace, but I vary my M.O. That's how most of the greats got caught, by using the same methods. When I'm working, I try and come up with new stuff all the time. On my own time, I'm doing a tribute, imitating the greats and their methods. I'm back to the great granddaddy," Charlie said.

"Manson?" I said. Charlie laughed.

"Manson? He's barely an uncle. I would have thought you would have guessed. You share the same name," he said. I couldn't come up with any serial killers with the name Gardner, until I remembered I was going by Frost. I still drew a blank.

"I thought Robert Frost was a poet, not a killer," I said.

"Poet! You're funny. Not your last name. Jack…"

"The Ripper," I finished.

"Bingo. I plan to go to Whitechapel in London in a week. I'll give the Brits a run for their money. I figured I'd do a warm up locally, just for the practice."

"When," I asked.

"Night before I leave, I guess," he said. That gave me six days to stop him. "Why? You interested?"

"What do you mean," I asked, confused.

"What I said before. Doing it with a partner. Always been a fantasy of mine. You seem like a cool guy. I can teach you a few thinks about doing it up close and personal," said Charlie, getting all shy and looking into his cola glass.

"Sounds like fun," I lied. "But the missus would probably get jealous of me working with someone else. You know how it is."

"Sure. Old ball and chain. Will you at least mention it to her?" That went without saying. Annie was never going to believe this. "Maybe ask her permission?"

"Okay, but I can't promise anything," I said.

"I understand. She could even come along, if she wants."

"It's nice of you to offer. I'll see what she says," I said, a sting operation already springing to mind. I stood up to go. "Speaking of which, I better go find her."

Charlie stood up and shook my hand. He had a grip like a dead fish.

"Let me know, and don't forget about the Bach thing."

"I won't," I said.

XV

The Entrepreneurial Killer. Learn new sources of income. For example, see a victim's family not as grieving but as a possible paying employer. Vengeance is big. You can give it to them wrapped up with a bloody bow, without the risk of getting caught themselves.

ANNIE HAD A busy day, which she filled me in on later. I was surprised by Annie's choice of seminar. I expected her to be interested in one on marksmanship or firearms, but she wasn't. They were all too basic, she said. Be kind of like teaching your grandmother to suck eggs. Not something I'd ever think of teaching grandma, or anyone else, for that matter.

Annie had hopes of learning some new marketing tricks. I had some qualms using the same marketing as killers, but Annie pointed out that we sometimes overlap in client base. It was true enough. Besides, we were doing as well as we were by diversifying.

The seminars were set up like almost every lecture. A podium in front, with rows of chairs facing the speaker. The chairs were almost all full. Annie managed to find a seat one away from the edge of a row, next to a gorgeous woman. She was the only other woman in the room and Annie was surprised one of the men hadn't snapped it up. Annie planted her lovely behind in it.

"Hi," said the woman. "I'm Rose."

"I'm Annie."

"Pleasure. Looks like we're outnumbered here," said Rose.

"Just a bit. It's a man's business, but as a consolation, for us to be here, we're probably twice as good as any man in the room," said Annie.

"Without a doubt," agreed Rose.

At that point, the lecturer walked in and introduced himself as Clinton Adams.

"Thank you all for coming. We only have a short time, so let's get down to business. We all know what that business is, so there's no need to state the obvious. What we need to look at is the traditional way the business works.

"Basically, someone wants someone else dead, but doesn't want to kill them directly. The reasons for this are many. Lack of skills is one of the biggest, but the most common is the need for an alibi. If John Smith is seen eating lunch in front of a hundred witnesses, he obviously couldn't have done the hit on Joe Jones, so Smith gets away with it.

"Who are the largest employers in our business? Those with money who work outside or above the law. Organized crime and governments, respectively. Problem for the freelancer is these folks tend to have their own people for most of their jobs. Now, for sensitive jobs where their own people would be too well known, organized crime is willing to hire out for the same reason as John Smith. For an alibi. For someone who knows how to keep his—"

"Or her," said Rose.

Adams glared, but continued on. "Or her mouth shut, this is an excellent source of income, but it is usually done through a middle man who takes a cut. Caution needs to be used when offered a similar deal from a government, particularly the bigger, more 'respectable' ones. Very often, they are looking for a patsy to pin the deed on.

"There is also some work available in the corporate world, but typically they prefer accidents to hits. If you can make a death look like an accident, you have a solid future ahead of you.

"The problem with these markets, is there is an overabundance of talent and the competition, if you'll pardon the pun, is cutthroat. It involves putting in time and paying dues. It can take years. Who needs it? There is an untapped market out there: the private individual.

"What are the most common reasons for someone to be killed? Anger, hate, jealousy, revenge, and greed are biggies. These are things the common man," Adams said. Turning to Rose, he continued, "and woman knows as well as the rich and powerful. Let's use an example. A woman finds out her husband is boinking the secretary. She wants to kill them both, but she doesn't own a gun, and her husband outweighs her by fifty pounds. If she did it and got caught, the neighbors would know, and so would all her friends and family. Besides, she doesn't want to go to jail. In the typical situation, she swallows her emotions and sues the guy for divorce. Best case scenario, she gets half, but has to watch as he shacks up with the floozy even before the divorce is final. She ends up looking like a chump. Don't you think if there was another option, she would take it?

"That's where you come in. If he's dead, she doesn't have to settle for half. She gets it all. Life insurance pays off, too. If she wants the secretary, too, you get double. The problem is, how do you hook up with her?

"The Internet is a biggie. Set up a website. For the right price, it can be done anonymously. Website do's—explain the service you offer and the benefits. Also what regions you are willing to work in. Website don'ts— don't list past jobs or anything that could connect anyone to you. Don't use your real name, ever. Don't list prices. Instead, try to get an idea of what they can afford, then milk them for every cent.

"Other pointers. Never meet in person. This way, they can't identify you, in case guilt makes them break down and confess to the police. Also, you avoid the inevitable sting, with the police playing the part of the client. All business can be conducted by e-mail and disposable cell phones, including pictures of the victims, along with schedules, etc. This also protects you from surveillance at a post office box, picking up your mail. You just need to be careful choosing your website host. Do not use your home computer. Use public ones, and vary the locations. Never the same place twice. Also, never let the client know exactly when or where the hit is going to be. This way, there are no last minute pangs of conscience or authorities to deal with.

"Always get the money up front, or as much of it as possible. Many people have a 'half now, half when it's done' policy. This isn't as risky as it sounds. Most people are too afraid of being caught to try and pinch pennies. If they do try to withhold payment, first threaten exposure. If that doesn't work, follow through. Then threaten to give them the same treat-ment they gave to the dearly departed. Then follow through. By doing the exposure first, you send a message that hitmen are not to be messed with. Or should I say hitpersons?" Adams said, directing his comments to Rose.

"Hitperson doesn't work for me. How about assassin?" said Rose.

Adams laughed. "Assassin, then. One other thing you may be tempted to do is try to blackmail a client. I don't recommend this. It's bad business, and you won't be regarded as trustworthy. Word will get out, and other larger clients won't go near you with a ten foot pole. Also, the former client may try to put a hit out on you.

"Another way to meet the disgruntled spouse is to make friends with a divorce lawyer. They can direct many clients to you."

Annie chuckled to herself, thinking she would have to mention this to our office mate, Bill.

"Read the papers for stories of rape, molestation, murder. Remember, most people are not like you, and are too scared or ignorant to take vengeance into their own hands, which makes them feel helpless. Helpless victims are full of rage. Send anonymous notes to crime victims and their families, mentioning your services and listing your website. Remember to never touch the paper or envelope directly. Never lick it, as that leaves behind traces of DNA. Wear latex gloves and a rubber bathing cap. You will look ridiculous, but it will prevent fingerprints or hair from being left on the letter and later used as evidence against you.

"Rage will help negotiations from your point of view. Angry people tend to not haggle much over price, as long as they can afford it. When you get their personal information, try to get a social security number, and then order a financial report. Use this to set your fee."

Adams shared his marketing wisdom, enlightening the masses in the process. A couple of hours later, it was over.

"What did you think?" Rose asked Annie, as the crowd stood and moved like cattle out the back door, into the main ballroom.

"He had some good ideas, but it seems like it would be a lot of exposure for a limited pay off," said Annie.

"I'd have to agree with you. Penny ante stuff, although I suppose it would help pay the bills. Makes me happy that I don't have those kinds of worries. Most of my headaches come from running a business."

"What kind of business," Annie asked.

"I own a brothel on the outskirts of Las Vegas, the Preying Mantis Ranch," explained Rose.

"You're a madame? Then why…"

"Am I here? Madame is my day job. I was an assassin first."

"I've gotta hear this story," said Annie.

"Not much to tell. I just invested my earnings in the PM Ranch. Smartest move I ever made. Look, I'd love to talk shop, but first I have some business to take care of. I noticed some local street talent last night, but couldn't stop to talk. I wanted to see if I could find her tonight."

"So you are not only an assassin, but a madame and a hooker talent scout," asked Annie.

"Pretty much. In Nevada, prostitution is legal. At most brothels, it's a job. Salary, benefits, bonuses, and a health plan. I even offer dental. In the rest of the country, it's more like slavery. I like to help out with freedom when I can."

"A sex industry underground railroad?"

"Exactly. Plus, if I'm recruiting, I can deduct the trip. I certainly don't want to claim KCON on my taxes."

"Aren't you worried about the pimps coming after you," Annie asked.

"Hardly. It would be their funeral. I usually try to sneak the girl away. If I have to, in order to make things run smoother, I'll give a pimp a 'recruitment fee' to give up any claims on the girl. I know talent, girls who will enjoy the work and not become too cynical and jaded. Based on looks alone, you could make a fortune," said Rose.

"Thanks, I think. You offering me a job," asked Annie.

"No, you don't have the right temperament. You already seem content. Boyfriend, husband, or girlfriend?"

"Husband."

"You in love?"

"Very much."

"Happy?"

"Deliriously."

"I envy you. I've never been in love," said Rose.

"Never?"

"Almost never. In my line of work, it's difficult. Is your husband here?"

"Yes."

"I'd like to meet him."

"I'm sure that can be arranged. He's around somewhere."

"First, I need to finish my recruitment. Care to tag along? I'll tell you the rest of my story when we're done."

"Why not? Might be interesting."

XVI

THERE WEREN'T THAT many working girls around the Hotel Royale. For one thing, where it was located was no longer the heart of the hotel district. That time of the evening, the only ones hanging around the outside were some cabbies hoping for a fare who wanted to see the Inner Harbor, grab a bite to eat in Little Italy, or experience what passes for vice on the historic Baltimore Block.

Howard Street really wasn't an ideal location for a self-employed pavement princess. North of the hotel was Maryland General Hospital, where all the beds were put to a healthier purpose. South was the theater district, with the newly restored Hippodrome Theater as its shining centerpiece. The police patrolled that area a little more heavily than most, City Hall not wanting a random mugging or the indecent sight of a hooker to ruin anyone's expensive night out.

But like most creatures of the night, the girls were there, you just had to look for them. Around the corner and up the street there were small businesses that closed every evening, leaving only dark streets and convenient doorways. Midway between the hotel and hospital, there was a parking garage that served hospital patients and visitors by day and another clientele by night. Walk a little ways west and the outdoor stalls of the Lexington Market had a variety of sins for sale.

Chandra was a seventeen-year-old girl working the streets. The girl had no horror story that led her down this path. She was a young woman on her own, and she needed money to live. Chandra made no excuses. She did what she did to survive, but kept her eye on getting somewhere better.

Unlike most of the girls, Chandra worked the hotel—not out of it, just in front of it. The nighttime doorman knew her, and so did the bell captain, both of whom were always glad to steer her some business and look the other way if a customer wanted to show her his room. It meant kicking back a little money, and the occasional freebie, but it kept her out of the usual hooker haunts. It was a matter of feeling safe.

The majority of her customers were nobody dangerous, just family men looking for a little out-of-town thrill. Most of what they thought was kinky was relatively tame, usually things their wives wouldn't do. With the white and Asian ones, sometimes just being with the dark-skinned Chandra was kinky enough, having sex with a black chick being part of their big-city experience.

Chandra didn't care what they thought or wanted, as long as they paid. To her, it was a simple business arrangement. She provided the thrill, the men provided the cash, and everyone was happier for it.

When Chandra saw the brunette and the redhead leave the hotel and come toward her without pretense, she shook her head, thinking that it took all kinds.

"Evening, ladies. What'll it be? A little threesome," asked Chandra.

"It's not like that," began Annie, but Rose waved at her to relax.

"Of course not. Kinky is extra, and the price is per head," said Chandra.

"If that's true, I can only assume your rate for women is half that of men," said Rose.

"Cute, but I charge by the big one, not the little one."

"We're not here for us," said Rose.

"Oh, a thing for your boyfriends? Or your boss? If it's a bachelor party, the groom and best man are included in the price. Anybody else is extra," explained Chandra.

"As I said, we're not here for us. We're here for you," said Rose.

"Obviously."

"We want to talk to you," said Rose.

"Talk or screw, I still get paid," said Chandra.

"For you not to listen will cost you. I'd like to offer you a job," said Rose.

"For the night or the week?"

"Indefinite."

"Like as what? Some guy's mistress?"

"Same line as now, just better working conditions."

"What are you talking about?"

"I want you to come work for me."

"You sound just like Chunkie."

"That your pimp?"

"He's the pimp that thinks he controls the neighborhood. I don't work for him, and it pisses him off something fierce. Even then, I gotta give him a cut for street rights," said Chandra.

"Why don't you work for him," asked Annie.

"I ain't no dumb whore, giving some man all my money that I earned with this," said Chandra, rubbing her hands from breasts to thighs. "I ain't giving up any more than I have to. Not to Chunkie, and not to any white bitch who thinks she's a pimp."

"I'm no pimp. I'm a madame."

"Pimp with a fancy name is still a pimp. I ain't working for you or Chunkie."

"Why doesn't this Chunkie force you," asked Annie.

"He's tried. I just take a week or so off. I ain't living no hand to mouth existence. I got some bucks in the bank. My vacation hurts Chunkie. Just his cut is as much as any three of his junkie hos take. Don't get me wrong. I don't screw three times as many guys, I just make more."

"So, you don't do drugs," asked Rose.

"Hell, no. I ain't putting that shit in my veins. I got more respect than that. Chunkie gives his girls heroin. Makes them easy to manipulate, but he can't manipulate me like he can them," said Chandra.

"I'm sure." Rose smiled. "What do you think, Annie? She clean?"

"Eyes are clear, no track marks on the arms or legs. She's probably telling the truth," said Annie. Rose grabbed her by the wrists and pulled, paying close attention to her hands.

"I'd say she is, too. It ain't enough to check arms and legs anymore. Addicts will shoot up anywhere, including under the fingernails," Rose explained to Annie. Turning back to Chandra, she added, "Still, I have to be sure. I do require regular blood tests, both for drugs and disease."

Chandra jerked her hands away.

"Let go of me. Chunkie don't mess with me for a reason, and you don't want to find out what that reason is," threatened Chandra.

"Probably the gun in your purse," said Annie.

"How'd you know that," asked Chandra, pulling the purse close.

"Your body language announced, for anyone watching, that you were carrying something in your purse. Judging by the bravado, it was a weapon. Knife wasn't enough of an edge, so it had to be a gun," said Annie. "Besides, it's my job."

"And my job as a madame is to make both my girls and my customers happy."

"You got a whorehouse somewhere, do ya?"

"Some call it that. I call it the Preying Mantis Ranch."

"Ranch? Where the heck you have a ranch around here?"

"It's not around here. It's about twenty-five minutes outside of Las Vegas."

"Vegas?"

"Yep. Your line of work is legal there. No worries about cops. No freebies to keep them from busting you, either." Rose looked back toward the hotel. "Or for sending you business. You'd have your own parlor at the ranch, so no street corners. The customer comes to you."

"A parlor? What's that?"

"A couple of rooms you set up, with some advice from me and the other girls. You design it to feel sexy, to both excite the men and put them at ease."

"How do I get paid?"

"The client pays me, I pay you. It's a fifty-fifty split."

"Half seems like an awful lot for doing nothing," said Chandra.

"Expenses like rent, advertising, and benefits come out of my half. Of course, money from the bar helps pay the bills. We get ten bucks for a glass of beer. I get the customers, I make sure nobody gets hurt."

"Chunkie says the same thing."

"In my place, someone has always got your back. All Chunkie has got is his hands in his pants holding his wallet. Besides, I doubt you'll complain about your cut. What do you make now?"

"Whatever I can get. Anywhere from seventy-five to two hundred if I'm lucky."

"Your cut would be two to two fifty per hour. Plus all tips are yours to keep."

"What's the difference in price?"

"I give regulars a better rate. Helps the repeat business."

"Why me?"

"I like what I see. You mentioned before you get more than Chunkie's girls. Why do you think that is?"

"I don't know."

"I do. Look at how you're dressed. Sexy, maybe a bit slutty, but not whorish, like I bet Chunkie's women dress. Your makeup is strong, but not overbearing. Also, addictions tend to lower the asking price. Junkies have a different look, rarely wholesome. You ooze wholesome. Guys are excited by you, but still feel safe. That's why you get more buck for your bang."

Chandra was letting things sink in.

"So I'd have to move to Vegas?"

"Probably be best. A commute from Baltimore would be a killer. Is that a problem?"

"No."

"Is what a problem?" said a male voice, approaching the trio of ladies. The dark-skinned man was around five foot nine, but he had to weigh two fifty. His rotund frame was draped by baggy jeans and an oversized Ravens jersey. A backwards Yankees cap sat on his head. His eyes were covered by dark shades. A gold chain thick enough to lock up a bicycle was wrapped around his throat.

"Chunkie, I presume?" said Rose.

"Either that, or a gangsta rapper has lost his way," added Annie.

"You think you're funny, lady?" asked Chunkie.

"Yep. Hey, Chunkie, where's your dog?" asked Annie.

"I ain't got no dog."

"How about your cane?"

"What the hell do I need a cane for?"

"Cause you're blind. It's obvious, with those dark glasses. Any person who could see would have realized it was dark out and taken them off."

"Lady, you're treading on dangerous ground. Chandra, these lesbos giving you any problems," asked Chunkie.

"No. As a matter of fact, this lady just offered me a job at her ranch," said Chandra proudly.

"What are you going to be, a cowboy? Get real. She ain't got no ranch, she just wants in your pants. Besides, you work for me."

"Wrong, I work with you."

"You dissing me in front of strangers? You need a lesson in manners, bitch," said Chunkie, pulling back his fist to whack Chandra's face. The fist froze in mid-swing at the sound of three clicks.

Each of the ladies had pulled a gun and cocked the trigger while they were pointed at Chunkie.

Instinctively, Chunkie's hands went to the front of his pants. Annie lowered her gun to follow it.

"Reach into your dip and I'll blow off your dippy," she warned.

"Shit," said Chunkie, raising his hand and using his open palm in a gesture of submission. "I was just kidding."

"Really? Well, I can joke, too," said Rose, as she stepped toward the pimp. Chunkie stepped back.

"Hell, I ain't scared of you. You ain't even got a real gun. That thing and the gun the redhead has are toys."

"Place we're spending the week has metal detectors, so we got plastic handguns, moron. It's real enough to put a big enough hole in your hide to end you."

The looks in three pairs of eyes told Chunkie that none of the three women were playing. He dropped to his knees, ready to beg for his life. "Hey, I said I was just kidding."

"And you said it with all the sincerity fear can bring a scumbag like yourself. I'm going to teach you a lesson. The moral is: don't hurt women. Say it," demanded Rose.

"Don't hurt women," repeated Chunkie.

"Very good. Now to make sure you don't forget it…" Rose moved closer. Annie stepped in, ready to stop her if it came to that.

"Tough bitch with a gun. You wouldn't be so tough without it," challenged Chunkie, trying to get back a little of his manhood.

"Actually, I was about to put it away." Rose returned the gun to its hiding place. "Go on, stand up."

Chunkie did, and swung his fist, this time at Rose. Rose caught his fist with one hand and grabbed above the elbow with the other. Lifting her knee up, she brought the pimp's arm down on her leg the same way a child would snap a twig. It had much the same effect.

"You bitch, you broke my arm. You fucking broke my arm."

The gun was suddenly in Rose's hand again, pointing at Chunkie's eyes.

"You got off easy. Next time I hear about you hurting a woman, I'll kneecap you, then shoot off your dick. Got me?" said Rose.

"Yes," whispered Chunkie.

"Yes, what?"

"Yes… Ma'am."

"Now get out of here," ordered Rose.

"I'm hurt," said Chunkie between clenched teeth.

"I broke your arm, not your leg, although something could be arranged," said Rose.

Chunkie got up and left in a hurry.

"Why don't you come into the hotel restaurant with me, and we'll talk business. I'll even buy dinner," said Rose.

"I can pay for dinner," said Chandra defensively.

"But I can deduct it. Learn a lesson from Chunkie and don't argue with me," said Rose with a wink. Chandra couldn't tell if she was joking or serious. Neither could Annie. The trio went back into the hotel proper. "Annie, care to join us?"

"I'd like to, but I've got to find the old ball and chain," said Annie. Personally, I resented that remark. In the past we'd had a ball using chains, but that was a whole other story.

"I understand. Chandra, why don't you go in and get us a table. I'll be along in a minute," said Rose.

"Sure," said Chandra, not even saying good-bye to Annie.

"Earlier, I promised to tell you the rest of my story. I'll give you the condensed version. I come from a long line of assassins."

"How long," asked Annie.

"Goes all the way back to my mother."

"And you were able to keep track of that? Pretty amazing."

"Yes, it is. My mother is retired now, but in her heyday, she was known by her codename, The Black Widow. That pretty much tells you how she worked. She'd have sex with a man, and then kill him."

"Charming."

"She was hot stuff, back then. She was the backup assassin for JFK, although instead of asking about the grassy knoll, they'd be asking questions of a much different nature. Mom perfected a method of applying poison during the act of sex, that wouldn't take effect until minutes or hours later. It depended on the dose."

"How'd she do it? Poison lipstick?" asked Annie.

"No. Mom had to use poison she could take an antidote for, but even antidotes can only do so much. Lipstick could be used occasionally, but not on a regular basis. Anything powerful enough to be used in lipstick would eventually start hurting her. Either that, or the lipstick would have to be gobbed on, and who'd want to kiss that? She needed a way to apply the poison without being exposed to it herself, at least on a regular basis. She came up with the perfect solution. Can you guess what it was?"

"Condom?"

"Bingo. Mix the poison with the lubricant, and they went out with a bang."

"What did your father have to say about what your mother did?"

"Not much."

"Didn't he know?"

"I'm sure he did in the end."

"In the end?"

"I never knew my father. He was one of my mother's hits."

"What happened?"

"An old story. The condom broke. Mom taught me how to do the tricks for my trade, and I took over for her."

"So call yourself the Black Widow?"

"Nah. Mother became famous enough to have imitators. The name was being used by everyone. My codename is Mantis."

"Which explains the Preying Mantis Ranch."

"Exactly."

"The mantis kills and eats her mate."

"I stop short of cannibalism."

"Glad to hear that. Tell me, would you ever just shoot somebody for a hit?"

"Like a sniper? No, not my style. Too many variables I couldn't control. I hear you're quite the shooter, though."

"That I am."

"Would you ever kill my way?"

"No."

"So, have I shocked you?" asked Rose.

"Yes."

"Wow, someone honest enough to admit it. Being one of a handful of women, the boys mostly know who I am and what I do. They play it cool, to keep up those macho boy images, but I can tell I make them nervous."

"I guess that makes you drop dead gorgeous."

"I guess it does. You better go find your husband," said Rose.

Using my impeccable sense of timing, I chose that moment to walk up.

"Speak of the devil…" said Annie.

"A handsome devil, I hope," I shot back.

"Of course," Annie said, leaning over to give me a quick kiss. I made it a longer, more passionate one.

"I love you," I said, fulfilling my earlier promise to myself.

"What's that all about?" asked Annie.

"Hotel almost blew up. I defused the bomb. So, how was your day?" I asked.

"Not as interesting as yours. I made a new friend though. Let me make introductions. Rose, Jack. Jack, Rose."

We shook hands.

"A pleasure," she said.

"Likewise," I replied.

"You really defuse a bomb?"

"Yep."

"Impressive. Annie, you could be right in keeping him. I hope you'll forgive me, but my dinner date awaits. Annie, let's hook up later. Maybe tomorrow at the Assassins' Ball?"

"Sounds good," said Annie. We all waved goodbye. "I'm beginning to worry."

"Why?" I asked.

"She's a killer."

"And?"

"I liked her."

"I hear you. I find myself liking that guy Rao I told you about. Nice guy, but a nice guy who can kill with his bare hands. You think Rose might be who we're looking for?"

"No. She's not a shooter by trade."

"You sure?"

"Yep, her methods are something altogether different."

"Like what?"

"I'll tell you about it later. Just promise me something."

"What?" I asked.

"If you ever cheat on me, promise me it'll be with Rose."

XVII

AFTER HOOKING BACK up with Marty for dinner, the three of us went to the ballroom for Annie's demo. Marty left us as soon as we walked through the door. "Gotta talk to more of the staff," he said, adding, "you never know." He was turning into a decent detective. I just hoped he played it safe.

During an earlier break in the day, I had run by a nearby branch of our bank for the money I owed Jacob the gunsmith, plus a little walking around cash. I went to pay the man. By the time I finished, Annie was almost done with her setup. She had pulled a sizeable crowd around the makeshift shooting range. Most of the crowd was men, and not all their interest was in the guns.

Annie had changed into tight jeans and a tank top. She was looking very hot, if I do say so myself. Annie used to work the carnival in a sports bra-style bikini top. She says having as little between her and the gun as possible improves her aim. Once when she worked QRT, it got her in a bit of trouble. They asked her to make an impossible shot from a ridiculous distance. Hostage lives were on the line, so she stripped down out of her uniform top and vest, to just her bra. The perp with the gun was about to put a bullet in some teenaged girl's head. Annie put a bullet in his head first. Problem was, a news crew got a glimpse of her taking the shot in her bra. The usual media nonsense followed. Annie became a brief Internet darling, with the image of her in her bra aiming her rifle becoming the most downloaded photo of the week. She had offers to do posters, T-shirts, and *Playboy*. Several national periodicals asked for interviews, and *Guns and Gals* magazines offered big bucks for an eight-page photo spread. Unfortunately, spread was the operative word, so Annie declined.

Naturally, various groups consisting of self-appointed guardians of morality demanded that the BPD "do something" about this "immoral" act. Just what it was they wanted done varied, from Annie issuing a public apology to the department firing her.

In the end, nothing was done. After all, Annie was the commissioner's daughter, she had made a shot nobody else on the force could have, and the mother of the woman she had saved stated publicly that she didn't care if Annie had been naked, she was just glad her daughter was safe.

"God, I'd love to take a shot at her," said some tall, dark bozo, who was practically drooling over my wife. When a guy is married to a beautiful woman, he learns early on that there are some men who see a wedding ring as an added thrill. The end result is that Annie gets hit on a lot. There are various ways to handle this, the most common of which is Annie has to hit back. While punching in some guy's face has a certain satisfaction, there are more fun ways.

"You think she's good looking?" I asked.

"Good God, yes. Look at that body and that face. Most girls have one or the other. She's got both."

"So why are you standing here talking, when you could be putting the moves on her," I asked. This kind of guy kind was usually all talk, going into action only if drunk enough.

"I heard she's got some bad ass husband, who'll just as soon blow you up as look at you. He took out a bomb with his bare hands the other day." Sometimes I loved the rumor mill. "Guy's so bad he has drinks with Hanson Bach," he said.

"Bad ass husband, huh?" I said. Looked like I was developing a rep. "She is a real babe, though. I might take a shot at her myself."

"Yeah, right," he sneered.

"You don't believe me?"

"I guess you might have a death wish. Besides, even without a husband, girls like that don't give guys like us the time of day."

"I'm gonna do it," I said.

"I'll bet you crash and burn."

"Yeah? How much?" I said.

"A thou if you get anywhere," he said, pulling out a roll of cash.

"A thousand bucks? Done," I said as we shook on it. I walked over to where Annie was.

"Hey, gorgeous. Busy after the show," I asked.

"Sorry, buddy. I'm a married woman," Annie said back, smiling all out. I looked back over my shoulder. My betting buddy was smiling, already counting his chickens.

"I hear he's a bad ass," I said.

"Where'd you hear that," she asked.

I pointed to my betting buddy. "Guy back there told me."

"It's true," Annie confirmed.

"That's okay, I don't care about that. I'm just looking for some wild sex," I shot back.

"Well, you are kinda cute. Promise you won't tell my husband?" said Annie.

"I won't if you won't. I'll even spring for dinner," I said.

"Who cares about dinner? Why don't we just go to your room and get naked?"

I turned and gave my betting buddy a thumbs up. His jaw dropped.

"How about a kiss for luck," Annie asked.

"My pleasure," I said. We embraced like a couple of love-crazed teens. We got some catcalls from the crowd. One guy even yelled "Get a room!"

Annie broke our clinch first. "Well, gotta get to work," she said, more than a little breathless.

"Go get 'em," I said, walking back to the man foolish enough to bet me.

"That was unbelievable," he said.

"Yeah, my wife is something, isn't she?" I said.

The guy did a double take. "You never said she was your wife."

"You never asked," I said.

"I'm not going to pay," he said.

I looked at his name tag. "No problem, Mr. John Mall. I'll just pass along the information that you welshed on a bet at KCON."

"To who?" Mall asked, a little nervous. I simply smiled. "You wouldn't tell Hanson Bach, would you?"

I kept smiling. "If you don't think it was a fair bet, then don't pay," I said, and turned to walk away.

Mall chased after me.

"No, no. It was a fair bet. Sorry. Here, take the money," Mall said, shoving the cash into my left hand. "What happened to your hand?"

"Lost a bet," I said.

"And you let them just cut off your hand?"

"I lost," I said. "When one gambles, one has to take the consequences. Besides, if I welshed, it would have been worse. Any bettor knows that."

Mall was looking frazzled, convinced the big bad Bach boogie man was going to get him. He put the money in my good hand. "Please, take it."

"Are you sure?" I said.

"Sure, I'm sure. And this little bet is just between us," he asked.

"If that's the way you want it," I said.

"That's the way I want it," he said.

"Done."

"Thanks," he said, then moved off in the opposite direction.

Annie's show had started. Shots were ringing out. So far, Annie was going pretty traditional in her shooting style. The professionals in the crowd started looking past Annie and watching her skills and the quality of the guns. Most were impressed. Two were not.

They stood on opposite sides of the range. Everyone else gave them a wide berth. One was dressed in a two-piece suit that cost more than most people made in a month. His short black hair was slicked back and, even inside, he wore dark black sunglasses. He was too tough to crack a smile. He looked like the poster child for the mafia. The other guy looked like a heavy metal singer. He wore blue jeans, T-shirt, and a long brown trenchcoat. He had long blond hair down to his shoulder blades. This one smiled, but it was the smile of a sadist, the look of someone who enjoyed another's pain.

I eased up to Jacob.

"Who are those two," I asked.

"Top shooters in the business. The guido is Antonio Tomaso. The escapee from MTV calls himself Reaper, as in The Grim. Neither ever misses," explained Jacob.

"Legends in their own minds, huh?" I said. If they were half as good as Jacob thought, either could be our shooter.

"And in everyone else's. They are the best."

"Who's better," I asked.

"Depends on who you ask. The two have a running feud. There's actually a pool for who'd die if they went head to head."

"Who's the odds-on favorite?"

"Tomaso. He's a bit more systematic. Reaper's more of a wild man."

"They buy guns from you," I asked.

"I wish. I'd be set. Be like an endorsement from the gods. Each has a personal gunsmith, works just for them."

"So they aren't here to check out the wares," I said.

"More likely checking out the new blood competition."

"Meaning Annie?"

"You got it. She's good enough to make them nervous. If you think my attitude toward women gunners is bad, wait until you see theirs," said Jacob.

"Annie can handle herself," I said.

She had finished her target practice. Jacob removed the target and passed it among the onlookers. Tomaso grabbed the target and tossed it back to Jacob. Reaper got it next.

"Not bad, for an amateur," said Tomaso.

"You think you can do better?" challenged Annie.

"Yes," said Tomaso.

"I could do better with my eyes closed," said Reaper.

"Could you?" mocked Annie.

"You better believe it, babe," said Reaper.

"I doubt it. By the way, babe is about ten years out of date," Annie said.

"You're not going to lecture me on calling you a babe?" asked Reaper, disappointed that he hadn't gotten a rise out of her.

"I don't care about what you say or think. Why should I bother?" replied Annie.

Tomaso laughed.

"You think you can do better with your eyes closed, too," asked Annie.

"Sure," said Tomaso.

"Great," said Annie, picking up a long piece of cloth. "Who's going first?"

"What's that?" said Reaper.

"A blindfold. You both just challenged me. Time to put up or shut up. We just have to determine the stakes," said Annie.

"This is ridiculous. I'm not shooting with a blindfold," said Tomaso.

"Me neither," said Reaper.

"Fine. I had mistaken you for real men, not a couple of windbags full of hot air," said Annie. She had done this routine hundreds of times at the carnival, getting the macho men to put up a hundred bucks that they could outshoot her. Annie never lost. Back then, it was just straight target shooting. Assuming the crowd here was more skilled than your typical carnival crowd, Annie made adjustments, going straight to her trick shooting routine. She still practiced every day, which is why we have to live out in the country. Otherwise, she'd be taking out the neighbors.

"What are you trying to say," asked Reaper.

"That the pair of you are chicken, scared of little old me," Annie said. There was a collective gasp from the crowd, which gave Annie pause. She didn't realize the reputation of the men she had challenged.

"Better watch what you say, little lady," said Tomaso, taking umbrage at the insult.

"Why," asked Annie.

"People could get hurt," said Tomaso.

"Don't threaten me, asshole. I'll put a hole between your eyes before your gun even clears your holster," said Annie. She wasn't exaggerating. Besides all her carnival shows, Annie has also won seven national quick-draw championships.

"Bullshit," said Tomaso.

"Let's go," said Annie.

"You're nuts," said Tomaso.

"What's your point," asked Annie.

"You may have a gun, but I don't. House rules," said Tomaso. "Not exactly a fair fight."

"How about we do it for fun? Jacob carries a full line of paintball pistols, complete with holsters. We can slap leather, and you'll get to walk away," said Annie. Apparently, it wasn't just for weekend warriors anymore. Real killers trained with the stuff, to get practice in without the messy corpses.

"What about you," asked Tomaso.

"I'd walk away, even if they were real," said Annie.

"Fine, let's have some fun," said Tomaso.

"If you really want to have some fun, put your money where your mouth is," said Annie.

"A bet?"

"Yep. You name the price," said Annie.

"Not money. I win, you get on your knees and kiss my feet, tell me I'm the greatest," said Tomaso.

"Okay. If I win, you've got to do the same to me," said Annie.

Tomaso laughed. "Sure, if that happens."

Annie walked over with two gunbelts. "Choose your weapon."

Tomaso picked the one on his right. He took out the paintball gun, getting the feel for it. Annie just put on the gunbelt, having already checked it out. Annie was left handed. Sometimes when she did this bit, she'd shoot right handed just to even the odds a bit. Today, she wasn't taking any chances. Her gun was on the left.

"Want goggles?" asked Annie, putting on a pair herself. She had learned way back that the only way a paintball can hurt you is if it hits you in the eye. With goggles on, there was no fear to make you do something you didn't plan to.

"Don't need them," said Tomaso, pointing to his shades. Satisfied with his inspection, Tomaso put on his belt.

"Ten paces, turn, and shoot?" asked Tomaso.

"Naw. You stand there, I'll stand here, and we shoot when we get a signal." The crowd backed away from the lines of fire, so as not to get spattered by a paintball.

"What signal?"

"Jacob fires a gun at the range." Jacob nodded he was okay with that. "As soon as you hear the shot, draw. Agreed," asked Annie. The gunshot signal was a trick. No matter how prepared most people are, the sound of a gunshot startles them for a fraction of a second, slowing them down. At 16, Annie had spent months getting rid of that reflex, just practicing this and other everyday things while random gunshots went off. She's worked to keep it that way.

"Agreed," said Tomaso.

Seconds ticked by. Tomaso tried to stare Annie down, but she didn't pay him any mind. It would divert concentration from the task at hand.

Jacob gave the gunshot signal. After that fraction of a second delay, Tomaso went for his gun, but he was already too late. Before the bang stopped ringing in her ears, Annie threw herself backwards. She got off three shots before her back landed on the floor. Tomaso fired once, the paintball missing because it was aimed at her chest while she was still standing. Tomaso was so intent on shooting that he never moved, so all three of Annie's shots hit their target. The first took him between the eyes on his forehead. The second was on his chest, and the third nailed Tomaso in the crotch. Red paint dripped from the mock wounds. The crowd erupted in laughter.

Tomaso wiped the paint off his face with a handkerchief. He was so furious I half expected to see steam coming out of his ears.

"Well," asked Annie.

"Well what?" barked Tomaso.

Annie stuck out her foot and wiggled it.

"Not a chance."

"Don't pay your debts, huh?"

Tomaso's voice was a cold whisper. "I pay my debts, and I owe you big time. Next time, you are a dead woman."

Annie shrugged, as if the threat was so much air. "I doubt it."

"Why's that?" barked Tomaso.

"Next time, I'll be using real bullets," said Annie, with a smile.

Tomaso threw down his reddened handkerchief, turned on his heel, and left. The crowd gave Annie an ovation. She gave a little bow.

I pulled her aside.

"That was great, Annie, but you should probably know who you just humiliated. His name's Antonio Tomaso, and according to Jacob, he's one of the best two shooters here." After a look from her I added, "Best three shooters."

"Great. We'll just have to watch our backs," said Annie. "Not like we don't do it now. Anything I should know about this other guy?"

"Goes by Reaper. He's the other leading contender," I said.

"It just gets better and better."

"On the plus side, you may actually be as good as you think you are," I said.

"No, actually I'm better. I'll prove it in round two," Annie said, walking back to Reaper. "Don't think I've forgotten about you. You ready?" Annie was waving the blindfold.

"Sure. What's the game?"

"Best score from one clip, at the target. Part two is skeet, best of two pigeons. All blindfolded," said Annie.

"Clay pigeons seem a little too easy. How about something smaller?" said Reaper sarcastically, not realizing he was playing into Annie's hands.

"Sure. A roll of quarters, thrown up by hand. We use a rifle or pistol for both, your choice."

"Rifle for the target, pistol's fine for the skeet."

"If I can interrupt," said Jacob nervously. "We are in a hotel ballroom. The range is designed to absorb bullets. The ceiling is not. Bullets are going to do damage, and I don't want to pay for it. Any chance you could use the paint ball guns for the skeet?"

"Okay with me, if it's okay with him," said Annie.

"Fine with me. What's the stakes," asked Reaper.

"Cash, unless you have a better suggestion."

"Hell, yeah. We play for shirts, mine against yours," said Reaper.

"Doesn't seem fair to me. Put up your pants and trench coat, and you got a deal," Annie said.

"My pants and trench coat against your bra and top," said Reaper.

"You never mentioned the bra. That'll cost you your underwear," said Annie.

"I don't wear any," said Reaper, using the line as a come on.

"That's more than I really need to know, but deal," said Annie, shaking Reaper's hand. "You can go first."

Reaper walked up to the firing range, his paper target already in place at the end. Making a mental note of distance and placement, he put on the blindfold. Annie checked to make sure it was on good and that he wasn't peeking. Reaper emptied the rifle's clip. He hit the target with every shot. Impressive.

He used the clothes line to pull the target back and held it out for Annie's inspection.

"Beat that," he said.

"I will," said Annie, positioning herself before applying the blindfold. Reaper checked it. Annie emptied her clip into the target. I could tell she hadn't missed the target, but had she scored more points than Reaper? I was not thrilled with the idea of her paying off this bet.

Annie reeled in her paper target and handed it to Reaper, without even looking at it.

"Ta-da," she said. She had gotten two more bull's-eyes than Reaper, and her overall point score was higher.

"Amazing. I concede. You win part one," said Reaper. "But we still have part two."

"True enough," said Annie.

"Ladies first, this time."

"Okay," said Annie, sliding her blindfold back on. "Jack, would you do the honors?"

"My pleasure," I said, picking up a roll of quarters that Annie had left out. This is a routine I had helped with before. There wasn't much to it except to time it with her voice. I knew where she'd fire and I would throw the quarters in a wide spread over that area in order to let her hit the most quarters. When we've switched places, I've managed to hit some. I find it more impressive that Annie, with a revolver and her eyes open, can shoot a quarter out of the sky.

"Pull," ordered Annie. I threw the coins high, and they showered down. Regular quarters from heaven. Annie got off a half dozen shots, although the sixth was too late to do any good. The other five hit change and spattered. She got paint on fourteen of the forty.

Reaper took the blindfold.

"You throw them for me the same as you did for her," he asked.

"Sure," I said. He looked at me for a moment, deciding whether or not to believe me. He decided to. I would throw them the same, otherwise Annie would be mad at me for helping her win. She's that way, prefers to win these contests on her own.

Reaper wrapped the cloth around his eyes. "Pull."

Once again, coins filled the air. Reaper was a quick study. He had watched Annie closely, and did the same. He fired seven times but the last three were a waste of paint. When the final count was made, he had splattered ten coins. Annie won.

Reaper seemed to be a good loser, and offered Annie his hand.

"Good work. Congratulations."

"Thanks. I hope you aren't planning on wimping out of our wager like your friend did," said Annie.

"He's no friend of mine. Don't worry. I'll pay up. One question first. If you're this good, how come I've never heard of you before?"

"I had an exclusive for most of my career," she said truthfully, if you count the Baltimore PD.

"And now?"

"Strictly freelance."

"And out to make a name for yourself, Ms. Frost," said Reaper.

"You got it, and it's Mrs. Frost," Annie said.

"Well Mrs. Frost, it's time to pay the piper," said Reaper, tossing Annie his trench coat as he began a striptease dance. It started out Chippendale, but ended as more Jerry Lewis, as he tripped trying to take the pants off. He didn't lie. He wasn't wearing any undies.

Reaper was unfazed by the fall. He stood and handed his pants over with a flourish, bowing in the process, and thereby mooning half the audience.

"A pleasure doing business with you, Mrs. Frost," said Reaper as he turned to leave. He actually went back to his room through the hotel proper. Apparently, he made a scene and offended no end of women. The hotel wanted to kick him out, but Reaper convinced the manager it would be a bad idea to tick him off.

"Impressive show," I told Annie.

"I'll say," said Jacob. "Look at the line!" He moved off to wait on his new clients.

"All in a day's work," said Annie. More quietly, to me, she added, "I've really missed the competition."

"You beat two of the best. You should be proud," I said.

"I am."

"What do you think of them as suspects?"

"Can't cross either of them off the short list, that's for sure," Annie said.

"I have to agree with you there, but I have a bone to pick with you. I always said you could charm the pants off any man. I just thought you would only try on me."

Annie leaned over and kissed me. "If it makes you feel any better, you're the only man who can charm my pants off."

"I'd like a chance to prove that," I said.

"How about now?" suggested Annie. Winning is an aphrodisiac for my wife.

"Works for me," I said.

Marty, of course, chose that moment to join us.

"Annie, that was incredible," said Marty.

"Thanks," said Annie.

"What's next on the agenda," he asked.

"You have some free time. We're taking another break," said Annie. Marty gave us a frustrated look.

"Again? You people are married."

"Exactly," I said, pulling Annie by the hand toward the elevator. We never made it to the room. We hit the stop button and covered up the video camera with my shirt.

XVIII

W̲E RETURNED TO our room a bit disheveled but in a very good mood. No sooner had we walked in than the phone rang. Annie answered it, but the caller hung up. Minutes after that, there was a knock on the door. A man in a dark suit and sunglasses handed each of us an invitation to a very exclusive party. He also cautioned us not to tell anyone about it, it was a "need to know" affair.

"Nice to know that our tax dollars are going to entertain paid killers," Annie commented, once she'd closed the door.

I didn't answer at first, being slightly distracted checking out our room, making sure no additional monitoring devices had been added, and that the surprises I had planted were all still in place. Satisfied, I said, "Cutbacks are everywhere these days, honey. Maybe their black ops section was shut down, and now they have to outsource their hits."

During Annie's demo, the mini-computer I still refer to as a cell phone had twice vibrated. I was about to check for messages when I noticed that Annie had stripped off her tank top and jeans, and was now down to a strapless top and panties.

"If we're going to party with spies, I should take a shower."

"Wait a minute," I said, messages forgotten for now, "I'll join you."

Thirty minutes later we were dripping wet, squeaky clean, and in an even better mood. After Annie chased me out of the bathroom so she could get dressed without further interruption, I got back to my forgotten messages.

There were two, one each from Sarah and Maggie, both to my email with attached files.

Maggie's was her report on Marty's gun. No match to the bullet from Joey's body. That was what I had expected, but it was a relief to know that my client probably wasn't playing me. Maggie's report went on to verify that the bullet was a 9mm, as we had believed, but could not be identified to a specific type of weapon; that the striations on the bullet caused by its passage through the barrel did not match up to any of the guns commonly found on the street. She suggested that the gun might be an import, an exotic, or one especially made.

I thought at once of Tomaso and the Reaper, each with his own gunsmith. I thought of all those specialty weapons in the dealers' room. And I thought of Mozzano's five-shot cane, and wished that we had taken that along with his gun.

But there was more to Maggie's report. In it, she made some suggestions as to why the room had been given an extreme make over, and told me what to look for. Kicking myself for not thinking of them myself, I decided to start looking right after I checked Sarah's message.

Best laid plans and all that. I had just finished reading about what Sarah had found when two things happened. Annie came out of the bathroom wearing a long hotel bathrobe, her hair and makeup done as well as any professional beauty shop could have managed. And no sooner had she asked the eternal question, "Now what am I going to wear to the party," then there was another knock, this one from the door between our room and Marty's.

"You guys decent," he asked in a hesitant voice.

"Not for the last five years or so," Annie called back. "Come on in."

The door opened slowly, as if Marty was giving us one last chance to cover anything that we didn't want him to see. Once in the room, he gave it a professional once over. I got a questioning look when he looked at the painting with the fake timer and real explosive. I gave him a quick shake of my head to let him know I hadn't played the joke yet.

Satisfied that all was well, Marty sat in a chair by the window.

"I'd have been up sooner, but there was a problem with the elevators. One of them had gotten stuck between floors, and they wanted to check them all out."

The quick glance and smile Annie and I shared did not escape Marty.

"Aw, geez, that was you guys? You act like you're not married or something. Anyway, I got nothing from the staff. Some of them said there was some kind of commotion the other night, but none of them got pulled into it. All they knew was that the next morning, the room was closed off, and a four-man crew brought in. Carlos, he's one of the bellhops, said that he saw their van. It wasn't marked in any way, but it had Virginia plates."

"Out of town help," Annie observed. "Bach's smart."

"Maybe." Then I gave voice to Maggie's suggestions. "Maggie thinks that the reason the walls were painted was to either hide marks from wiping blood off the walls, or because a bullet hole or two had to be patched."

Annie shook her head. "There wasn't that much blood, and the bullet stayed in the body."

"That's what I thought, too, but who says only one shot was fired? And Joey may have had time to shoot back. The attacker may have been in this room, and a stray shot or a through-and-through could have broken the window."

"You think," Marty asked.

"Who knows, but you'll have plenty of time to check it out. Annie and I will be out tonight. If you have no other plans, see if you can find any trace of a quick spackle job." The look on Marty's face told me that he'd rather do anything else. "It's a long shot, I know."

"Yeah, so where will you guys be while I'm having all this fun?"

"At a party."

"Who's giving it?"

"We'd tell you, Marty, but then we'd have to kill you."

"No, we wouldn't, Jack," Annie corrected, then turned to Marty, "but someone would."

Marty nodded. "Oh, you mean the government guys."

"You know about them," I asked in surprise.

"Everybody does. They never could keep a secret."

That was my opening to bring up Sarah's report. "Speaking of keeping secrets, Marty, what do you know about Joey that you haven't told us?"

Marty looked confused. "Nothing. The boss said not to hold nothing back, so I told you everything. Why?"

"Yes, Jack, why?"

"At lunch, after you left, Marty told me that Joey had a taste for the ladies. What he didn't tell, and I'm guessing he didn't know, was that Joey's tastes ran to the dark side." I had their attention. "Simply put, Joey sometimes likes to play it rough, the rougher the better, it seems. Seven arrests in the past two years, all for aggravated assault, all on women. Three were ex-girlfriends, four were hookers."

"And those were just the ones we know about," offered Annie.

"Yeah, there's probably at least that many we don't, unless Marty can enlighten us."

Marty was pale. "I didn't know," he said, shaking his head. "I swear I didn't know. Mr. Mozzano, he never discussed things like that with me."

I believed him, mostly because I wanted to.

Then Annie asked, "What happened with the charges?"

"Joey's the grandson of a mob boss; what do you think? Two of the girlfriends dropped the charges, so did one of the hookers. Paid off probably, although Sarah couldn't find any record of it. Two of the hookers just never showed up in court, and the other girlfriend just disappeared, probably a 'Jane Doe' in some county's Potter's Field."

"That makes six, what about the other one?" Marty's voice was shaky, and he looked even paler. He knew the people he worked for were crooks and gangsters, but this may have been the first time someone had turned over the rocks to show him what was crawling underneath.

I gave it to him straight and hard. "She's in a Nevada nursing home. Someone beat her so badly that she's in a coma she'll probably never come out of."

Marty was now almost physically ill. "Joey did that?"

"No, someone else. Four days after she filed charges against Joey. With no grand jury testimony and no other evidence, Vegas PD had to drop the charges."

"You don't think Mr. Mozzano…"

Annie took pity on the big ape. "Your boss probably wasn't involved, Marty. He was in jail while most of this was going on, and he says he's been straight since. Has he?" Marty nodded. "But Joey hasn't, or wasn't. He's been mobbed up all his life, he has his own friends, his own connections, people who owed him favors."

"I guess," Marty said after a long pause. "You know, I know Mr. Mozzano hired you two to find Joey's killer, but right now, I don't care if you do or not."

Neither did I, and if wasn't for two things, I would have suggested dropping the dime on Bach about the planned Lady Liberty bombing, then going home and sleeping in my own bed. The one was that when we took the job, we knew or should have known what kind of person Joey was. The other was…

"The orphanage," Annie said, echoing my thoughts.

We nodded in agreement. We'd stay and get the job done.

XIX

THE INVITATION-ONLY PARTY was held in a suite that more than rivaled Bach's, only without the women. This one was filled with men in dark suits, who looked so much like government agents as to verge on stereotypical. There had been no formal mention of who was throwing the party, just dropped hints and an occasional mention of "The Agency". There was an overabundance of men with the last names of Smith and Jones.

"This is interesting," I said.

"Yeah, I've never been wined and dined by the CIA before," said Annie.

"I just hope they aren't expecting me to put out. I'm not that kind of guy," I said.

"Sure you are," said Annie.

"True, just don't tell anyone."

"Your secret is safe with me," said Annie, kissing me on the cheek. We got a couple of stares from the suits.

"I guess we are the only ones who thought to bring a date," I said.

"Probably not a big make out spot."

"I wonder if they have any of their little spy gizmos lying around, and if we get any just for showing up," I asked. Annie and I had already noticed the camera behind the mirror. They barely did a better job of the set up than a department store.

"Maybe they'll have goody bags or door prizes," said Annie.

"But I didn't get a raffle ticket."

"Oh well."

"At least the caviar is good." It was, but I was hardly an expert. I only had the stuff when I was at a party where someone else was serving it. Besides, with my paranoid mind, I had to watch someone else eat it first. Once I was sure the fish eggs hadn't been poisoned, I had some.

One of the Smith brothers approached us.

"Mr. and Mrs. Frost, how good of you to come," he said.

"Several times, actually. Have you been spying on our room?" I said. Annie elbowed me, but Smith surprised me by having a sense of humor.

"No, but we do monitor the elevator cameras. You should remember they are wired for sight *and* sound," Smith said with a smile.

"Thanks, I'll keep that in mind," I said. Smith motioned us to a love seat opposite a chair which his butt claimed as its own.

"Please, have a seat. Before we begin, may I ask how you lost your hand?" said Smith.

"Sure, go ahead," I said, egging Smith on.

"Cute. How did you lose the hand?"

"Sad story, really. Went deep sea fishing with some buddies and landed me a blue shark. Nothing like *Jaws*, only about four feet long. Took me almost an hour to get him in the boat, but I did it. One of my buddies decided it would make a funny picture if I put my head in the shark's mouth. Luckily, I decided to put my hand in instead. We were going to pretend it was eating my hand. No sooner had I shoved my hand in, then the damn thing twitched and clamped its jaws down hard. The SOB wasn't all the way dead, and had torn my hand off with its teeth. While I was screaming like a baby, one of my buddies put a tourniquet on my wrist, while another one beat the shark to death with a club. It had swallowed my hand, so the same buddy who used the club gutted the beast and took it out. We tossed the beer out of the cooler and put the hand in the ice, then headed for shore. But we were a few hours out, and by the time I got to a hospital, they couldn't reattach the hand. That's it in a nut shell."

"That's quite a fish story."

"Yep. I got the thing stuffed and mounted. It's hanging over my fireplace."

"The hand or the shark," asked Smith.

"Both, actually," said Annie, grinning.

"Must make for interesting decor. You are probably wondering why you were asked here."

"Not really. I assume it's in regards to work," said Annie.

"Yes, it is, but I was referring to certain kind of work," Smith answered politely.

"I thought you weren't allowed to operate domestically," I said. Smith smiled.

"We're not. That's where you come in. You are private citizens, and what you choose to do on your own time is your business. If you happen to take care of a problem we are concerned with, so much the better. In gratitude, we would reimburse you for any expenses incurred, plus a generous interest payment. You have both impressed us with your escapades at KCON. We would like to enter into negotiations, especially you, Mr. Frost."

"Why me?"

"Your specialty, explosives. Domestically, we are facing violent militia movement attacks on home ground targets. These are terrorist attacks on American soil. Because they are domestic, military strikes are out. The FBI and other agencies deal with arrests after the fact. Wars are not won after the fact. They are won by striking fast, first, and fierce. We want to give these domestic terrorists a taste of their own medicine, see how they like being blown up. We need it to look like accidents, that they blew themselves up while building a bomb. Publically, that will be the story, but the militia groups will know the real deal. It should discourage all but the truly hardcore."

"That would involve more than just planting a bomb. I would have to go deep undercover, join the group. It would take months of 24/7 work days. That's more than I'm willing to do. I have a life," I said.

Smith pushed a piece of paper across the table. "This is what we are willing to pay."

I unfolded the paper. All the zeroes would have made my eyes bulge, if I hadn't received Bach's offer. The CIA was only offering five million. I showed the paper to Annie.

"I'm sure you don't get offers like that every day," said Smith, smiling at me, confident I was sufficiently impressed.

"No, I don't, but I have had a higher offer this week for a single bombing, no undercover work," I said.

"How much higher," asked Smith.

"More than six times," I replied.

"Impressive. I'd be very interested to find out who made the offer."

"Truthfully, I don't know. It was done through an intermediary."

"Who?"

"I'm afraid I can't tell you," I said. I wasn't sure how closely they were connected to Bach. For all I knew, this was a test, with death as the penalty for failure.

"How about I take a guess and you just nod?"

"Guess all you want, but I won't tell you anything," I said. I was still trying to come up with some way to take out Bach. When I did, I would talk with Matt Reily, my buddy in the FBI about the rest.

"We haf vays of making you talk," said Smith with a German accent.

"You mean make me disappear, interrogate me with drugs, take me for a little waterboarding, and such?" I said.

"Pretty much."

"You could try, but then I'd have to kill you," I said with the utmost sincerity.

"How would you do that," he asked.

But I was a cop. I know enough to keep my mouth shut. "If I tell you, the element of surprise would hardly work in my favor, now would it," I asked.

"I guess not," Smith said, smiling.

"You touch my husband, and *I'll* kill you. I won't tell you how, but I will tell you it will involve the loss of both testicles," said Annie.

"Sounds good. You two are my kind of people. What do you say, Mr. Frost?"

"I don't take separation from my wife for extended periods well, so no. If you just need a simple bomb planted and blown, I'm your man," I lied, hoping they wouldn't have any such work handy. I lucked out.

"Nothing like that in the works, but if it comes up, I'll keep you in mind," said Smith. "Mrs. Frost, we would like you to do some basic hits for us in the domestic sphere. We'd arrange time, place, weapons— everything you need."

He pushed a piece of paper across the table again. The number was significantly lower than my offer.

"First off, I don't have a set price for a hit. My fee varies by the difficulty of access to the target and risk of capture. Second, I figure expenses and travel into my price. Third, this is hardly an impressive offer, especially considering your track record of using your assassins as patsies, framing them, and then killing them with one of your own people before they can make an official statement to civilian authorities. When and where I do my job is as much a surprise to the client as it is to the target. I certainly would not feel comfortable doing hits on demand for an agency with your kind of a track record," said Annie convincingly. The seminars had been doing her good, because she sounded like a real assassin talking.

"So do you believe every conspiracy story you hear," asked Smith.

"No, but when I hear the same thing happening over and over, I lend it some credence," said Annie.

"So are you saying you won't work for us, Mrs. Frost," asked Smith.

"Under those conditions and for that price, no," said Annie.

"I see. Mr. Frost, are you sure you have nothing further to add on the matter of the intermediary," asked Smith.

"Nope," I said.

"Then we will have to talk again," Smith said, standing. "Please enjoy the rest of the party."

"Our tax dollars at work," said Annie. "How about we get out of here? I have a bad taste in my mouth."

"Works for me," I said. We stood and walked toward the door. At the same time a bellhop was coming in the door with a couple dozen lobsters on a cart, a layout fit for a king. I grabbed two by the claws with my right hand. Smith raised an eyebrow. "Just taking ours to go."

Smith walked over, picked up a metal bowl, and handed it to me. "Don't forget the butter."

"Thanks," I said. My good hand was full, and this was a bit too delicate for my other one, so Annie took the bowl.

"A little midnight snack?" I said.

"From the CIA?" said Annie, igniting my paranoia.

"Good point. Don't know what the intent was, meal or poison," I said, dumping them in the ashtray sand outside the elevator. Annie put the butter bowl on top. "Be free, little guys."

The elevator opened, and we stepped in. Annie was thinking hard.

"Did you realize the elevators were wired for sound," asked Annie.

"No. Didn't think it would be worth the bother, but I guess you never know what deals might be overheard. Wonder if it's just them, or if everybody has access?"

"I don't know." Annie was doing the same thing I was, thinking back to make sure we had said nothing incriminating in the elevator. We both came to the same conclusion. "Nothing we need to worry about."

XX

NORMALLY, AFTER A good night's sleep, things tend to look better. I was still waiting for that to happen. The early Saturday morning sessions had been a bust, and none of the late morning classes interested me. I did, however, find time to call the office. Bill answered. His was a one-man practice, so he frequently worked weekends.

"What are you guys up to?"

"Twice a day, three times if I take my vitamins. Did someone drop off a gun?"

"The babe in black? She sure did. Last night before Sarah and I left. Not bad looking."

Knowing Bill the way I do, I had to ask. "How'd you do?"

There was a sigh before he answered. "Never got the chance. She gave Sarah the gun and a bullet, then asked her to go for a spin. Next thing I knew, Sarah was asking me to lock the stuff in the safe, then she wheeled on out of here. Who knew she rolled that way?"

Having caught our secretary checking out Annie once or twice, I had suspected, but what and who Sarah did on her own time was her business. But I hadn't called to gossip.

"Bill, how would you like some billable hours? My client's paying."

"Is he rich?"

"Rolling in dirty money."

"Once again my rates have doubled. What do you need?"

I had a list of people we'd met at the convention. I asked Bill to find out what he could about them. Given that they were all professionals, I wasn't hoping for much. I also gave him the names of the Joey's victims and asked him to research their friends and family: if any of them had the resources to hire a hit and if they'd made any large cash withdrawals or transfers.

Of course I didn't say anything to Bill about a hit. Just asked him to check their financials.

It was a shot in the dark—no pun intended. Just maybe someone frustrated with the law's impotency had hired some private justice, and whoever took the job decided to mix business with, well, business.

I hung up and went downstairs to join Annie. That's when we got cornered.

"Don't they just make a darling couple, dear," the elderly woman asked her husband.

"Yes, dear, they do," he replied.

Saturday afternoon wasn't going any better than Saturday morning had. Annie and I had been caught by a couple of senior citizens. I was having flashbacks to having my cheeks pinched by old people when I was a kid. One thing I could say about this couple was that they were sweet to the point of being frightening, even without knowing that they killed for a living.

They were Richard and Maude Gladstone, or at least, that's how they introduced themselves. Actually, Richard insisted we call him Dick. Both were happy, vibrant, and in their seventies. The treatment we were getting would normally be reserved for grown grandkids. Speaking of which, we had already been treated to the start of a private showing of Maude's wallet full of pictures of their seventeen grandchildren.

"Little Emmy's only two. She's just learning to climb all over the furniture. This is Rebecca, Margaret and Bob's first born. She's our oldest grandchild, a junior in college. Honor student, too, with an academic scholarship," said Maude.

"You must be very proud," said Annie, actually interested, or at least able to pretend to be sincere. I came across as tolerant. Then again, Annie comes from a big family, so maybe that increases the tolerance for pictures of total strangers.

Dick was a little more in tune with the male of the species. He knew he couldn't stop his wife, but realized that we could all be more comfortable during the picture show.

"Maude, how about we menfolk get some drinks while you ladies talk," said Dick.

"Okay, sweetie. I'll have a gin and tonic," said Maude.

I looked at Annie. "How about you, hon?"

"Orange juice, please," said Annie.

Dick and I made our way into the Cantina.

"You have to excuse Maude. The grandkids mean the world to her; she can't believe that everyone else isn't just as interested," explained Dick. He ordered the drinks for the ladies, and beers for the two of us.

"I appreciate the save," I said.

"My pleasure. My wife is quite taken with the two of you. I think when she sees you, she thinks of us when we were starting out," said Dick.

"When was that?"

"Don't you know it's impolite to ask your elders about their age? Suffice it to say, it was before you were born. Just thinking about it makes me feel old. Let's get back to the ladies," suggested Dick.

Taking our drinks and those of our respective spouses, we did as Dick suggested, and returned to our wives. Judging by the wallet going back into Maude's purse, the show was over. Guess I'd have to wait to see it on video. The ladies took their beverages of choice from us.

"Thanks, sweets," said Maude.

"Ditto," said Annie.

"Our pleasure, ladies. I hope Maude isn't boring you, Annie," said Dick.

"Not at all," said Annie.

"Do you have any kids?" asked Maude.

Annie got real quiet. Maude may have been a little long in the tooth, but she was sharp.

"I'm sorry, did I hit a sore spot," she asked.

"No," said Annie, breaking eye contact and staring at Maude's purse.

"Look, I'm sorry. I shouldn't have pried," apologized Maude.

"It's okay, Maude. It's no big thing. Jack and I held off having kids at first because of the type of work we did." That much, at least, was true. We figured it wasn't fair to kids to have two parents who were cops. Didn't want to leave any orphans. If it was a matter of who would quit, it would probably have been me. I was on the good side of the twenty-year mark.

"I can relate, dear. Dick and I were the same way when we first started out. We were so worried about getting caught that we didn't have kids for years. They one day, the Lord smiled on us. I got pregnant. It was an accident, but a beautiful one. Maybe you two will have a similar accident, huh?" said Maude. Annie made a half-hearted attempt at an agreement smile. "Oh, no. I stuck my foot in it again, didn't I?"

"An accident would be wonderful. We've tried to have kids, but no luck," explained Annie.

"My son-in-law Tommy and my daughter Melissa had that problem. Melissa got Tommy to switch from briefs to boxers. Upped his sperm count. Jack, which type of underwear do you wear," asked Maude.

"Maude…" admonished Dick, mildly embarrassed.

"It might help. You know it worked for Melissa and Tommy. They have two boys and a girl," bragged Maude.

"It's none of our business, Maude."

"I'm just trying to help."

"You don't ask a grown man about his underwear."

"Why not?"

"Because he might think you're flirting with him."

"So?"

"You might make me jealous," said Dick.

"Oh, you," said Maude, playfully slapping her husband on the arm. "Jack, I apologize if I embarrassed you, but still, keep what I said in mind."

"No problem, but it probably wouldn't help. I wear thongs. No panty lines that way," I said. Maude's eyebrows rose up before she realized I was joking.

"Actually, Maude, the problem isn't with Jack. It's with me. We've been to lots of doctors, and they all say the same thing. I have endometriosis," said Annie.

"Isn't that where the lining of the uterus thickens up," asked Maude.

"Among other things. I theoretically can have children, but it hasn't happened yet. We keep trying and praying one day we'll get lucky," said Annie.

"You have each other, just like Dick and me. That's pretty lucky, if you ask me," said Maude.

"I couldn't agree with you more, Maude," said Annie.

"How about we change the subject," suggested Dick. "Politics, anyone?"

"Oh, no you don't. Dick is a die-hard Republican. Thinks the liberals have led this country to hell in a hand basket," said Maude.

"Well, they have, and they made us working stiffs pay for it. Welfare should be abolished. Imagine paying people to sit around and do nothing all day. What is the government thinking? If we're paying these lazy good-for-nothings, at least put them to work picking up trash on the side of the road," said Dick.

"Then what would they make the drunk drivers do for their community service," I asked sarcastically.

"Give them to me, and I'll get rid of them. That'd be a real community service," said Dick harshly.

"A drunk driver killed our granddaughter, Susan. She was sixteen and out with some friends when he blindsided the car. It was his third offense, and his license had been revoked after the second," said Maude.

"What happened to him," asked Annie.

"The courts convicted him, but he only got a year in prison. Scum was out in eight months. Then it seems he met with a bizarre accident: someone forgot to set the parking brake on a truck, and it rolled down a hill. Back wheel went right over his head. Popped it like a melon," said Maude.

"The police didn't understand it. They said he had to have been drugged to have stayed in one spot like that," said Dick.

"Or drunk. Of course, they checked him for drugs and alcohol during the autopsy, but they didn't find anything," said Maude.

"True, but they don't typically check for tetrodotoxin," added Dick.

"You're right, dear. Comes from the puffer fish, among other places," said Maude.

"Yes. The Japanese eat the fish with just enough of the poison to give them a buzz, but not kill them. The right amount of that stuff would paralyze a man, but he'd still be aware of everything happening. Poor fellow would be helpless to stop it, kind of like the victim of a drunk driver. Plus, if his head was faced the right way, be forced to watch the tire bear down on him," said Dick.

"The police said his head was facing the right way," added Maude.

"It couldn't have happened to a nicer guy," said Dick.

"Poison is your specialty, then," asked Annie.

"Heavens no, but we know enough to get by. We always tried to vary how we did things. Killing is a lot like sex that way. Got to spice things up so it doesn't get boring," said Maude.

"When we first started out, we were just a couple of kids. It was the Fifties, and there wasn't a lot to be had. We started out rolling drunks.

Maude would play nice and distract them, then I'd sneak up behind them and knock them in the head with a sock," said Dick.

"A sock?" I asked.

"A sock filled with sand. Couldn't afford a blackjack, and the sock was easier to hide. Dump the sand and the weapon was gone. We made some cash that way. One night, this big shot sees us work over some drunk, and he offers us a deal. He'll give us a hundred bucks to do the same to a friend of his the next night. A C-note was a fortune back then, so we agreed. We waited outside the same bar, and Maude enticed his so-called friend into the alley where we laid him out. Apparently unconscious wasn't good enough, because the guy pulled out a knife and slit his friend's throat. Never did find out why. Maude and I were shocked.

"The guy turns and laughs at us, and throws us a fiver. I point out to him that he was ninety-five bucks short, and he laughs some more. Has the nerve to tell us we'll take his measly money and like it. What were we going to do about it, tell the police? I said we would. Guy laughed again. Told us he'd tell the cops we killed the guy and he was just an innocent bystander. Who were they going to believe, a couple of street hustlers or an upright citizen? We knew the answer, but that didn't mean we liked it. The guy said he might just tell the cops it was us just for fun. I slugged him, but he was older and bigger. He grabbed my arm and was about to slice my throat when my Maude hit him on the back of the head with the sock. It staggered him, but didn't knock him out. It was enough to make him drop the knife," said Dick.

"What happened? You get the knife," I asked.

"Nope," said Dick.

"I did," said Maude.

"That she did. My Maude is a quick learner. Just from watching the guy do his friend, she picked up how to slit a throat, and she did it. One quick, clean stroke, and the guy was toast. I'm not ashamed to tell you, I was scared. I thought Maude had gone crazy," said Dick.

"I managed to convince him that we had done the right thing. If we let the guy go, he would have finked on us to the cops, and we would probably get the electric chair. This way, he couldn't talk, and we were safe. Besides, he tried to rip us off for almost a hundred bucks. Guy got what he had coming to him. We emptied both guys' wallets and made about a hundred and twenty dollars. It didn't take us long to figure out some people would pay a lot to have certain other people eliminated and, as simple as that, we found our life calling," said Maude.

"We found that, working as a team, we could accomplish more than the guys who worked solo," said Dick.

"Plus, people underestimated me because I was a woman, and I used that to my advantage. I probably don't have to tell you about that Annie, do I," asked Maude.

"No, you certainly don't," replied Annie.

"In the beginning, we did a lot of our killing up close and personal. After I got pregnant, we started working smarter. We learned how to kill from a distance, mostly with rifles," said Maude.

"You still use the rifles," I asked, suddenly wondering if either had been in the building across from Joey's room.

"Heavens, no. Between these old eyes and my arthritis, I'd be lucky to hit an elephant, let alone a person. Nowadays, I use an Uzi. Get a good spread of firing power real fast. As we got older, we got sneakier. I gained another advantage, as did Dick. Young people don't take old people seriously. They discount us and figure we are harmless. They only find out a moment before they die," said Maude.

"Enough about business. How'd you two kids meet," asked Dick.

"On the job," I said truthfully. "It was love at first sight."

"Well, it was for him, anyway. It took me a bit longer to see the diamond in the rough," said Annie, winking at me.

"I think he's a cutie," said Maude. "If I was five years younger, and didn't have the old ball and chain, you'd have some competition, Annie."

"Guess I'll have to count my blessings, then," said Annie.

"I have a question for you though, Jack. I hope it's not too personal," said Maude.

"Maude, we've talked about my underwear. How much more personal do you want to get," I asked.

She smiled. "I was wondering about how you lost the hand," she said, whispering the last word, as if speaking of something she didn't want everyone to hear.

"Stupid thing. My lawn mower got jammed by a branch. I turned it over and pulled the branch out, but didn't get my hand out in time. It's mulch now," I said.

"How horrible," Maude exclaimed, making a face meant to express her horror and sympathy.

"On the bright side, I sued the manufacturer, and got some big bucks because they hadn't put a warning label on. I don't have to work anymore. I just do it because I enjoy it," I said.

"Same with us. We're retired, mostly. We just take on the occasional job to keep our hand in it," said Dick.

"When was your last job," asked Annie.

"Two months ago," said Dick.

Maude glanced at her watch. "Oh my, look at the time. The seminar on 'New and Exciting Ways to Dispose of a Corpse' is going to start in a minute. I really wanted to go to that one. I always like to see if our ideas are more original that other peoples'. One time, we mailed a body in five boxes to five people we picked randomly out of five different phone books. The hands and teeth we dumped separately, so they couldn't identify the body. Another time, we snuck into a funeral home, and stuck the body in a coffin that was buried the next day. We even kept a big tank of flesh-eating piranha to eat the bodies, but we had to get rid of them."

"Why," asked Annie.

"Two reasons. One, they didn't eat the bones, which we still had to get rid of. Two, the kids kept trying to play with the fish, and it got too dangerous. Not to mention what happened when the cat fell in," explained Dick.

"We really have to run to catch the seminar. You don't mind do you," asked Maude.

"It's okay. We understand," said Annie.

"Maybe we'll see you later. You two remind me so much of us. If the Lord is good to you, maybe you'll turn out as happy as we are. Bye," said Maude, her husband echoing her words a moment later.

"Well, I think we can cross them off our growing list of suspects," I said.

"I don't know. Remember what Maude said about discounting old people. Jack, promise me something," said Annie.

"Again?"

"If we ever turn out like those two, that you'll put us out of our misery."

"I'll blow us both to kingdom come."

"Good."

XXI

CHARLIE WAS A sick bastard. There was no other way to describe the man. In his mind, he just wanted to imitate his heroes. Sadly, his heroes were all stone cold killers many times over, and imitating them meant blood in the streets and bodies in the gutter. In the world of the professional killer, Charlie had developed quite a reputation for himself, not necessarily as the best, but he was reliable. If he promised that someone would die, they would. It was that simple, and he had some skill. He had over fifty kills to his credit, and to date he hadn't been caught; he'd only been suspected once. The hits he took for hire, for the most part, were made to look like natural accidents, so usually there wasn't even a homicide investigation to worry about.

So far, Charlie had been enjoying his time at KCON. It was his first time, and he was learning a lot. He was networking, and in one day, had managed to get enough work to fill up the next four months of his schedule, but in his heart, he was disappointed. He wanted more than just business out of this convention.

Charlie had always considered himself an outsider. He knew early on that his dark, murderous desires set him apart from most people, so he felt he never quite fit in anywhere. He had hoped that by coming here, he could meet kindred spirits, folks who knew how he felt and knew how he thought. So far, that had been a bust.

It was just like back in school: there were cliques that stuck together and didn't admit outsiders easily. Even among killers, he was still alone, and no matter how much he loved his work, it didn't make the loneliness go away. It did, however, usually make him feel a little bit better. So Charlie decided to push up his plans to do his tribute to The Ripper.

He'd go out on the streets of Baltimore, maybe down to The Block. Get the lay of the land so to speak, then tomorrow night, he would claim his victim. After that, he would be ready to head to London and Whitechapel, and do it for real five times over, one for each of The Ripper's victims.

Charlie stepped onto the dark street outside the Hotel Royale. He had walked maybe half a block when a teenaged girl accosted him.

"Looking for a good time?" she said with a smile. It was a nice smile, not the half-hearted one Charlie had seen on other hookers. The girl was probably still new to turning tricks. She looked sixteen, maybe seventeen. Very pretty. She was African American, Charlie thought to himself. He might be a killer, but he tried to be politically correct, more to be facetious than anything else. Charlie wasn't prejudiced. What concerned him was that Jack the Ripper's victims had all obviously been English women.

"Maybe," said Charlie, smiling back. "What's your name?"

"Chandra," said the girl. Not exactly an English name, Charlie thought, but what the hell, she had chosen him. This was an opportunity too good to pass by, he decided finally.

"Are you new at this?"

"A little. Actually, I'm moving out to Vegas this weekend. Got a job lined up out there."

"Need a little spending money?"

"Something like that. Not that I'm not enjoying your company, but I am a working girl. Do you want a good time or not?"

"Sure, Chandra, I'd like a good time. What does a good time go for around here," asked Charlie.

"Two hundred will get you almost anything you want, as long it's not too kinky," said Chandra.

"It's not terribly kinky. I don't think you'd have any objections," said Charlie, adding silently to himself, "At least not for long."

"So shall we go back to your room or..."

"I don't think that would be necessary. How about right here in this alley?"

"Oh, that's the not terribly kinky part," said Chandra, as she took Charlie's hand and walked into the deserted alleyway. "Doing it where you can get caught is a common fantasy."

"Well, that's not all I had in mind," said Charlie. Once he had gotten down to the end of the alley, Charlie made sure he positioned himself between Chandra and the only way out, which was toward the street. He had a large knife, the kind hunters use to gut deer, hidden in the small of his back. Charlie pulled the blade out with such casualness that Chandra didn't even realize what he had done until the knife was already at her throat. She barely had time to scream before Charlie sliced her open.

In bloody silence, Charlie completed his work. By the time it was done, thoughts of loneliness had fled from his head, at least for the time being. Chandra lay on the ground of the alley, dead, her innocent expression transformed and forever frozen into a look of terror as her life blood flowed away down a drain.

Taking a step back, Charlie inspected his handiwork. He was very critical, especially of himself. That's why he took a practice run before moving on to Whitechapel. He saw it was a good thing he did. The way he had cut Chandra was not quite in the same pattern that The Ripper had used. It differed just enough to make it look like it could have been just a slashing instead of a tribute. That's the hardest thing about using a blade, Charlie thought. If the victim won't hold still, you never know what you're going to end up with as the end result. The cuts were bad, but not unfixable. Charlie made a mental note how to correct them, then turned to walk out of the alley. That's when things began to fall apart.

"You there, stop. Police," said the uniformed officer. Realizing everything was about to hit the fan, Charlie's mental wheels began to spin furiously.

"Officer, thank God you're here. I was walking by, and I saw this woman lying in the alley. I called to her, but she didn't move, so I came down to see what was wrong. I think she's been murdered," said Charlie, tucking the bloody knife back into the sheath hidden in the small of his back. "You have to call an ambulance." The officer had drawn his gun, and had it trained on Charlie.

"You keep your hands where I can see them and don't move," ordered the officer. He keyed the radio mike on his shoulder. He described the situation, saying there was a woman down, and gave the address, called for an ambulance and also for backup for the suspect he had cornered.

"Put your hands against the wall, keep your legs spread apart, and don't move," said the officer. He started to frisk Charlie one handed. In half a second his hand would find the knife. Charlie snapped his head toward the alleyway.

"Oh my God, he's got a gun," he screamed, putting his hands over his head in a frightened gesture. The officer turned his head for a split second. Charlie hit the cop's hand, knocking the gun to the ground, then took off for the mouth of the alley, running. The officer quickly picked up his gun and gave chase.

XXII

A BOUT THE TIME Charlie was getting ready for his big night out, Annie was primping for the Assassins' Ball, and I was checking the results of Bill's very expensive research. The SOB really had doubled his rates, but he had come through. Not with the assassins: for obvious reasons, they kept rather a low profile on the web. But I had full info on all of Joey's victims, along with the names and addresses of husbands, brothers, and fathers; even cousins, uncles, and boyfriends; just about everyone the police had talked to until Joey's contacts could get the investigations shut down.

It was a lot of information, but none of it was any immediate help, nothing jumped off the screen yelling, "This is the guy." Maybe I'd been hoping for too much, like one of the hookers having worked at the Preying Mantis Ranch, or Rao being reported in the same city as one of Joey's other unfortunate playmates. As much as I liked the guy, Joey's crimes made him just the right target for an "ethical assassin." And maybe the girl in the Vegas case was one of Rose's, only she kept that info out of the records.

I hated to admit it, but we were running out of time. With what Sarah and Bill had dug up, the case was solvable, maybe not for a court of law, but enough to satisfy Mozzano. The problem was that it would take another week or two of work, and we had only tonight and part of tomorrow before the convention was over.

I was half tempted to forgo the night's festivities and concentrate on finding something, anything that would give me a solid lead. But who could turn down attending the Assassins' Ball? Anyway, it was the probably the last time all my suspects would be in the same room together. Maybe something would happen.

XXIII

"I FEEL LIKE a princess," said Annie sarcastically. "Who'd have thought that a little girl from Baltimore would one day grow up and be able to go to the Assassins' Ball?"

"Dreams do come true. We'll have to thank your fairy godmother," I said.

"Given who hired us, it's more like a fairy god*father*. You're not going to turn back into a pumpkin at midnight, are you?"

"No, a cucumber. More phallic."

"Works for me."

The program was right. The Assassins' Ball was the social high point of KCON. This was the one part of the convention that outsiders—discretely invited, of course—were allowed to attend. After all, when most of your attendees are male, it doesn't leave room for much dancing, and then Bach would have wasted all the money he spent on the twenty-three-piece orchestra.

All the conventioneers were decked out in their homicidal splendor. Truth be told, I was disappointed. Not one person was wearing an ammo belt draped around their chest. Apparently it was against the dress code. The whole thing was black tie only. I had to run home in the limo to get a gown for Annie and my tux. It was left over from when I was in a buddy's wedding party. I got the thing when I found out it was only fifty dollars more to buy it than to rent it. This was the second chance I'd had to wear it since that wedding.

It was a basic black, single-breasted jacket and matching black pants. I had a high blue paisley vest, which Annie claims brings out the color in my eyes. The shirt had a Manchurian collar, which basically meant no real collar at all. I topped off the ensemble with a decorative gold and black cover over the top button, which was a fashion plus because I hate ties. I have an eighteen-inch neck, but only a thirty-six-inch waist. All the tailors in the world had gotten together one night and decided that anyone with my neck size should have a waist somewhere between forty-six and fifty inches. This meant that even fitted shirts off the rack were baggy around the middle. In retaliation, I learned how to sew, so I can take in my own shirts, and I refuse to wear a tie unless absolutely necessary. When I first made detective, I had no choice, but when I got onto the bomb squad, I managed to use the excuse that it would only get in my way. My lieutenant bought it, or at least overlooked my breaking of the dress code.

Annie was a vision in white. It was a simple white gown, no sequins or patterns, but it brought out the best in my wife. It was a strapless number. It hugged her curvaceous figure every bit as intently as I did, except I couldn't go walking around doing it: people tended to stare and point. Community standards can be so inhibiting sometimes.

Most of the usual suspects were in attendance. The CIA's Smith brothers were escortless and huddled around the punch bowl, trying to blend in. They were failing.

Rao was over in the corner in a traditional black tux, sans cummerbund, talking with Annie's friend Rose, who everyone else called Mantis. Annie was still promising to explain later.

Rose was the lady in red, wearing a silk gown that left little to the imagination. Most of the men couldn't take their eyes off of her. She was a beauty, but still not as good as my Annie. Reaper was in the corner, a woman on each arm, and he was back to wearing pants.

Tomaso also had a date. Petite thing in a black cocktail dress. He didn't overtly do anything, except he kept giving Annie dirty glances out of the corner of his eye. He was still not happy about her showing him up. Bach and his ladies were milling about the crowd, pressing the flesh and making sure everyone was having a good time. There were several people noticeably not in attendance. First was our sidekick Marty who, when he found out he'd have to wear a tux, chose the better part of valor, and decided he would stay in his room and watch pay-per-view. Glemmer and Doc were nowhere in sight. I also didn't see my "friend" Charlie and his serial killer impersonator road show. The guy didn't seem to be overly gifted with social graces, so maybe he opted not to come.

The band was good, not my typical kind of music, but for the novelty alone, it was nice. The affair just oozed class.

We drifted over to Rao and Rose to say our hellos. The pair seemed to be getting along well, which only made sense, I suppose. After all, they were both in the same line of work; it gave them something to talk about.

"Evening, folks. Everyone enjoying the party," I asked, trying very hard to mask my suspicions, even while looking for a way to bring Joey and his sins into the conversation.

"Not bad," said Rose, "At least the company is good, and it's getting even better with the two of you joining us."

"Rose, you sweet talker, you. It's enough to make a man blush," I said.

"Rose can say a lot of things that can make a man blush," said Rao, obviously coming out of a reddened face himself.

"It's a gift. So, why are you two so late," asked Rose. Like I said, I had to run home and get the clothes.

"Ah, we just wanted to make an entrance," said Annie. "I didn't know you two knew each other."

"We don't, really. Rao here was trying to hit on me, but he did it in such a sweet, non-obnoxious way that I didn't shoot him down. At least, not yet," said Rose. "Besides he's got enough of a rep to keep the other wolves at bay."

"I'm ever ready to help a damsel in distress. However, I don't think you need much rescuing, ever," said Rao.

"You're probably right about that," said Rose. Rao pulled me slightly aside.

"Jack, I've poked around a little bit, but I still haven't found out anything that would be of any use to you yet. Sorry. Have you had any luck on your own," asked Rao.

"Any luck with what," asked Rose.

"The Frosts are playing detective and trying to locate who among us did in one of our fellows the other night," said Rao.

"Annie, shame on you. You didn't tell me about this," said Rose.

"Sorry about that, Rose. I would have mentioned it, but you had that recruiting to take care of first," said Annie.

"It's okay, I'm not mad. Just think, it might be fun to try and see how the other side works. What happened," asked Rose. Annie related the details.

There was nothing out of the ordinary in Rose's reaction. If she'd ever heard of Joey Mozzano before, she didn't let on.

"Interesting, but it doesn't sound terribly specialized. Probably anyone in the room could have made such an easy shot with the right equipment," she said.

"Now you see why we're having trouble," said Annie.

"Especially since KCON ends tomorrow. Can I join your crime-busting team, too," asked Rose, "That is, if I'm not a suspect."

"Well, technically everybody is a suspect, but we already crossed you and Rao off of our short list," said Annie.

My wife's almost as good a liar as she is a shot.

"That's good to hear," said Rose.

"Me, too. There's such an abundance of things I've done, it would be a shame to waste time on something I wasn't guilty of," said Rao.

"So, Rose, do you have any suggestions?" asked Annie.

Rose looked around the room. "You have your basic mafia types like Tomaso. Must be a few dozen here, and that was the world your Joey was involved in. Of course, why do it here, then?"

"To throw off suspicion?" said Rao.

"Convenience," I suggested. "Why hunt him down if you knew he was going to be here, knowing Bach would likely cover the whole thing up?"

"Maybe. Over in the right hand corner, you have a bunch of Triad boys. Your Joey have any problems in Chinatown," asked Rose.

"None that we've heard about, but that doesn't mean anything," said Annie.

"It would have to be an order from on high, because those boys don't blow their noses without permission. Neither would the two Yakuza on the opposite side of the room," said Rose. The gentlemen in question wore tuxedos, but dragon tattoos could be seen peeking out from their necks and sleeves.

"They are guilty of many things, but I can account for their whereabouts on the night of the murder," said Rao. I looked at him, but the glance he gave me screamed, "don't ask."

"The guys on the right side of the dance floor are Organizatsiya, Russian mob. They tend to put their bullets in the head, not the chest, so you could probably overlook them. Those guys drinking at the bar worry me more. A couple of ticking time bombs," said Rose, indicating a white and a black man talking.

"Why? They seem buddy-buddy," I said.

"White guy's the strong arm of The Aryan Sword, a white supremacy group. Black guy is the hitman for The Ebony Vipers, a black hate group.

The only people they hate more than Jews and WASPs are Aryan supremists. Yet, here they are, palling around. It worries me," said Rose.

"I can tell you what they are talking about," said Rao.

"You can hear them from here?" asked Annie.

"No, but I can read lips," said Rao.

"So can I, but I'd need binoculars to see them," I said.

"We'll just have to get you a pair of glasses," said Annie. "Rao, what are they saying?"

"They are discussing the common enemy, the Jews, and teaming up to eliminate them, then dividing the country in half," said Rao.

"That's a realistic goal," I said.

"Might want to tell Eve over there," said Rose, pointing to one of the few other women who were attendees, not guests. "She's Israeli secret service, Mossad. Be interesting to see what happens."

My time as a PI gave me an inspiration.

"I have a better idea. Video the two of them acting all chummy, and then send a copy each to the head honchos of the Aryan Sword and the Ebony Vipers. It would be more interesting to see what happens then," I said.

"I like the way you think," said Rao.

"Me, too," said Rose.

"What the heck. I like it too," said Annie.

"Aw, shucks, guys," I said in a goofy voice. From across the room I noticed the elder statescouple of the assassin set, the Gladstones, making their way toward us.

"Um, if you excuse me, I think I'm gonna ask my wife to dance," I said.

"Why the sudden rush?" said Rao, looking around and not sensing any danger.

"See that older couple making their way toward us?"

"Yes."

"They're the Gladstones. Nice people, but they'll talk your ear off. If they see you two here, they will probably try to fix you up, get you married, and then move onto children. Since we were already together and married, they only worked on the kids part. You've been warned. You stay wallflowers at your own risk."

"Shall we?" I said, bowing to Annie in a courtly manner, indicating the dance floor with the wave of my hand.

"Sure," said Annie.

As we walked away, I heard Rao ask Rose to dance, and she accepted. The dance floor was fairly crowded. Seeing all the killers, hitmen, and assassins in one place sent chills up and down my spine, and reinforced the enormity of figuring this thing out.

"You know this is practically impossible. We're never going to find out who did it," I said to Annie, as I pulled her closer. The band was playing a slow jazz tune, the type where any dancing you needed to do involved holding on to your honey and rocking back and forth.

"Don't get all defeated on me now. We knew this wouldn't be easy when we started, so if we don't figure it out, it's no big deal, but if we do manage to, we'll be legends," said Annie.

"I'm already a legend, but I guess you're right."

"Of course I'm right. I'm always right. Haven't you learned that by now?" said Annie.

"I guess I'm a little dense sometimes," I said.

"But you've gotten much better. You use to be dense all the time," said Annie.

"And now I dense the night away," I punned.

"Jack, sometimes you should leave well enough alone, but I still love you," said Annie.

"You always know the right thing to say, you sweet talker, you," I said.

"Like Rose said, it's a gift," said Annie. We danced in silence for a while. As we were turning around in circles, I noticed Tomaso still leering daggers at us from the corner. His date had apparently moved on, because she was nowhere to be seen.

"Tomaso is still pouting. Better watch your back," I said.

"That's what I have you for. It never ceases to amaze me how fragile the male ego is," said Annie.

"And you're saying I'm a little dense?" I said. I made a mental note to make sure I knew where Tomaso was for the rest of the night… and the rest of the convention, for that matter.

A loud bang and a loud buzzing caused me to turn my head. The buzzing was coming from the metal detector. The ballroom doors had been smashed open by a running man who plowed his way through the crowd of killers. He was looking for someone, and apparently we were it. When he ran right between Annie and me, I recognized who it was.

"Charlie?"

"Jack, you gotta cover for me. I started a little bit early on that Ripper thing. Sorry, I didn't call you, but the Ripper worked alone. One of the boys in blue saw me standing over the body. Be a pal and distract him long enough for me to disappear," said Charlie.

"But—"

"Thanks. Appreciate it," said Charlie, running with an obvious plan of leaping on the stage, then running behind the curtain and disappearing out the back door. Before he could act on it, a uniformed cop came in the door, his gun drawn. "Freeze! Police!"

The next thing that happened was as sudden as it was reflexive. Close to forty people in the crowd pulled out plastic handguns and pointed them at the cop. Breathing suddenly became the loudest sound in the room. The poor guy's eyes went wide, and all color drained from his face. It was a cop's nightmare. Alone, without backup, facing down a mob of gun-toting killers. He didn't have a chance, and then I realized I had yet another reason to feel bad for the guy.

"Oh my God! It's Glen," whispered Annie. I'd recognized her brother just a second after she did. Glen was the youngest of the McHale clan. He had graduated the academy two years ago, and would be on the streets for a while yet. Far from granting favoritism, Chief McHale was harder on his kids then he was on the rest of the force. That way there could be no accusations of favoritism.

"They're gonna kill him. Looks like it's time to blow our cover," I said.

"No, then we'll just end up corpses alongside him. I have a better idea. Play along with me," said Annie, pulling out her plastic handgun.

I took a moment to look at Bach; he was not a happy camper. He had eased off security slightly for this event, not forcing frisks on the assassins and their guests, but still, everyone went through the metal detector. The new plastic handguns couldn't be detected by a mere metal detector.

Everyone was still frozen. No one wanted to be the first to move. With me in tow and her gun pointed out, Annie casually strolled the distance between her and her uniformed brother. Glen recognized us, but the look in his eye, combined with the fact that Annie had a gun pulled out, convinced him not to make that fact public.

"Oh my goodness. I think he's a real cop," said Annie, "Are you a real police officer?"

"Yes ma'am, I am," said Glen.

"Oh my God. I'm so sorry. This isn't what it looks like. You see, we're playing a game. One of those murder mysteries that you have to solve. We thought you were part of the show," said Annie.

"Then what's with all the guns?" said Glen.

"Oh, that's part of the game. They're only plastic toys. See," said Annie, handing her gun over to Glen for examination. "They look real, but they're only made of plastic. Certainly having a toy gun is no a crime, is it, officer?"

"But pulling a gun—even a toy one—on a police officer is, and having a toy gun that looks like a real gun is also illegal," said Glen, looking around. The crowd had relaxed, but the plastic handguns had not been put away. Glen noticed this and added, "And it could get someone accidently shot."

I could see the rest going through his mind. *And it could get me shot if those aren't toys.* He gave Annie a glance that only a sister (or her husband) could interpret, one that said, *Get me out of this and quick.*

"Oh my goodness. I'm so sorry. I didn't know. We're just playing a game. You have to trust me on this Officer…"

"McHale, and I don't care if this was a game. You people just helped a murder suspect get away. Give me one good reason I shouldn't arrest the lot of you, and run you in for obstruction of justice?"

"Because it was quite an innocent mistake. We thought you were part of the game. Besides, is arresting a hundred and fifty people going to serve any purpose other than to cause a lot of paperwork and a lot of wrongful arrest lawsuits? I think that could all be avoided," said Annie, taking back her gun and putting it back in the thigh holster underneath her dress. The rest of the crowd followed suit, making the guns disappear from whence they came.

"That still doesn't help me get my murder suspect back," said Glen. Charlie had never stopped when Glen yelled freeze, and was long gone.

"I feel bad about this whole thing. I was one of the organizers of the game. If it will help matters, my husband and I will go with you and answer any questions you have. We'll do anything we can to help you, Officer McHale," said Annie, her eyes pleading with her brother to go along.

"Fine, but I want everyone to stay in this room. I've already called for backup, and we'll want to question everyone to see if anyone got a good look at his face. Police sketch artists will be along shortly," Glen announced to the crowd. He then pulled his sister and me aside, and spoke to us in quiet and private tones.

"What the hell is going on here?" demanded Glen.

"I can't tell you, at least not right now," said Annie.

"Why the hell not?"

"Because if I did, you'd try to do something about it, and the people in there would kill you, then make you disappear. No one would ever see you again," said Annie.

"I think we better end this conversation. Bach's on his way over," I warned.

"Who's Bach? And what's—"

"Glen, you just have to trust me. Please," begged Annie. "Your life depends on it."

Glen was silent for a minute, mulling it over. "Okay, but you'd better explain this later. I take it I'm still not supposed to know either of you," said Glen. Bach was too near for her to answer, so she just nodded.

Bach swooped in like he owned the place, which I guess in a way he did.

"Officer, my name is Hanson Bach. This is a horrible, horrible tragedy, and I am at your disposal to help you in any way I can," said Bach, shaking Glen's hand. "Perhaps we could talk outside."

The backup had arrived, a squad of uniformed and plain clothes cops. Bach was moving to damage-control mode.

"Excuse me for one second," he said to Glen, stepping back to where Annie and I were.

"Quick thinking," said Bach and, without so much as a "thank you", moved on to the officers who were invading the hotel.

We turned and went back into the party, which had sobered considerably. Despite Glen's orders to stay put, more than half the guests had already disappeared. It was a safe bet that at least part of the crowd was wanted by the police, so any close scrutiny would be a very bad thing.

We looked out into the lobby, where Rao and Rose were walking arm in arm, past the police to the street outside.

"Where are they going," I asked.

"Maybe they have records," suggested Annie.

"Maybe, but they didn't look like they were trying to get away, looked more like they were trying to have a look at what's going on." I said. "I think we better go keep an eye on them. I don't want the police bothering Rao. He could probably kill two or three of them before they could shoot him, if he wanted to."

"Do you think he'll want to," asked Annie nervously.

"He didn't strike me as the type, but let's not take any chances."

We followed them out and around the corner. An alley had already been blocked off with crime scene tape. It had three patrol cars surrounding it with their lights flashing, unintentionally signaling crowds of morbid onlookers to come see what was happening. Rose was at the corner of the crowd, looking into the alleyway. Her face dropped at whatever she saw inside. She tried to push past the police barricade and go into the alley. Inside, someone put a sheet over a dead woman's body.

"Excuse me, ma'am, you can't go in there," said a uniform I didn't recognize.

"You have to let me in. I think the woman in there may have been a friend of mine," said Rose. Her outfit alone practically demanded a double take from any male with the strength to breathe. The officer was already on his triple take of looking Rose up and down.

"The woman in there was a street hooker. You don't look the type to have known her, ma'am," said the officer.

"She and I were talking about getting her out of that profession. She had agreed. We were supposed to fly out Sunday night."

"Well, if it is your friend, I'm sorry. It looks like she didn't stop turning tricks, despite your offer," said the uniform.

"Can't you let me in there just to set my mind at ease? Please?" pleaded Rose.

"No, ma'am. This is a crime scene. I can't disturb anything until the detectives get here."

That's when Annie stepped in.

"You'll need someone to identify the body, won't you, Officer? And if you escort her in, just for a second of course, she can get a look at the victim's face. It might save you a lot of work later on," said Annie. The uniform was debating about going along, because, quite simply, what Annie said made sense. The problem was, he didn't have the authority to do it. Luckily, a couple of plainclothes detectives came over, intending to inspect the crime scene.

"I can't let you in, but they can," said the uniform, pointing to the detectives, efficiently passing the buck.

Rose strolled over, effectively stopping both men in their tracks.

"Can we help you, miss?" asked one of the detectives. It was obvious the type of help he wanted to offer had nothing to do with police work. Rose explained the situation.

"There's a dead woman down there. This is not going to be pretty. I don't know if you would be able to handle it, ma'am," said the detective.

"I can handle it," Rose said simply. The detective was wavering, but Rose turned on the charm. There was a slight chill in the air, and Rose was not wearing anything under the silk, so certain attributes were prominently noticeable. Rose didn't exactly say anything, she just changed her body language. Putting one hip a little higher, tilting her head slightly and batting her eyelashes, she tossed her hair. The detective looked like a deer caught in her headlights, and it was over. He was putty in her hands. The guy would do whatever she wanted, with hopes that maybe later on he'd have a chance to console the grieving friend and maybe get a little something extra for his efforts.

"I can handle it," repeated Rose, "I need to know if it's her. Please?" The detective nodded, and lifted up the police yellow tape to let both of them climb underneath.

"Just take a quick look, tell me if it's her, and don't touch anything," said the detective, walking her down the alley.

"Thank you," said Rose.

"I'm not so sure you're gonna thank me after you see the body."

The detective gently pulled back the sheet, just enough so Rose could see the face. Rose's eyes started to tear up.

"It's her," said Rose.

"I'm sorry to trouble you in your time of grief, but can you give me a little more information? Her name and where she lived, maybe," asked the detective.

"Her name was Chandra Summers. I can't tell you where she lived, but I could give you her phone number. You could track down the address from that, couldn't you?"

"Sure. We have a crisscross directory that could do that," said the detective. Rose gave the detective all the information she had on Chandra. Then the detective took down Rose's fake personal information, so he could contact her with any further questions and maybe an offer of a date. He put the sheet back over Chandra's face, stood up, and wrapped a consoling arm around Rose's shoulder, escorting her out of the alley.

Rose thanked him for his help, before she stormed away from the alley, daring anyone to stop her. Rao, Annie, and I moved alongside her, not willing to take the dare. The woman was mad.

"She had a chance to get out of this. Some sick bastard took it away from her just to get his jollies. I'm gonna kill him. Did you see who that guy was," asked Rose.

"Yes." I said. "The guy's name was Charlie."

"The little weasel of a guy who kept to himself," asked Rose.

"Yes," I said.

"You two are the ones playing detective. Do you have any idea how I can catch him," asked Rose.

I did some soul searching. I severely doubted that the authorities would be able to find and stop Charlie before he finished his tribute to Jack the Ripper. If my memory served, he killed five women.

I was even more sure that Charlie had cleaned out his things and was already far away from the hotel. If I told Rose, she wouldn't just stop him, she would kill him. He was a killer. By ending his life, she would save those of other innocent women. In the end, I couldn't live with their deaths on my conscience. I could live with Charlie's.

"He's planning to leave for London in seven days. He's going to Whitechapel. He's planning to do a tribute to Jack the Ripper there, killing his victims the same way the Ripper did." I said.

"Thanks, Jack, I'm gonna take this guy out. He's too loose a cannon," said Rose. I nodded.

"This is an evil man. He should be killed. If you wish, I will help you with this," said Rao.

Rose looked up at him and smiled, then she leaned over and kissed him on the cheek.

"What was that for?" said Rao.

"For treating me like a peer," said Rose. "Thanks for the offer, but this is personal. I'll take care of him myself, but I would like to get to know you better."

"Me too," said Rao.

"And I'll keep you two abreast of what happens as well," said Rose.

"Thanks," I said.

For better or worse, Charlie would now be taken care of. That was one killer down, who knew how many to go.

XXIV

THE ASSASSINS' BALL had been interesting, but it couldn't hold a candle to the post party Annie and I held in our room. It was a private bash, only two guests, and it had been excessively explosive and athletic. I was lying down, doing my best to recoup, and loving every minute of it.

I just love the afterglow. That's that moment right after you make love, where everything is kind of warm and fuzzy, and all is right with the world. I could have stayed lying there naked, with my arms around my wife, for what I wished would be forever. Unfortunately, Annie had other ideas.

"Come on, lazy bones, we got work to do. What do you want to do, just lie here and sleep," asked Annie.

"Actually, that sounds good to me," I said.

"Tomorrow is the last day of the convention. We still don't have any idea who killed Joey Mozzano, and we're not gonna learn anything else by just lying here in bed," said Annie.

"Yeah, but at least we're enjoying ourselves here," I said. Naked, Annie walked over to the wet bar, and pulled out a can of soda.

"Want one?" she asked.

"Those things are six bucks a piece."

"Yeah, but we're not paying for it," Annie said.

"In that case, I'll have two," I said.

"We're gonna sit down and go over everything, then maybe we'll come up with some clue we missed somewhere. I've got no trouble taking Mozzano's money, but I want to make sure we at least do the best job we can," said Annie. She took a glass from on top of the wet bar and poured her soda into it. She lifted it to her mouth and took a sip.

"Yech, this stuff's warm. Needs ice," said Annie, picking up the ice bucket and jiggling it. It was empty.

"I'll go get you some ice," I said, as I slowly sat up on the bed.

"Don't trouble yourself. Rest up. We're gonna need to take lots of breaks tonight. I need you to be able to keep up," said Annie, as she threw a T-shirt over herself, then picked up one of her Berettas and the ice bucket.

"You're only going to the ice machine," I said.

"Why take any chances in this place?" said Annie. "I'll be back in a minute."

Annie walked out the door and shut it behind her. I laid back down on the bed. A couple minutes passed, and I was beginning to wonder if Annie had gotten lost. Maybe the ice machine was broken and she went to another floor. I was debating between whether to relax or put on a pair of pants and go look, when someone kicked the door in.

It was a beautiful redhead, but it wasn't Annie. She had a forty-five automatic in her hands, and it was pointing at me. I rolled to the opposite side of the bed. Thank goodness for paranoia. Whenever we stayed somewhere, Annie would stash guns in different parts of the room so we'd have easy access in case we were ever caught with our pants down, literally in this case. For my part, I had picked up two bed holsters from the dealers' room. These are holsters that could be hooked on to any bed. One of my better purchases.

When I rolled off the bed, I grabbed a thirty-eight revolver that was holstered there. The redhead had already gotten off two shots by that point. One took out my pillow and the other part of the mattress where I had been lying.

I started firing without looking up, so my head wouldn't become a target. I assumed she was still in the doorway and fired all six shots from the revolver in the general direction at different heights in case she had ducked. I don't care what you see on TV, when you're in a gun fight, you don't stop shooting until you're out of bullets. I didn't hear any movement, but I wasn't taking any chances. Annie had put another thirty-eight revolver behind the nightstand, which I crawled over to and retrieved.

Slowly, I stood up. There were red stains on the door frame and the nearby walls. The redhead was lying in a pool of her own blood on the floor. It looked like I had hit her with four bullets. The first thing I did was walk over and kick the gun out of her hand. I can't tell you how many people get dead from a perp who they thought was out of it, but still had a gun in his, or her, hand. I checked for a pulse, but couldn't find one. She was gone.

I recognized her. She was the redhead in Bach's suite when we visited him. Whatever she did, she was doing under his orders. Her gun had a silencer, so the two shots she'd gotten off had made little more than a puffing noise. My six shots were much more likely to bring attention to what had happened, at least in a normal hotel. In this place, everyone else on my floor was an assassin. Once they were sure this wasn't affecting them, they would ignore it. The Gladstones were the only ones who bothered to come out and investigate.

The elderly couple came up to the door, him with a forty-five and her with a compact Uzi. For senior citizens, they carried their weapons with an amazing ease. Maude looked at the situation and then looked at me. She smiled and raised her eyebrows. I realized I was still naked, so I opened the bathroom door, pulled out a towel, and wrapped it around my waist.

"You and the missus have a falling out?" asked Maude, looking at the bloody redhead.

"This isn't my wife," I said.

"What you folks do in your personal life is your own business," said Dick.

"She just tried to kill me," I said.

"She's breaking Hanson Bach's rules," said Maude.

"She works for Bach," I said.

"Ah. This is not good," said Dick.

"Did either of you see Annie in the hallway?" I said, rushing out to the ice machine, gun still in hand. No Annie, only an ice bucket on the floor. I ran back to the Gladstones.

"We haven't seen her," said Maude.

"Something happened. She's missing," I said.

"Any sign of foul play, son?" said Dick. "Besides the dead woman on your floor, that is."

"The ice bucket she was carrying was lying down by the ice machine, but there is no blood or other sign of a scuffle," I said, as my mind raced. "Now that I think about it, I don't think the redhead was trying to kill me, just frighten me. She waited till after I moved before she fired off a shot, and she only fired two. If she wanted me dead, she should have kept shooting." Anyone who worked for Bach would know that much.

At the end of the hallway, we heard an elevator ding. The three of us all pointed our guns in that direction. Rao turned the corner, saw us, and slowly put his hands over his head.

"What's going on," he asked.

"Bach had one of his girls take a couple of shots at me, and I think he grabbed Annie," I said.

"What are you going to do about it," asked Rao.

"Going to go get her," I said, marching toward the elevator.

"Uh, if I could make a suggestion," said Rao.

"What?"

"You might want to put on some pants first," said Rao.

"I'd have to agree," said Maude.

I looked down at the towel I was wearing, which was hardly the way to strike fear in a man who brokered out hired killers.

"I'll be back in a minute," I said. I ran into the room, threw on some clothes and sneakers, then ran back out toward the elevator. Rao gently put his hand on my shoulder, stopping me.

"You can't go off half-cocked. You need a plan. You go charging after Bach, and you're going to end up dead. That's not going to do you or Annie any good," said Rao.

He was right. I went back into the room, stepping over the bloody body.

"Why don't you guys come in?" I said.

Rao and the Gladstones walked in, each gently stepping over the body. All of them were careful not to touch anything, so as not to leave fingerprints or physical evidence at the scene of a murder. They were professionals, after all. I loaded up on weapons.

"Anyone need anything? Gun, ammo, knife," I asked.

"What are you planning to do? You're only one man, you know," said Rao.

"I'd prefer to rent out an army, but it's kind of hard to get one this time of the day and on such short notice," I said.

"I don't know about an army, but you got some people right in front of you that you can ask for help," said Dick.

"You guys would help me out against Bach? I thought he's the one broker killers didn't cross."

"I've never done work for Bach," said Rao.

"We're retired, dear. I told you that. Bach doesn't scare us. We were around before he was, and from the look in your eye, we're going to be around long after he's gone," said Maude, in a grandmotherly fashion.

"Thanks. I need all the help I can get," I said. With that in mind, I banged on the dividing door between our room and Marty's. It took Marty a minute to open up. He'd been sleeping and hadn't heard a thing.

"What do you want?" growled Marty, his hair disheveled, squinting against the light.

"Bach's kidnapped Annie. We're gonna get her back. Wanna help?" I said.

"What the hell are you talking about?" said Marty, as he opened his eyes. He noticed the dead and bloody redhead on the floor. "Oh, crap. You're serious, aren't you?"

"Yes. Look, I know you're afraid of him. You don't have to, but—" Marty shut his door.

"Well, I guess that answers that," I said. All those monkey jokes were coming back to haunt me. About a minute later, the door opened up. Marty's hair had been combed. He had put on a holster, and was putting on his jacket to cover the gun.

"What's the plan?" said Marty. I extended my hand to him, and he shook it.

"Thanks," I said.

"I ain't doing this for you. I'm doing this for Annie," said Marty. I nodded.

The wheels in my mind were already turning. I had a couple of ideas. "Here's the plan."

W E DIDN'T BOTHER to knock, and the CIA spooks didn't take too kindly to us invading their hotel suite. They went for their guns. Fortunately, we already had ours out.

"Good evening, gentlemen. I'm here to make you a deal," I said.

"Sorry, we don't make deals with killers," said my dear friend Smith.

"Bullshit. You *are* killers, but I'm not here to quibble. Like I said, I'm here to offer you a deal. You wanna know who offered me that contract, here's your chance. Let me throw in a bonus. It was to blow up the Statue of Liberty. I'm willing to hand over that information to you," I said.

"What do you want in return?" said Smith dubiously.

"It's simple. I want to review your surveillance for the elevators for the last hour. Somebody kidnapped my wife. If your surveillance tapes from the elevator or somewhere else show me who did it, and where they took her, I give you a name. They don't, we walk out," I said.

"And if we refuse?" said Smith, in his best tough-guy voice.

"Then you'll disappear, never to be seen again," said Maude, pointing her compact Uzi directly at Smith. She was a professional: she held the gun at her waist, close to her side, so it couldn't be knocked out of her hands, and stayed far enough away from Smith so he couldn't jump her before he got shot. It was the things like that that they don't show you in the movies, things that make the difference in the real world. As far as tough voices go, Maude may not have had a lot of grit in hers, but I believed every word. So did Smith.

"Get them what they need," barked Smith to another man, who had also identified himself as Smith earlier. It took a couple of minutes for them to get the right drive plugged into their laptop. Meanwhile, the CIA spooks were trying to decide if they could take us. After all, there were just five of us, two of whom were collecting Social Security. There were nine of them. Problem was, we had our guns drawn. They didn't, and that made all the difference.

"As long as you're sharing, do you have anything from our room for the two nights before we arrived," I asked.

"We don't have anything on the Mozzano killing. He was more paranoid than you two, and had all the mirror-cams covered," said Smith. So much for a quick solution.

There were actually four elevators in the elevator bank nearest our room. It took a while to review everything, even at high speed. In elevator number three, we had a winner. It showed Annie, still in just the large T-shirt, being held at gun point by a familiar face. Hanson Bach was standing by his side.

"The Reaper," I growled in some surprise. I had been half-expecting Tomaso. The video kept running. Reaper and Annie got out at the tenth floor. Hanson Bach pushed the button for the penthouse.

"What's the Reaper's room number?" I demanded.

"What makes you think I'd know that information? We're just simple recruiters," said Smith, with a smile and a sarcastic tone.

"I love sarcasm as much as the next guy, but don't mess with me right now," I said.

"What's it worth?" he said.

"Your life."

"Frost, you're just no fun anymore. He's on this floor, just down the hall in 1014."

"Thank you," I said.

"I believe you owe me some information," said Smith.

"Fair is fair. Bach offered me the hit. He never told me the country, but he implied it was Middle Eastern," I said.

"What makes you think we're going to let you live after this?" said Smith.

"Simple: this is a business for you, plain and simple. We just gave you something that's gonna make you look like heroes to your superiors. It doesn't pay. Besides, you never know when we might be useful again," I said. Another possibility was to blackmail him, but his type usually responded to that by killing, so I would only use that option as a last resort.

"Besides, the bastard took my wife. I want to kill him for you."

"No, we need him alive. We need that information. As a matter of fact, we'll take care of him for you," said Smith.

Nine CIA spooks saddled up and went out the door, heading for the penthouse. They had no interest in saving Annie, only in nailing Bach. We were still the rescue detail.

The door opened, and another Smith stuck his head back in.

"You might want to have an idea about what you're charging into. Punch 1014 in the console, and the cameras will show you the inside of the Reaper's room," said Smith. "Not everyone picked up on our surveillance as well as you and your wife did." He winked at me, and headed out again.

"Anyone know how to work this thing," I asked. I could figure it out, given time, but that was too precious a commodity to waste right now.

"I've used something like it," said Rao, fiddling with some controls. He managed to figure it out. We were able to get three separate views of the Reaper's room. One was at an angle that looked like it was outside the window. All that one showed was curtains. The second was from the main mirror in the bedroom area, and the other was from the mirror in the bathroom.

In keeping with the melodrama, the Reaper had bound Annie to a chair, but instead of using rope, he restrained her with duct tape. From the look of things, he had more on his mind than just keeping her captive. He was lifting the bottom of her T-shirt, trying to bring it up. I felt my blood begin to boil. Before I could even speak, he made the mistake of getting too close, and Annie head butted him between the eyes, stunning him for a second. He slapped her across the face. Annie spit in his. He pushed the chair down, on its back. I took off out the door, running. Rao tackled me in the hall.

"Jack, I hate to keep pointing this out, but if you don't have a plan, you'll kill her. If you want, I'll tape a note saying that to your shirt," said Rao.

"The son of a bitch is about to rape my wife, and you want me to have a plan? I can't even see straight," I screamed. Rao shushed me.

"Think about it, Jack. The whole time we watched, he never put his gun down. If you barge in, he'll be able to put a bullet in Annie before you can put a bullet in him," said Rao.

I forced myself to start thinking like a cop again. Hostage situations are probably the toughest conditions to work under, especially if you are emotionally involved. If I was still on the force, they wouldn't let me near this. I even considered calling in the boys and girls in blue, but it would be too late to do any good. I broke it down as I saw it.

"The Reaper has the doors locked and the curtains drawn, so we couldn't sniper his hide. He's on the tenth floor. The windows don't open, and attacking from outside in would as likely hurt Annie as him. There are two doors leading in, but he'd hear us before we got either open. I could blow the doors, but again, the blast could hurt Annie. If it didn't, he might be stunned enough for us to charge in and shoot him. If we had some sort of gas, maybe we could either knock him out or flush him out. Problem is, all my ideas are too complicated, too many things can go wrong. Simple works best, but I don't have a simple plan," I said.

"I do," said Maude.

XXV

"YOU STUPID BITCH," the Reaper said softly, as he casually slapped Annie across the face again. He had pulled the chair back up to an upright position, but was having second thoughts about it. "You thought that just because I put on a good show in the dealers' room, I wouldn't be looking for payback. Well, you've seen mine and now I've seen yours, most of it, anyway. And when I'm ready, I'll see the rest, just before I humiliate you like you did me. How do you like that?"

"A whole lot better than having to look at you," said Annie. Her left eye was beginning to get puffy and swollen. There was blood dripping out of her left nostril.

"Oh yeah, real funny. You're missing out on the chance to have a real man."

Annie laughed. "If what I saw was real, you should go for an extension. Now I know why you carry a big gun."

"Just wait, you'll see and feel how big my gun gets."

There was a knock at the door. The Reaper looked up. Obviously, he wasn't expecting company.

He made his way carefully to the door, but didn't use the peephole right away. It was an old hit man trick. Stare right in the peephole and as soon as you saw someone on the other side block the light by moving in front of it to look, you pulled the trigger and blew them away through the door. The Reaper had used a piece of duct tape to cover up the peep hole and carefully pulled it away using his hands to make sure no light shone through. It was only a little old lady. She knocked again, and started yelling loudly.

"Henry! Mildred! Open up, it's me," Maude kept repeating. She kept knocking and yelling. She was bringing too much attention to his room. He couldn't just shoot her, because someone might see the body or blood, and Bach wouldn't like that.

Realizing that his best option was to just make her go away, the Reaper opened the door to the room slightly, just enough to stick his head out, but not wide enough so the old lady would be able to see anything in the room.

"I'm sorry. I think you have the wrong room," he said, straining to be polite.

Ignoring him as if he wasn't there, Maude tried to look past him, and kept screaming. "Mildred? Henry? Are you in there?"

"Listen, lady, you got the wrong room. There ain't nobody named Mildred or Henry here," growled the Reaper.

"Don't give me that, young man. Mildred told me her room number was 1014, and that's what it says on this door," said Maude, tapping the numbers with her finger, "This is Henry and Mildred's room. What have you done with them?"

Maude pushed open the door enough to get her shoulder and foot wedged in.

"Listen, you old bat, you're gonna be sorry if you don't get out of here now."

"I'm not leaving," said Maude.

"Yes, you are."

"You either let me in, or I'm gonna scream," threatened Maude.

The Reaper shook his head and sighed in resignation. He was going to have to kill the old crone. Might as well let her come inside, so there wouldn't be a body in the hall.

"Fine," he said, opening the door just enough to let the old woman in. He pointed the gun at her face. "I told you, you'd be sorry."

"Not as sorry as you," said Maude, gesturing down with her head. The Reaper looked down to find a large caliber derringer aimed at his crotch.

"What the hell?! You better put that down, lady, or I'm gonna kill you," he said, his voice trembling only slightly.

"Go ahead. I'm an old woman, I've had a good life. I gotta go sometime. Head shot, I'm pretty much dead. You, on the other hand, will probably survive, although your family jewels will be blown clean off. You could shoot me, but we'd both know that even if you do, my fingers are going to squeeze the trigger. I'll be comfortably dead, but you're going to have to live the rest of your life as a eunuch. I think it'd be best if you handed that gun over to me. Don't worry, take your time. I'll give you to the count of three to decide. One, two…"

The Reaper took his finger out of the trigger and handed the gun to her, butt first. Behind him, he heard the door that adjoined his room to the one next door being broken down. He turned his head slightly to see Marty walking in, holding a marble coffee table in his hands as if it was a shield. The next sight was Dick, providing cover. He had traded in his .45 for an Uzi. Rao and I rushed past to grab Annie, chair and all.

Maude's plan had worked beautifully. Part one was for her to distract the Reaper and disarm him, if possible. That part had gone well. Just in case she wasn't able to do it, we would have whisked Annie back to the next room, which thankfully had been empty. Dick would have been trying to kill him before he killed us.

Marty dropped the marble coffee table. Holding it up had been a strain. The thing was heavy, and we hoped the CIA wouldn't mind that we stole it from their suite. The marble coffee table was the only thing we could find that was remotely bullet proof.

Since Maude had pulled off part one, we were able to put Annie down and take the duct tape off. It wasn't a pleasant experience. Annie screamed as we took it off her arms.

"Don't be such a baby," I said, covering my relief by being obnoxious.

"Let's rip off all the hairs on the back of your arms and see how you like it," said Annie. As soon as her arms were free, she wrapped them around my neck and kissed me. Then she turned to everyone else and said, "Thanks."

"Our pleasure, dearie," said Maude. "Can't let this piece of trash take out such a beautiful young lady. Besides, you still gotta keep trying to have those kids."

"But if you're really feeling grateful, you could always name them after Maude and me," said Dick, with a smile and a wink.

Annie laughed. "I'll honestly think about it."

"Now, what was all this about," I said, glaring at the Reaper.

Annie answered for him. "From what this asshole here blabbed to me, Bach gave him fifty grand to kidnap me. The rape was his idea. Bach planned to use me as a hostage, to blackmail you into doing a job. As near as I can figure, it's gotta be the Statue of Liberty job."

Annie picked up her Beretta from where the Reaper had lain it on the dresser. Knowing her, she felt more naked without a gun than without her clothes. Though she did technically have the T-shirt on, it didn't cover a whole lot, especially if she breathed in too deeply.

"I guess he figured to save you, I'd do it for free, and he could keep the whole hundred million for himself," I said.

"Wait a second, you're saying you turned down a hundred million-dollar job?" said Dick unbelievingly.

"Yep," I said.

"A man with standards that money can't buy. A patriot, even. I'm impressed," said Rao.

"Me, too. Maybe there's some hope for you young people after all," said Maude.

While the rest of us were making small talk, the Reaper reached back behind his head to where he had a twenty-two pistol hidden in a neck holster just under the collar of his jacket. He pulled it out, planning to shoot Maude, then the rest of us.

Problem was, he was just too slow, at least compared to Annie. She had the Beretta up and fired before his gun even cleared the top of his head. Maude and Dick with their Uzis hadn't even had a chance to react yet.

"I saved you. You saved me. Looks like we're even," said Maude.

"I still owe you one. I owe all of you. Thanks again. It's not enough, but how about we take you all out to eat? We can call it a late supper or an early breakfast," said Annie.

"Food works for me," said Rao.

"Way to a man's heart is through his stomach," said Dick.

"Don't believe him dear, it's a little bit lower than the stomach," said Maude with a wink.

Something struck me, which I had overlooked in my concern for Annie's well being.

"We've got two dead bodies. What are we going to do about that," I asked.

Annie and I knew each other well enough to know what the other was thinking. If this had happened in a normal case, we would have called the cops and let them take care of everything through channels. There was a problem doing that here. For one, we already knew that Bach had some cops in his pocket. Two, we'd have to reveal the involvement of our new friends. I had no way of knowing if any of them were wanted by the police. To get them in trouble with the authorities, after they had just saved Annie's life seemed ungrateful. Besides, there was nothing for the system to be brought in to solve. We knew who the killers were. We were them, so there was no reason for an investigation, and we knew it was justifiable homicide.

"You mean you've never cleaned up after your own hits before?" said Dick, "I guess being a bomber, you wouldn't have to. Don't worry about it, I have a friend here in the hotel who can take of it for you, he owes me a favor. He's a fixer."

A fixer was someone who made the evidence of crimes disappear. He'd get rid of the body, the carpet, paint over everything, so that there would be nothing to tie us to the crime. As far as that went, there would be no evidence that a crime had even occurred.

I looked at Annie; she nodded. This would be easier. Then we both got the same idea at once.

"Ask him if he did any work for Bach a few days ago."

"I will. I'll give him a call, and we'll meet in the lobby for that meal in about an hour," said Dick.

Annie and I agreed, then went back to our room to change.

XXVI

THE DOOR TO our hotel room made a sickening squishing sound as it opened, pushing against a carpet that was saturated with blood. I had rolled the body over, so the door could open and close without hitting the redhead in the back of the skull.

"What a mess. I can't leave you alone at all, can I?" said Annie. "I wasn't gone five minutes, and you had another woman in the room."

"Honey, I can explain. Rumors of my prowess had leaked out, and she wouldn't take no for an answer, so I had to shoot her," I said. There is something about death that made both of us try harder to laugh, kind of like remaining defiant in the face of an overwhelming enemy.

Things were a mess. But the fixer would have this body out of here long before that happened, and have the room cleaned up so the hotel would be none the wiser. I started to step over the crimson areas of the carpet, using the sections that were relatively untouched. I was looking down to make sure I put my foot in the right spot, when I noticed a foot print that hadn't been there before.

"Get out of here," I said, shoving Annie toward the door, but it was too little too late. Bach stepped out from his hiding spot, just inside the bathroom.

"I would advise against that. Mr. and Mrs. Frost, please come in," said Bach. He was holding a forty-five magnum. The macho part of me thought about just jumping in front of the gun and letting Annie get away, but a magnum would blow a hole all the way through me and still get her. Luckily, the part of me that wanted to survive held those emotions in check long enough for me to assess the situation. We did as we were told.

"Mrs. Frost, please close the door," said Bach. Annie did as she was instructed. "You would not believe what has happened to me. Then again, maybe you would," growled Bach.

"The maid shorted you on the towels?" I said.

"Maybe room service messed up your order?" said Annie.

As we walked into the room, we moved toward opposite corners. It was basic flanking maneuvers. It meant he could only shoot one of us at a time, which meant the other one would probably be able to get him. We didn't want to force a confrontation, as the results would be far too bloody for our side, but it increased the odds that one of us would walk out of here.

Bach was familiar with the tactic, and he pulled a second, smaller thirty-eight revolver out of his pocket to counter it. I was to his right and he trained the magnum on me. Annie was to his left, with the revolver pointed at her.

"Nice try, but that's not going to work here. Both of you, please take out your guns slowly and throw them on the bed," said Bach. He didn't say anything about knives, so I left the blade I had hidden in my sleeve. I put three guns on the bed: one from my holster, another from my waistband, and one from the small of my back. I still had another one hidden in the small of my back, and a special toy in my pocket. I assumed, correctly, that Bach wouldn't risk getting close enough to me to frisk me.

I could see in Annie's face that she was upset. Normally, she packed at least four weapons: two Berettas, a thirty-eight revolver in case one of the Berettas jammed—as automatics can sometimes do—and a twenty-two in an ankle holster. This time, she was only carrying the Beretta, and wearing just a T-shirt. There was no place else for her to hide another one.

"Should we read the guns a bedtime story now," I asked.

"Enough with the funny business," said Bach.

"Okay, then, why don't you tell us what this is all about," I asked.

"Simple, really, I offered you a reasonable job for more money than you're ever going to see in your miserable life, and you turned me down," said Bach. Looks like we had guessed right.

I knew better than to try to appeal to his patriotism again. "Why me?"

"Originally, I was going to use Glemmer, but then you showed him up, so I figured I'd use you instead. You've never done any work for me before, and there is nothing to trace you to me, which couldn't be said for Glemmer. Besides, my end of the contract obligated me to make sure the bomber didn't live to testify if he got caught. Glemmer had done work for me for years and he was reliable, although the incident with the painting caused me to doubt his competence. This was too important a job to have doubts on.

"You had the advantage of being good and meaning nothing to me. Plus, you managed to piss me off several times. Hell, I was debating having you killed even if you didn't get caught. I was even going to approach your wife to see if she'd be willing to do the deed. After all, with you dead, all that money would be hers. The bitch wouldn't even talk to me about it. It didn't matter; it just meant I was going to have to pay for a little extra something out of my cut to see the deed done," said Bach.

"That's another thing I was having a hard time believing," I said.

"What's that?"

"That you were offering the full amount. A guy like you tells me the price is a hundred million less twenty million for your commission, I figure the real price was at least a hundred and fifty million," I said.

Bach smiled. "Closer to two hundred. I'm a millionaire many times over, and I have power: power that men who could buy and sell me fear, but they still have more money than me. With this one job, that injustice would be corrected. That much money is more than even I could spend in a lifetime."

"So you sell out your country?" said Annie.

"What's my country ever done for me? Pick up the garbage? Provide police protection? They don't do it for free. I have to pay taxes for that, which the damn IRS is constantly auditing to make sure I'm not hiding anything. I guess I'll move to another country and pay someone else to pick up my garbage. I never wanted law enforcement anywhere near me, anyhow."

"So why kidnap me and kill Jack?" asked Annie.

"Sondra…" said Bach, indicating the redheaded corpse on the floor. I looked down, and a sick thought came to mind. With all the blood from the head shot over her face and hair, she was more of a redhead now than she had been when she was alive. "…was supposed to scare your husband and then bring him up to see me. He'd find out that we had you, and the only thing that he could do to get you back was do the job. That way, I kept all the money for myself. Speaking of your kidnapping, if you're here, I can only assume the Reaper is dead," said Bach.

"You mess with us, you pay the cost," said Annie. Her tough guy voice was better than the Reaper's, even when he was alive. I can't imagine he'd be doing a lot of talking now, or any time in the near future. "Even the Reaper has to pay me."

"Looks like Sondra was a little too slow in dealing with you, Mr. Frost. Good help is so hard to find, and I find myself without a staff at all.

It seems for some reason, the CIA came calling and killed my other girls. They were babbling some nonsense about wanting to know about a bombing. I can only assume I have you to thank for that, Mr. Frost," said Bach.

"No need to thank me. All part of the service," I said. Bach cocked the trigger on the magnum. I could hear the ocean rushing through my ears from my blood pressure pounding in my head. One little twitch of his finger, and I was a dead man.

Annie talked to Bach, distracting him.

"So what happened to the spooks," she asked.

Bach turned his head to answer. "They're next. I wanted to make sure of you two first."

"But if you kill Jack and me, who's going to do your little bombing," asked Annie.

"Glemmer will have to do."

"Sounds like you're in need of a new bodyguard. I'd like to apply for the job," said Annie, turning on the charm and taking a deep breath to make her two biggest assets much more prominent.

"You're just saying that because you don't want me to kill you."

"You're absolutely right. I don't want to die. I'd much rather work for you."

"Even if I kill your husband," asked Bach, amused.

"I prefer that you didn't—I'd miss him, but in a choice between him and me..." said Annie letting her unfinished sentence hang in the air.

"Nothing like loyalty, eh Frost?" Bach said to me. For once in my life, I kept my mouth shut. "There's no reason I should trust you. How can you prove to me that you're serious about your offer?"

Annie smiled, ran her fingers through her hair, and did her famous head toss. Slowly, she reached down to the bottom of the T-shirt she was wearing, and pulled it up over her head. Annie dropped it gently on the ground and stood naked in front of Bach. He forgot I existed. His entire concentration was focused on Annie.

Slowly, she walked up to Bach. With her right hand, she slowly traced little zigzags down his chest. She reached out with her left hand and uncocked the magnum. She pushed him down so he sat on the bed, and took the magnum from his hand. Bach pointed the thirty-eight caliber directly at her, but she just dropped the magnum. He had a big smile on his face.

While that was going on, I didn't go for my gun, which is what I think Annie was expecting. I had a better idea.

I still had the painting with the plastic explosives from Glemmer's lecture hanging on the wall. I hadn't gotten a chance to show it to Annie yet. I only hoped that the fake radio detonator switch would fool Bach.

I took the painting down, threw the phony switch, and saw the little light come on. I had a tiny bottle of mace which I carried on my key chain. It looked enough like a detonator for what I had in mind.

"Bach…"

"What's the matter, Frost, can't handle the sight of a real man with your wife?" said Bach, wrapping his free hand around her waist.

"That's not it," I said.

"Don't worry, I'll kill you in a minute," said Bach.

"No, you won't, not unless you want to die, too," I said. Bach turned and stared at me, then at the picture with the fake detonator on the back of the frame. Annie stepped back from Bach.

"Took you long enough. Now I'm going to have to shower to get the stench of his touch off me," said Annie, moving to get her T-shirt. Bach pointed the thirty-eight at her, and picked the magnum back up.

"Don't move, Mrs. Frost," said Bach. Turning his attention back to me, he said, "That's the picture you took from Glemmer, isn't it?"

"Why, yes it is. It's outfitted with a little radio detonator, which is attached to this dead man switch in my hand."

"You're full of shit. Why would you put something like that back together again and keep it in your hotel room?"

"Simple: I wasn't planning to keep it here long. I had a job to do later tonight, and it saved me some expenses."

"Job for who?"

"For Mozzano," I lied, but he'd believe it. "There are a couple of people he wanted to make an example of while they were having dinner at a nice little restaurant. I was going to switch this painting with one of theirs tonight, when no one was around. Then tomorrow, during the appetizer, boom. I hit the plunger and watch them die," I said with what I hoped was enough sincerity to fake blood-thirstiness.

"How much," asked Bach.

"Fifty grand."

"You take a job for chicken feed and turn down one for millions? Your priorities are all messed up," said Bach.

"No, not really. My way, some bad people die. Your way, some innocent tourists and their kids bite the big one."

"I don't believe you," said Bach.

"Fine, then we all die," I bluffed.

"Fine, I don't want to go alone anyway," said Bach as he shot the detonator. Luckily, there was no spark to set off the explosives.

"You're just not crazy enough to pull that one off," said Bach. He wanted to gloat some more, which gave us maybe two more minutes on this planet.

Bach hadn't bothered with silencers. The noise got Marty's attention, and he opened the door between our rooms.

"Guys, everything okay in here," asked Marty, before he saw Bach with the two guns and Annie standing naked in front of him.

"Everything is not okay, but this doesn't concern you. You will turn around and go back into your room. You will pretend like nothing happened, and I'll let you live," said Bach, without even looking at Marty.

Marty stood silent and unmoving.

"I said get out," said Bach, not even bothering to stand up from his perch on the bed.

"Okay, Mr. Bach," said Marty, as he pulled his gun out from the holster under his jacket and laid the muzzle right above Bach's left ear. "Not."

My bomb scare tactic hadn't worked, so I pulled out the gun from the small of my back.

"Drop 'em, Bach. It's all over," I said.

"Not from where I sit. You and your pretty wife are still gonna be dead," said Bach.

"So are you," said Marty.

"Oh, well," said Bach. He took the gun off Annie and bent his elbow backward so the thirty-eight was now pointing at Marty. "Betcha I could kill all three of you before any of you pulls the trigger," said Bach.

"You don't want to do that. You'll lose anyway," said Marty.

"Why is that," asked Bach.

"Because Annie's the Baltimore police commissioner's daughter. That's more heat than even you can handle," said Marty.

Bach laughed. "The commissioner's daughter is a killer? Ah, I'm gonna own this town."

"She's no assassin, she's here undercover," said Marty, but he had over-played his hand. The thought of the police chief's daughter as an assassin was amusing. The fact that someone had infiltrated his world was an insult. His face turned red. I'm not sure exactly what happened next. All I know is I saw the finger on the gun pointed toward me twitch.

I needed a distraction. Fortunately, I had one already set up. I reached for the toy in my pocket.

There was a beep, then a gunshot from nowhere. It didn't hit anything but the wall, but it drew Bach's attention just long enough.

I dove for the floor, firing at the same time. A bullet flew mere inches over my head. My shot hit him in the chest. At the same time, he must have pulled the trigger on the thirty-eight, it took Marty in the left shoulder, but Marty's shot blew out Bach's brain, which unfortunately splattered all over me. Annie had hugged the floor, and wasn't hit, thank God. I got both guns out of Bach's dead fingers. With a hole in his head like that, I don't see how he could still be alive, but I wasn't taking any chances. Then I helped Marty.

I had had EMS training. It was years ago but, I still remembered the basics. I kicked Bach's body onto the floor, pulled off the comforter that was covered in blood and brains, and tossed that on the floor. I laid Marty down on the bed, then pulled off a couple of pillow cases to put pressure on the wound.

"You're lucky. The slug went in one side of your shoulder and out the other. You're gonna be fine," I said. Annie was throwing on some clothes in the closet and talking on the phone at the same time.

"I don't feel so lucky. It hurts like hell," whined Marty.

"It's going to hurt for a while. Marty, I take back every bad thing I said about you. You are one tough son of a bitch," I said.

"That mean I'm gonna ruin your image of me if I start to cry from the pain," he asked, forcing a smile.

"Not at all."

"I need to go to the emergency room," said Marty.

"That would be a bad idea. If we take you to a hospital, they're required by law to report gunshot wounds. Your wound is serious, but not life threatening. I'm sure we can come up with another solution," I said.

Annie stepped back into the room.

"We already did. I called Dick and Maude, and told them we'd be late for dinner. Their fixer friend is going to get a doc up here who won't file the official paper work. Think you can hold on that long," asked Annie.

"I think so."

Annie came over and took over my job of putting pressure on the wound with a couple of towels she'd grabbed out of the bathroom. She pushed me away.

"You're filthy. Go take a shower and get that gunk off of you. Do I have to tell you everything," she asked. "You'd think you didn't have a brain."

"Actually, I seem to be wearing an extra," I said.

"Go," she ordered. I moved, and she leaned down and kissed Marty on the forehead. "Thanks. "

"My pleasure. Hope you didn't get dressed on my account," he said.

"Sorry, but I did," said Annie. I was in the shower by this time and crooning. "I'm in love with the jerk singing, 'If I Only Had a Brain' in the shower. That sight is reserved for him."

"Bach make you get naked," Marty asked.

"Not exactly. We needed a distraction to keep him from pulling any triggers. I hoped stripping and playing up to him would do the trick."

"Would have stopped me in my tracks," said Marty, with a smile.

"You're sweet," she said. I was out of the shower, dressed in a robe, and going through the closet for something to wear.

"I leave you alone for five minutes, and you have a man in our bed," I said, turning Annie's earlier line back one her. I could see that Annie had stopped most of the blood flow. All we had to do was keep his mind off the pain until the fixer's doc arrived.

"Honey, I can explain. Word of my prowess has gotten out and—"

"Yeah, yeah. Marty, don't get any ideas. She's mine," I said.

"There was never any question of that. However, if you ever wise up and want to trade him in for a younger, handsomer model, keep me in mind, okay?" said Marty.

"Okay," said Annie. "But don't hold your breath. Jack's like a fine wine."

"He gets better with age," asked Marty.

"No, he's worth more," said Annie.

"I can feel the love," I said.

"So do I. You haven't made one monkey joke," said Marty.

"After what you did for us twice today, I was thinking of stopping the monkey jokes," I said.

"Completely?"

"Actually, I was thinking more like the rest of the day," I said.

"It's better than nothing," said Marty.

"Actually, Marty, if it wasn't for you, we'd be dead. That's two I owe you."

"Okay, if you really owe me and wanna pay off, tell me something," said Marty.

"What," I asked.

"I must have heard you tell fifty different versions of how you lost your hand. Tell me the real story."

I nodded okay.

"Back when Annie and I were still on the force, we responded to a call. Some psycho had planted a bomb in a day care center. Apparently his wife had left him for another guy, and he was going to get even with her by killing their daughter. He came into the place with a bomb and a gun. He handcuffed his three-year-old daughter to the bomb. We couldn't get near the place. The negotiator had managed to talk him into getting pizza for the kids. Figuring a woman would be less threatening than a man, Annie dressed up as the delivery person. When she went inside, she got a chance, and she took the guy out. She got everyone out of there, except the little girl, who was still chained to the bomb. The handcuff was some sort of S&M job. Our keys wouldn't open it.

"I went in trying to defuse the thing. It was on a timer. I had less than three minutes, and bolt-cutters to clip the handcuffs wouldn't be there in time. Annie wasn't about to go anywhere. She had a flak jacket thrown over the little girl, and then one over herself. Annie threw herself over the little girl. I tried to explain to her that the bomb would blow both of them away as easy as it would one, but you know Annie. She wasn't budging.

"I didn't have enough time to shut down the clock on the bomb, so I separated the clock and the detonator from the secondary explosives. The problem was, the detonator was still an explosive, just on a smaller scale. We had blast-proof boxes that we put bombs in to explode. I tried to put the detonator in one across the room, but I didn't make it in time. As I was dropping it into the blast box, it blew, taking all of my fingers and part of my wrist with it.

"I was out for a while, but refused to let them kick me off the force on disability. The only reason I was able to get away with it was because I was the best bomb guy they ever had. Before the accident, I had even taught a class at Indian Head," I said.

"What's that," Marty asked.

"The best bomb disposal school in the world. It was at the Indian Head Naval Base, here in Maryland, in Charles County. They just closed it down and moved it to Enlin Air Force Base in Florida, but for fifty years, it taught military and federal bomb specialists how to defuse everything from a torpedo or a landmine to a nuclear missile. Even other countries sent their people to Indian Head."

"You must have made a fortune teaching there," Marty said.

"Kind of. My price was tuition. I went through the school myself. For the most part, local cops don't rate admission. I was one of ten they made an exception for. Simply put, with that kind of knowledge, I was too valuable to put on disability. Even knowledge didn't make up for losing a hand, so they assigned another cop to be an extra set of 'replacement' hands. Sad part is, not too long after that, I ended up quitting anyway."

"You can really defuse a nuclear bomb?"

"Yes."

"That's the straight story," asked Marty.

"Yeah. I'm sure you understand that it's not exactly one I could share with the folks here," I said.

There was a knock on the door. It was the fixer, a guy by the name of Dean. He was in his sixties, but Maude and Dick said he knew his stuff, and that was good enough for me. The doctor was with him, and went over to take care of Marty. Guy had a luggage handcart full of boxes that turned out to be equipment. The doctor snapped on a pair of latex gloves and did a quick check on the wound, then complimented us on our first aid. The guy had a mini-lab with him, and managed to type Marty's blood in under a minute. He opened a cooler which was filled with IV bags of blood. Pulling out the appropriate bag, he hooked the bag to the wall with a thumbtack. The needle end went into Marty's right arm to replace the blood he had lost. Then the doctor started to sew up the hole. Guess he didn't want the new stuff to go right out the bullet hole in the left shoulder.

Eventually, he announced that Marty was going to be fine.

Dean had already moved around the room, and was shaking his head. "I thought there was only one body to take care of," said Dean.

"Well, this is our busy season," I said.

"You wouldn't believe how busy I am tonight. I got another job making some other bodies disappear."

"In the penthouse?" I said.

"Yes," said Dean, looking at me suspiciously.

"Bach hire you for that one?"

"No, a couple of guys named Smith and Jones."

"Bet you already did this room on Tuesday," said Annie.

"No," said Dean.

"No?" said Annie.

"No, I won't bet you, because you're right," said Dean.

"Mind if we ask you a few questions about the body," asked Annie.

"Won't do you any good."

"Confidentiality," asked Annie.

"No, Bach had already removed the body before I got here," said Dean.

"Did he do it," asked Annie.

"Don't think so, judging by his mood. He was more worried about what would happen if word got out. Had he arranged it, his mood would have been more pleased with himself," said Dean. "Listen, I owe the Gladstones a favor, so I'll do either the guy upstairs or these two for free. The other one, I have to charge somebody for."

"Well then, do the two down here for free. How much for the guy upstairs," I asked.

"Fifty thou."

"Sounds fair," I said. Annie looked at me like I was crazy.

"You never don't barter. Besides, at that price, it might be worth it just to play it straight," said Annie, meaning to call in the cops.

"I don't think so. Bach lived in that suite up there. A man like him has to have a safe."

"So? You don't know how to crack one," said Annie.

I bent down and picked up the picture with the bullet hole on it. I peeled back the paper and removed about two square inches of C4.

"I don't know about that," I said with a smile and a wink.

XXVII

B Y THE NEXT morning, our room looked brand spanking new. You would never know that three people had been killed in that room in the last week. Of course, I had some questions for our new-found friend Dean, the big one being what the room looked like the night Joey was killed, and why the full paint job.

"All part of the service," he explained. "It's just easier to fully paint the room than worry about missing something. In that case, like this one, this room needed it. There was a bullet hole in the wall there." Dean pointed to spot next to the door. "And a dent in the plaster up there," he said, now pointing to the wall above the bathroom door.

A thought suddenly occurred to me. "Did it look anything like that?" I showed Dean the wall just next to the door to Marty's room, right where I had placed my diversion. I then picked up something from the floor. "And did you find one of these?"

"Yes, and yes. I wondered at the time, but in my business, you don't ask questions. What is that thing?"

"Maybe the key piece of a puzzle."

While Dean worked, we spent the night with Marty in his room, or rather, Annie did. Doctor's orders, someone had to sit up with him. Annie got the job, dozing the best she could in a chair. Me, I had work to do.

The first was a trip back to the CIA's temporary Baltimore HQ. They were more than a bit upset at our killing Bach before they could question him, but their ransacking of his room more than made up for it. They not only got a good lead on who wanted Lady Liberty blown to bits, but found info on several other operations Bach had been brokering.

Since they were going to take all the credit for this intelligence coup, they had no objection to my checking their surveillance video for the day before Joey was killed. What I saw, or rather, what I didn't see, convinced me my theory was right.

And for the record, they also didn't have any objection to my blowing open his safe. They were going to do that anyway. We split the money.

From the CIA rooms, my next stop was the alley below our window. After scaring off several rats and a homeless couple, it took me only a few minutes to find a match to the distraction that had saved our lives in the room above.

It was near four in the morning. Marty was sleeping peacefully, Annie snoring softly in her chair. I was wide awake, still cruising from the adrenaline rush that had started earlier in the evening and was kept going by the knowledge that I was close to solving the case.

One last thing. I pulled up the files Bill and Sarah had sent, this time looking for and finding one name in particular.

Done and done. Finally able to relax, I wanted to curl up next to Annie, but the chair wasn't wide enough. And even if Marty wasn't taking up the whole bed, he was far from an acceptable substitute. Taking a spare blanket and pillow from the closet, I made do with the floor.

XXVIII

MARTY CHECKED OUT before we did. His instructions were to tell Mozzano to meet us at our office the next afternoon. There I'd make our final report.

"You solved it? Whodunit?"

Annie wanted to know too, but I shook my head. "Sorry, Marty, you've been a big help and a great partner, but you still work for Mozzano. He deserves to know first. I wouldn't want you, shall we say, jumping the gun, and doing something we'd all regret."

I could tell his feelings were a bit hurt, but he understood how things were, or at least said he did.

"Now that he's gone, tell me," Annie demanded.

"I don't know, would Holmes tell Watson at this point?"

"Since when are we Holmes and Watson? I thought we were more Steed and Mrs. Peel."

"They weren't married. I think we should go for Nick and Nora."

Annie shook her head. "We don't drink enough. Let's settle for Annie and Jack."

I couldn't argue with that. "As long as it's not Batman and Robin."

"Why not? You didn't object on your birthday. And we still have the costumes."

"That was Batman and Wonder Woman. But that's still no reason to tell you."

"I haf vays of making you talk," Annie said, doing a much better Colonel Klink than had one of the Smiths. Then she pounced on me and showed me a few of the ways.

I talked, after which we loaded all our bags into the limo and checked out of the hotel. That done, we went into the dealers' room one last time. We swung by Jacob's table to pick up all of Annie's new guns and my special order. Apparently, Bach's disappearance hasn't made the gossip mill yet, because we didn't hear anything. Jacob pulled me aside first.

"I got your hand ready. Here," he said, giving it to me. For a guy who was a gunsmith, he had done an impressive job of making a prosthesis. Looked like any other prosthetic I had ever had, not counting the hook.

"I sure could have used this last night," I said.

"Why's that," asked Jacob.

"Long story. Show me how it works."

"Sure," he said, taking off the middle finger and the index finger from the prosthetic. I gave him a funny look.

"That's so we don't damage them. I'm only giving you five extra of each finger. After that, you're going to have to buy replacement parts," said Jacob. I nodded, and took off the hand that I was wearing. I put on the new one. It was a little rough in parts, but I'd been through that before with hands. If they don't fit right, you can get skin breakdown and skin ulcers, all sorts of nasty stuff, but that was something I didn't need Jacob to fix. I'd just replace the socket where my stump slid in with that from an old prosthesis.

"Okay, how does it work," I asked.

"Real simple. To make the stiletto pop out, you pull the pinkie back and twist clockwise 180 degrees. If you don't twist it back counterclockwise, it becomes pressure sensitive, and the moment you tap the top of the finger against something, the stiletto blade pops out. If you twist it around clockwise to 270 degrees, it'll pop out, then it can be used for stabbing as opposed to surprise. Go ahead and try it," said Jacob.

I did what he said. Pulled the pinkie back and twisted it clockwise. He'd gotten a cantaloupe, and held it up for me. I brought he hand up and pushed the middle finger against the center of the cantaloupe. The stiletto blade popped out, impaling the melon.

"Impressive. Now how do I put it back in," I asked

"Just take a piece of metal and push down gently. When you hear it click in place, you're set. The click should also put the pinkie back into position. That's your safety. If the pinkie's in a normal position, the stiletto can't come out. Now, as for the twenty-two caliber portion, you have to spin the thumb around backwards. That unlocks the safety. If the thumb isn't in the reverse position, you can't fire. I managed to get five bullets in there. You pull the trigger by bending the ring finger down towards the palm," he said and motioned me toward the firing range. "Take it for a test drive."

I spin the thumb around, aimed for the target, and pulled the ring finger back. It fired just like a gun. I did it five times, just to get the hang of it. I actually hit the target twice. I didn't have to worry about long distance; this was more of a close-in, surprise kind of weapon.

I was very impressed and said so.

"Thank you. I aim to please," said Jacob, bowing modestly.

"How do you reload," I asked.

"You twist the hand clockwise so it's faced outward, and then pop it toward you. That opens up the inside. You have to load each bullet individually, but the storage mechanism is similar to that of an automatic. You can get a sixth bullet in there if you want to carry it around in the chamber, but I wouldn't recommend it. You bump the hand too hard and it might go off. Easy way to lose a toe."

"Thanks for the advice. I've lost enough body parts," I said, handing him the envelope with the balance of his payment. As I reloaded my hand, he took the envelope, opened it, and counted out the cash.

"No offense."

"None taken."

As soon as he verified that it was all there, Jacob thanked me, and then moved on to go over all of Annie's hardware with her. While I waited, I picked up one of his pocket assassins, thinking, "Little sucker saved my life." It was also what had killed Joey Mozzano.

Knowing that someone might be gunning for us, I had bought a pocket assassin along with the bed holsters, setting it up at an angle to our room door. The dent it made on the wall when it went off was, according to Dean, identical to the one he found when he cleaned up after Joey's murder. Only Joey had bought two of them—one placed in much the same way I had, and the other on the window, hoping to trap whoever broke into his room in a crossfire. Only it didn't work out that way.

Annie and Jacob had finished their business.

"Guess we're done here," he said, giving us a merchant's smile. "You guys coming back again next year?"

I didn't tell him that with Bach dead, there wouldn't be a next year. Instead I said, "We're not quite done, Jacob." I laid a photo of Joey on the table. "Remember him? You sold him two of your pocket assassins."

"I sold lots of those things. You bought one yourself."

"That I did." I looked over at Annie. She had taken up a position behind Jacob. There were a lot of guns on the table. Annie's hand was on her pistol, just in case. Then I showed him another photo, one I had printed last night.

"Remember her?" It was one of Joey's victims, a girl from Cleveland. She had just entered college when she made the mistake of dating Joey Mozzano.

Jacob froze. His eyes went to the guns on the table. I pointed my loaded hand at him. "Annie's behind you," I warned.

"Her name was Emily Woodward. Officially, she's missing. The Cleveland PD thinks she's dead, and that Joey Mozzano likely had her killed. He certainly put her in the hospital."

All Jacob had to say was, "So?"

"So her mother's maiden name was Holland, same as yours. And in addition to this little sideline, you run a legitimate gun shop in Cleveland. What happened, Jacob? Get tired of waiting? Or was the sight of Joey walking around free while your niece was rotting in an unmarked grave just too much for you?"

It was all guesswork based on a few pieces of evidence, but Jacob didn't deny it. He didn't admit it either. I went on.

"Here's how I figure it. You saw Joey cruising the dealers' room, figured this was your chance—maybe your only one—at justice for Emily. Your first thought was to hire one of the hitmen attending the convention to do the job, then Joey came to you. He bought two of your little toys. And then you didn't need a hitman. You sold him two of your specials, the ones with the remote cameras, and made sure you had remotes for them. Then you waited, and when he was lined up, did the job yourself. And to get rid of the evidence, you fired off both of them, the one on the window breaking the glass and falling down into the alley."

"This Joey was mobbed up. How do you know someone else didn't do it? Like I said, I sold lots of those things. Someone could have planted one in his room."

I thought back to the surveillance video, and what I hadn't seen, which was anyone but Joey going into his room. That left only one possibility. But I didn't tell Jacob that. Instead, I said, "I can't blame you, really. If scum like Joey had hurt someone I loved, I'd take him out." I didn't bother adding that I had done just that the day before. "But here's the thing. Joey's grandfather paid us to do a job. Giving him your name is part of that job. Part of me feels bad about that. If anyone deserved to die, it was Joey. But there's another part of me that says that you and your toys have been and will be responsible for lots of deaths. So how does that make you any better?"

Except for a long, drawn-out sigh of surrender, Jacob had no answer. "So what happens now," he asked. "You and the missus take me somewhere quiet and do the job? You gonna shoot me with your new toy? With the hand I made you?"

Annie spoke up from behind him. "If we wanted you dead, you'd be gone by now. Or we'd would have skipped this conversation and just given Mozzano your name. Jack and I talked it over, Jacob. We're giving you a chance to get out."

"What will it cost me?" From the sound of his voice, he was willing to pay anything.

"Just your life, Jacob," I told him. "Just your life."

XXIX

IT WAS APPROACHING high noon on Monday. We were just waiting for Marty and Mozzano to show up, so we could give them our final report on the case. Bill was in court, trying a case, so we had the place to ourselves, and were just relaxing. Well, almost to ourselves. Sarah was there. When I asked how her date with Maggie had gone, she just smiled and went back to work.

Sarah was typing up a legal brief for Bill. When she didn't have any office work, she was studying. She wanted to get a private investigator's license, not that you have to study for that. Well, not as much as she did, anyway. You just need two thousand hours of experience in law enforcement, which working for us was giving her. The studying part was so that when she got the PI license, she'd be good at her job. I had no doubt of that.

The front door of the office opened, and Sarah stopped typing. Some words were exchanged, but not loud enough for us to hear. Sarah rolled in.

"Guys, there's a gentleman here to see you. He says he's not a client, but claims he's an associate. He said he helped you out with some ninjas. What's the deal? Is this guy nuts? Should I let him in," asked Sarah, "If it makes any difference he's got a build on him that you wouldn't believe."

I looked at Annie. "It couldn't be."

"After this week, I don't know if I'll be saying that phrase again for a while," said Annie.

"Show him in," I said. Sarah rolled out and told him to come on in. Rao walked into our office.

"Nice place you have here," he said, smiling.

"How did you find us?" I said.

"I told you I knew you weren't an assassin. You're not the only one who could solve a mystery, you know," said Rao, "I guess your main purpose at KCON was to solve the murder."

"That's how it started out, anyway," said Annie. "How it ended up is another matter entirely."

"Rao, I seem to remember you telling me that if I ever told you who I was, you would tell me a story about when your father found you," I said.

"True, but you didn't tell me," he said.

"Fair enough," I said.

"Maybe next time. This time, I can't stay long. I just wanted to stop by to say hi."

"Appreciate the visit. Where are you off to?" I said.

"I'm heading south of the border. Seems some drug dealers about a hundred and fifty miles outside of Mexico City are terrorizing a small village."

"And you're looking for six other guys to go with you?"

Rao nodded at the reference. "With or without others, I'll do what I can do to help out."

"By help out, you mean kill?" I said.

"Not as a first resort, but if I have to, yes," said Rao.

"I don't understand. There are other ways, you know," I said.

"Really, like there was with the Reaper, or Bach?" He had me there. "Life is difficult, there isn't always a way to wrap things up in nice, neat, little packages, so I don't get terribly upset when I can't find the giftwrap. I do what I can to try to make the world a better place. Maybe it works, maybe it doesn't. The important part is that I try, not unlike yourselves," said Rao.

"Can't argue with you there. Good luck," I said. Rao looked at me with a twinkle in his eye.

"Oh, you mean you're not going to try to stop me?"

"I couldn't stop you short of killing you, and I'm not sure I could even do that."

Rao laughed. "I think I'll be keeping in touch with you, if you have no objections."

"Not at all."

To Annie, he said. "Take good care of him, okay?"

"I will."

Rao turned and walked out of the office, plain as day, the same as any ordinary guy would. I was disappointed. Guess I was kind of hoping I'd turn around, then twirl back to find he'd disappeared somehow.

A little later, Sarah came in again.

"Your twelve o'clock is here."

"Send them in," said Annie. Mozzano came in first. Annie took his cane and patted him down for a gun, which she also took. Marty lumbered in behind him, his left arm in a sling. She didn't bother checking him, and Mozzano noticed it.

"What's the deal here? You frisk me, but you don't frisk him? He's the hired muscle, for Christ's sake," he said.

"Marty's family now," Annie said, smiling. Marty stood a little straighter, and smiled back.

"What did you do, adopt him? I don't give a crap about this family stuff. What I want to know is did you find out who killed my grandson?"

"Yes, we did," I said.

"Well, it seems like maybe I didn't waste my money on you after all. So, was it Bach?" said Mozzano. Chuckling, as an afterthought he added, "I love the way you turned it over to the authorities."

"If the guy we hired did his job right, the authorities will never find him. By now, he's been judged by a Court he can't bribe. But he didn't kill your grandson."

"So who did? Tell me his name so I can watch him die."

I didn't mention the fact that it would be in direct violation of our deal and his word. If everything worked out, it wouldn't matter.

I held up an envelope. "The name's in here." He reached for it, but I kept it just out of his reach. "Before I give it to you, before you open it, there's something you need to know."

"What?" Mozzano growled.

"Joey was sick, dangerously sick. He liked to hurt women, bad. But because he was your grandson, what he did was covered up—victims and witnesses paid off, threatened, or made to disappear. And that's what killed him."

"You saying it was my fault?"

I shrugged. "Doesn't matter whose fault it was. If Joey had done some time, maybe he could have been stopped. Maybe he would have gotten the help he needed. And maybe the family would not have looked for their own justice."

I handed Mozzano the envelope. "It's all in here. Name, address, all the evidence you need to convict. Read it after you leave. Just one more thing."

"What?"

"Right now, this is between us. If this guy or anyone in his family turns up dead, what we know goes to the authorities. They'll look at you first."

It was Mozzano's turn to shrug. "Let them look. If he turns up, there might not be anything for them to find. If he even turns up." He put the envelope away for further reading.

We had no further business. His checks, both for us and for the orphanage, had already cleared. We had nothing else to discuss.

"Let's go, Marty," he said, as Annie gave him his gun and cane back. He walked out toward the elevator. Marty stayed behind for a moment.

"Marty, what Annie said before was true, you are family now. Risking your life for us qualifies you. We owe you, and the Gardners pay their debts. If you ever want to leave Mozzano, we have a job for you here, at Gardner Investigations."

"Really?"

"Really. It's nothing glamorous. You would be an assistant, meaning you'd mostly get to take pictures and videos of cheating spouses. The pay wouldn't be much, certainly not what you're getting from Mozzano, but it would be honest work," I said.

"Plus, we can always use someone we know we can trust," added Annie.

"Could I become a private eye?"

"Eventually," Annie said, explaining that was what Sarah was doing.

"I'll think about it," said Marty. Mozzano was bellowing from the elevator. "I gotta go."

Annie kissed him on the cheek.

I pushed a brown paper bag into a desk drawer.

"What's that," asked Marty.

"Nothing," I said.

"Give it over," said Marty. I handed him the brown lunch bag. Marty opened it and pulled out a banana.

"I wasn't going to do it," I said, shrugging my shoulders.

"It's all right. I never told you my full name, did I?"

"No."

"Martin Joseph Young," he said.

"Marty Joe Young?" I said, unable to not laugh.

"Unfortunately."

"Your childhood must have been rough."

"I just thought I'd be old and senile before I had to endure a second one," said Marty.

Annie pulled out a gift-wrapped box and handed it to Marty.

"What's this?" he said.

"Open it," said Annie.

He did. Inside was the gun Annie had taken from him the first time he came to our office with Mozzano.

"My father's gun. Thanks, Annie," said Marty.

"You're welcome. It was Jack's idea," Annie said. Marty looked over at me.

"I'm not a jerk all the time, you know," I said, tossing him the limo keys.

"Thanks, Jack," said Marty. Joseph bellowed again. "Bye."

Marty left. I sighed and collapsed into my office chair.

"How long before Mozzano opens the envelope?" Annie asked.

"About ten seconds after his car pulls away. Five seconds after that, he'll be on the phone, ordering the hit. Doesn't matter now." I looked at my watch. "He's already twenty-four hours too late."

A NNIE AND I had helped Jacob pack up his wares and take them down to his van. Then we escorted him up to the rooms of Smith & Jones, spies and recruiters for the CIA and other governmental alphabet agencies. They were expecting us.

"This the guy," Smith asked.

"Yeah," I said, "he's no bomber, but he is a weapons expert. Those domestic terrorist groups you need infiltrated would love to get their hands on someone like him."

Smith looked at Jones, Jones looked at Smith. "Agreed," they said as one, then Jones added, "But what's his cover?"

"The truth," replied Annie. "This guy killed Joey Mozzano. What's his life expectancy if he doesn't go deep into the underground?"

"You got a point. You okay with this," Smith asked Jacob.

Forced to choose between the possibility of discovery and execution by the groups he was going to infiltrate and his very probable death at the hands of Mozzano's organization, Jacob did the only thing he could. He nodded.

"Tell them the rest," Annie prompted.

"The amount you offered me," I said, "that's what Jacob gets. Only he gets just a third of it. The rest goes to battered women's shelters in these cities." I handed Smith a list of cities where Joey's victims had lived.

It was decided that Jacob should disappear that very day, Smith and Jones taking immediate custody of him and his van full of lethal merchandise. Well, most of it. Annie and I selected a few choice items for brokering the deal.

"THAT JUST ABOUT wraps this case up," I said, trying not to think of what Mozzano would do once he failed to find Jacob.

"Not quite," Annie said.

"What do you mean?"

"We're having dinner at my brother Glen's tonight. And we promised we'd explain everything."

"Oh joy."

XXX

RAO DID KEEP in touch with us. He passed on our address to Rose, who also keeps in touch, so we found out what happened with Charlie. He had gone to England, as planned.

Charlie was loving life. He prowled in the dark streets, feeling every inch the predator. Sadly, London and Whitechapel had changed with the times. It was no longer the world of The Ripper. He didn't mind so much the changes in architecture, but he truly wished that there were still gaslights. That would have made everything perfect.

Charlie couldn't wear traditional nineteenth century garb either. He would stand out too much, and one thing he had learned in his career was that standing out was a bad thing. But he couldn't complain all that much. Just walking in the streets in his dark trench coat gave him goose bumps and chills up and down his spine. All of his other tributes had been contemporaries of a sort. They and Charlie occupied the same world, but this was different. This was like he was exploring another world and time traveling, all wrapped up into one neat little bundle.

Whitechapel had changed in one more way. It wasn't quite the red-light district that it was in Victorian times, and Charlie was having great difficulty locating a victim. Sure, he could just pick a woman at random, but it wouldn't be the same, it wouldn't be art. Just a sloppy, pale imitation. Better to give it up and wait until the time was right, than do it wrong.

Just when Charlie was about to give up all hope, a vision appeared at the end of the street. The Ripper must have been smiling at him from his place in hell. It was a beautiful woman, as out of place on these London streets as would be a rhinoceros. For one thing, she was dressed as though she had stepped right out of the Victorian era. Her long frilly dress with a low-cut neck line, puffy sleeves with frills and ruffles all around. Her hair was even curled up in a style reminiscent of that bygone time. She turned her head and saw Charlie.

The streets were deserted, and he feared that she might get nervous and leave. Far to the contrary, she smiled and made her way toward him.

"Evening, Guv'ner. Bloke like you looking for a date?" asked the women in a Cockney accent. A wave of ecstasy crashed against the shores of Charlie's soul.

"As a matter of fact I was, but I have to ask, what's with the getup?" said Charlie.

"Well, Guv'ner, I have a client who has a Victorian fetish. I'm meeting him in a little over an hour. He pays well, and he likes me to be in character. I figured I'd see if I could pick up a little business beforehand," said the woman.

"Very enterprising of you," said Charlie.

"Thank you."

Charlie looked at her face, and saw something familiar there, but it wasn't something he could place.

"Do I know you?" said Charlie.

"No, I don't think so. I'd remember a bloke like you," said the woman.

"I love the accent. You do it very well. What's your name?"

"Rose. And what should I call you?"

"Call me 'Jack'," said Charlie.

"Well, Jack, so what'll it be? Your place or mine?"

"Actually I was hoping you wouldn't be averse to a fetish of mine. I like doing it outside, under the stars."

"No problem. It's an extra twenty pounds, though," said Rose.

"I think I can handle that. How about that alley," asked Charlie.

"Behind the dumpster? Okay, I suppose, but it's not very romantic."

"What's romance go to do with it? I thought prostitution was just about sex."

"It doesn't have to be, but I think you Americans have a saying that the customer is always right. It's your money, so it's your fantasy."

"After you," said Charlie, bowing gallantly and using his outstretched arm to point the way into the alley.

"Jack, I hope you won't think me a timid little lass, but I'd prefer if you went in first. That close to a dumpster, I'm afraid there might be rats or something. I'd rather you scared them off, 'cause if one of them came anywhere near me, I'd probably run away screaming," said Rose.

Charlie nodded. "Sure, no problem." Charlie went into the alley, making just enough noise to scare any rats. There weren't any.

"There we go. All the rats have been scared away. It's now safe for you to come in," said Charlie.

"Thanks."

"Don't mention it," said Charlie. As he eased his hand into the small of his back, he felt his fingers close around the hilt of the knife. The erection he felt was perfectly in keeping with the character he was playing. He waited for Rose to step out of the light cast by the electric street lamps and into the shadow, before he pulled the blade all the way out.

"There's been a change in plans," said Charlie, putting the knife in front of him.

"I'll say there has."

He looked down at Rose's hand, and saw a nine millimeter pistol staring back at him. He cursed silently. He had been so confident that he didn't even bother to bring a gun.

"What happened to your accent," asked Charlie.

"What's that in your hand?"

"Aw, this thing? It's just made out of rubber. It's a play toy. It's part of my fetish," said Charlie.

"Well, this is real," said Rose as she squeezed the trigger. There was no way she could have smuggled a gun into the country. The nine millimeter had been hell to come by, and had cost twice as much as it would have back home, but it was worth it. The gun was outfitted with a silencer, so the only noise was a little pop of air as the bullet rocketed forth into Charlie's wrist, making him drop the knife and scream in pain. The large knife clanged to the hard ground.

"Sounds an awful lot like metal to me, Charlie. You wouldn't lie to me, would you," asked Rose.

"I never told you my name was Charlie."

"You didn't have to."

"Where do I know you from?" said Charlie. He was still defiant, and wasn't afraid. He had never imagined that he could die, so he was angrier at the indignity of being shot than fear.

"You've probably heard of me. They call me Mantis."

"The lady killer. What do you want with me? Someone put a hit out on me? It's bad form for professionals to go up against each other like this. I'll double whatever they gave you, as long as you give me their name, so I can take them out," said Charlie.

"No one ordered a hit. This is vengeance, pure and simple."

"Vengeance? What did I ever do to you," asked Charlie.

"Not to me, to a friend of mine. You remember a girl named Chandra?" demanded Rose.

"The whore from Baltimore?" said Charlie.

Rose altered where she was aiming the nine millimeter to a region between Charlie's legs. She squeezed the trigger one more time. The bullet went into and out the other side of Charlie's right testicle, pulverizing it. Charlie fell to his knees, screaming with a pain so intense that his anger faded and he began to feel fear.

"She wasn't a whore, she was a prostitute. There is a difference, not that it matters to you," said Rose.

"Please don't do this. I can make it worth it for you. Let me go," gasped Charlie through the pain.

"Maybe you could give me something, but you can't do anything for Chandra. Guess the Jack the Ripper thing was a bust for you, huh?"

"Please…"

Rose shook her head no, and brought the gun up to the center of Charlie's forehead.

"G'night, Guv'ner." The bullet made a pop and then a sickening, squishy noise as it sliced through brain and bone and came out the back. A huge chunk of Charlie's brain flew out the rear of his skull.

Rose threw the nine millimeter in the dumpster and proudly walked out of the alley.

XXXI

A FEW WEEKS later, we heard from Marty. Mozzano had put an open hit out on Jacob, but had made no real effort to find him. By then, I had met with Matt Reily at the FBI, and told him what I knew. Plans were made for me to consult with the FBI about the best way someone could blow up the Statue of Liberty, and how to prevent it. Reily was the one who dropped the word that there would be a KCON next year. This time it would be jointly, but covertly, sponsored by the FBI and CIA. It had been decided that the intelligence gathered at this event more than made up for any damage a gathering of killers could cause. Plus the fact that, once everyone checked out of their rooms, the FBI could send in its crime scene unit to gather hairs, fibers, latent prints, and DNA—all to use in past and future investigations.

Annie and I were invited, as guests of honor, of all things. We talked it over and decided that, whenever it was to be held, we would be busy that weekend.

That should have been the end of it. And for a time we thought it was, until about a month later.

I was on a missing daughter job. She had been attending college up in York, Pennsylvania, when she failed to show up at her student apartment one day after classes. After two days, her roommates called her parents, and they called me. I was on campus, trying to decide which boyfriend she had followed—the one from New Jersey or the one from Colorado—when it happened.

Annie was in the garage of our building, keys in her hand and heading for her car, when a familiar voice came from the shadows.

"As I said, I always pay my debts."

Antonio Tomaso stepped out of the darkness.

Dropping her keys, Annie was about to reach for her gun when she saw that Tomaso's hands were empty. He had, however, taken a gunfighter's stance.

"Here to kiss my feet," she asked.

"Not likely. Since that convention, work has been hard to come by. Word got out that I was shown up by a dame. Time to correct that."

"Your funeral," Annie said calmly.

"Or yours," Tomaso replied. "No toys this time. Real guns, real bullets."

"Works for me."

The two squared off, the only witnesses to the showdown a couple of pigeons nesting in the roof supports. For several seconds, neither moved, each of them studying the other's eyes, watching the other's hands. And then...

Back at the convention, Annie had bragged that she could put a hole between Tomaso's eyes before his gun could clear his holster.

Turns out she was right.

Printed by BoD™in Norderstedt, Germany